A Society of Novelists

The Twickenham Tales

Vol. II.

A Society of Novelists

The Twickenham Tales
Vol. II.

ISBN/EAN: 9783337137021

Printed in Europe, USA, Canada, Australia, Japan

Cover: Foto ©Andreas Hilbeck / pixelio.de

More available books at **www.hansebooks.com**

THE

TWICKENHAM TALES.

By a Society of Novelists.

⌇⌇⌇⌇⌇⌇⌇

IN TWO VOLUMES.

VOL. II.

LONDON: JAMES HOGG AND SONS.

LONDON : PRINTED BY W. CLOWES AND SONS, STAMFORD STREET AND CHARING CROSS.

CONTENTS OF VOL. II.

always got through four-hours' work by this time of day ; and now I have not begun ;—but those articles must be finished.'

'Good-bye,' said Verney. 'Good-bye,' said Mrs. Verney, and she looked at Rebow sadly, as he sat down to write his soul out.

The day was fine ; and all the others went out on the river. Every one took a hand at it—rowing, or steering, or making himself useful somehow, except Scott. He stopped in the middle of the boat and studied his boots.

When they had returned and dined, and the time came for Angerstein's tale—'In this case,' said he, 'a question of construction arises.' 'Oh! "shop!" "shop!"' they all cried except Scott. 'Fine him ! fine him !' 'No,' said Angerstein, 'that was the very point I was coming to—whether my tale is "shop" or not. The facts stand thus:—(renewed cries)— by the first resolution it is provided that the tale should not be drawn from the teller's personal expe- rience. Now during last "Long" I went to Corsica on a commission to examine witnesses in reference to a suit in the Court of Chancery—(cries of "Oh! oh!" a voice, "Oh no we never mention her;" counter cries, "Order, order !")—and while so engaged I fell in with a tale by Prosper Mérimée, one of the forty of the Académie Française, which is very popular in that island, and which I translated. I propose to read that translation to you, unless, inasmuch as I met with the tale on a professional journey, it should trench upon the aforesaid resolution.'

' My dear Angerstein,' said D'Aubrey, ' such a thing would never have occurred to the mind of any but a Chancery lawyer.'

' Well,' said Angerstein, ' Scott and I know that common lawyers are horribly personal ; but never mind, if you will pledge your professional reputation that a tale with which I so became acquainted is not obnoxious to the resolution, I am content.'

' I'll pledge my own and yours too.'

' Stop,' said Scott, ' I don't think there is anything in your fear about your tale being "shop," as the undergraduate's phrase is, but—but—isn't a French novel very objectionable on other grounds ? We always make it a rule in examining the undergraduates' rooms to burn the French novels, and I really think, Angerstein, if you could tell us some tale of your own it would be much better. How very disagreeable the light is !' and he pulled down the blind, and put his back to the window.

' Ah, yes,' said D'Aubrey, ' that's why it is that the undergraduates always keep the French novels in their pockets—as you don't search them ; a practice which they find convenient in chapel, when they slip the novel out under their surplices, and read it inside their prayer-book all chapel-time.'

' Will you give me the name of any undergraduate who does so ?' said Scott.

'Henry D'Aubrey, Senior Soph, Letter L, Old Court, Trinity.'

'Yes, no doubt you did it, and a great many other wrong things too, for which I am sorry to see you are not now properly repentant; but there is a great improvement since you left, and decorum is now bserved for its own sake.'

'Hem,' said D'Aubrey.

'As for the propriety of the tale,' said Angerstein, 'you may be quite easy on that head; it's nothing worse than a love-story.'

'Such subjects appear to me to be highly objectionable,' replied Scott. 'What a pity it is that they are allowed !'

'Well, never mind, old fellow,' drawled Graham; 'when Angerstein comes to the love passages you—aw—can go out of the room, you know—aw—and we'll call you in again for—aw—the descriptions, and so forth, you know—aw—and—aw—'

Angerstein said, 'You'll remember that Corsica, the scene of the following tale, is one of the departments of France, and that we consequently find there French laws and institutions mixed up with native habits and customs. Colomba, the Christian name of the principal personage, is, you all know, synonymous with Dove. The author speaks of the Irish people as if they were English; and as it's rather amusing than otherwise, I have not taken the liberty of altering it. There are several notes to the tale.

They are all by the author, except when I have put
the letters Tr. at the end of them, and then I am
responsible for them. I ought to apologise for giving
only a translated story; but then you know that a
Chancery man loses his imagination after the first
six months reading in a draftsman's chambers, and so
the alternative is between borrowed or none.'

'All right—go on,' said D'Aubrey.

Angerstein read on—

THE DOUBLE SHOT.

Pè far la to vendetta;
Sta sigur', vasta anche ella.
                VOCERO DU NIOLO.

AT the beginning of the month of October, 181-, Colonel Sir Thomas Nevill, an Irish baronet and a distinguished officer in the English army, arrived with his daughter at the Hotel Beauveau, at Marseilles, on their return from a tour in Italy. The continued admiration which enthusiastic travellers display in respect to that beautiful country, has produced a reaction ; and, in order to distinguish themselves from the crowd, many tourists of the present day take for their device Horace's *nil admirari*, never to admire anything. To this class of discontented wanderers belonged Miss Lydia, the Colonel's only child. In her eyes Raphael's Transfiguration was only so-so; and Vesuvius in eruption was hardly superior to the chimeys of the Birmingham furnaces. In short, her great objection to Italy was, that it was deficient in local colour, in character. Explain who can the meaning of those words, which I understood perfectly several years ago, but whose sense is now to me a mystery. At the outset, Miss Nevill flattered herself that she had discovered on the other

side of the Alps objects which no one had seen before
herself, and about which she might converse, as M.
Jourdain says, '*avec les honnétes gens*,' with respectable people. But finding herself everywhere fore-
stalled by her compatriots, and despairing of hitting
upon any single unknown thing, she soon threw herself into the ranks of the opposition. It is, in fact,
very disagreeable not to be able to talk about the
wonders of Italy without some one's saying to you,
'Of course you saw the Raphael of the Palazzo
* * *, at * * * *? It is the finest picture in
Italy.' And it is sure to be exactly what you did not
see. As it is much too long an affair to see everything, the simplest plan is to condemn everything
without exception.

At the Hotel Beauveau, Miss Lydia experienced a
bitter disappointment. Amongst her treasures was a
pretty sketch of the Pelasgic or Cyclopean gate of
Segni, which she thought had been neglected by
wandering artists. Now, Lady Frances Fenwick,
whom she met at Marseilles, showed her her album,
in which, between a sonnet and a dried flower, figured
this very gate in question, illuminated with a liberal
allowance of burnt sienna. Miss Lydia presented the
gate of Segni to her maid, and lost all esteem for
Pelasgic edifices.

These melancholy views were shared by Colonel
Nevill, who ever since the death of his wife, saw
only through Miss Lydia's eyes. For him, Italy had
the enormous fault of having wearied his daughter,
and was consequently the most wearisome country in

the world. True, he had nothing to say against the pictures and the statues; but what he could state with certainty was, that the sporting was wretched, and that you would have to walk five-and-twenty miles in the burning sunshine in the Campagna of Rome before you could kill two or three miserable red-legged partridges.

The day after his arrival at Marseilles he invited to dinner one Captain Ellis, an old adjutant of his, who had just been spending six weeks in Corsica. The Captain told with considerable skill a story of bandits, which had the merit of bearing no resemblance whatsoever to the tales of robbers which you hear so repeatedly on the road between Rome and Naples. At dessert the two gentlemen, left alone with their claret, talked of nothing but shooting, and the Colonel learnt that in no country in the world was there better, more varied, or more abundant sport.

'There is plenty of wild boar,' said Captain Ellis; 'but you must learn to distinguish them from the domestic swine, which are wonderfully like them; for, if you kill the pigs, you get into trouble with their keepers. They rush out of the copse-woods, which they call *mâquis*, armed up to the teeth, make you pay for their brutes, and then laugh at you. You have, besides, the mouflon, a very curious animal which is found nowhere else, hard to get at, but famous sport. Red-deer, fallow-deer, pheasants, partridges: it is not easy to enumerate all the kinds of game which swarm in Corsica. If you are fond of shooting, go to Corsica, Colonel; there, as one of my

hosts said to me, you may fire at every possible species of game, from the thrush to the human being.'

At tea the Captain again charmed Miss Lydia with
a story of *vendetta transversale*,* still more strange
than the former one; and he wound up her enthu-
siasm for Corsica by describing the wild and singular
aspect of the country, the original character of its
inhabitants, their hospitality and their primitive
manners.   Finally, he laid at her feet a pretty little
stiletto, which was less remarkable for its form and
its brazen handle than on account of its origin.
Captain Ellis had obtained it from a famous bandit,
with the warrant that it had been plunged into four
human bodies.   Miss Nevill gave it a place inside
her sash, afterwards deposited it on her bedside table,
and drew it twice out of its sheath before she went
to sleep.   The Colonel, on his part, dreamt that he
had shot a mouflon, and that the owner of the land
made him pay its value, to which he consented will-
ingly ; for it was a very curious animal, resembling
a wild-boar, with the horns of a stag and a pheasant's
tail.

'Ellis tells me that there is capital shooting in
Corsica,' he said, as he breakfasted tête-à-tête with
his daughter.   'If it were not so far I should like to
spend a fortnight there.'

'Very well,' replied Miss Lydia ; 'what is there to
prevent our going to Corsica?   While you are out
shooting, I can sketch ; I shall be delighted to enrich

---

* The vengeance which is made to fall on a more or less distant relation of the original author of the offence.

my album with the grotto Captain Ellis mentioned,
where Bonaparte used to go and study when he was
a little boy.'

It was, perhaps, the very first time that a wish
expressed by the Colonel obtained his daughter's approbation. Overjoyed at this unexpected event, he
nevertheless had the good sense to make a few ob-
jections, in order the more to excite Lydia's fortunate
caprice. In vain did he talk of the wildness of the
country, and of the difficulties a lady would have to
encounter in travelling there. She was afraid of
nothing; she liked above all things to travel on
horseback; it would be a treat to her, to sleep in
bivouac; she threatened to go to Asia Minor. In
short, she had an answer for everything, for no
Englishwoman had yet been to Corsica; consequently, she must go. With what satisfaction would
she produce her album when she got back to St.
James's Square! 'Why do you turn over that
charming drawing, my dear?' 'Oh, it is nothing.
It is merely a rough sketch of a Corsican bandit who
acted as our guide.' 'Really! have you been to
Corsica?'

Steamers between France and Corsica not being
yet in existence, they inquired for a vessel that was
on the point of sailing for the island, which Miss
Lydia proposed to discover. That very day, the
Colonel wrote to Paris to give up the apartments he
had engaged, and came to terms with the master of a
Corsican schooner bound for Ajaccio. There were
two cabins, such as they were. They sent provisions

on board. The captain vowed that one of his old sailors was an excellent cook, and had no equal for *bouille-abaisse;* he promised mademoiselle that she should be very comfortable, that she should have a fair wind and a smooth sea.

Moreover, according to the will of his daughter, the Colonel stipulated that the captain should take no other passenger, and that he should hug the shores of the island as much as possible, so as to enjoy the mountain scenery.

II.

On the day fixed for their departure, everything was packed and sent on board at an early hour. The schooner was to sail with the evening breeze. To pass the time, the Colonel and his daughter were taking a walk in the canebière, when the captain accosted them to ask permission to take on board one of his relations; that is to say, the second cousin of his eldest son's godfather, who, wanting to return to Corsica, his native country, on urgent business, could find no vessel in which to take his passage. 'He is a charming fellow,' added Captain Matei, 'a soldier, an officer in the *Chasseurs à pied* of the Guard, who would have been a colonel long before this time, if *the other one* still were emperor.'

'Since he is a military man,' said the Colonel.— He was going to add, 'I have no objection to his going with us;' but Miss Lydia exclaimed in English,

'An infantry officer!' (her father having served in the cavalry, she despised every other department of the army) 'an uneducated person, perhaps, who will be sea-sick, and who will spoil all the pleasure of the voyage.'

The captain understood no English, but he made a good guess at the tenor of her speech from the way in which her pretty mouth was twisted; and he commenced a set panegyric of his relation, which he concluded by assuring them that he was a man *très comme il faut*, belonging to a family of *caporali* or corporals, who would cause no annoyance whatever to Monsieur le Colonel; for he, the captain, would undertake to lodge him in a corner where no one should be aware of his presence.

The Colonel and Miss Nevill thought it singular that in Corsica there should be families whose members were corporals from father to son; but, as they piously believed that the party in question was an infantry corporal, they concluded that it was some poor devil whom the captain patronised out of charity. If it had been an officer, they would have been obliged to speak to him, to mess with him, but with a corporal there was no occasion to put themselves out of their way; he was a creature of not the slightest consequence, except when he came with his detachment, under arms, to escort you to some place where you had no mind to go.

'Is your relation ever sea-sick?' inquired Miss Nevill, in a dry tone of voice.

'Never, mademoiselle. His stomach is as firm as a rock, out at sea as well as on land.'

'Very well! you may bring him,' she said.

'You may bring him,' echoed the Colonel, and they continued their walk.

About five in the afternoon, Captain Matei came to fetch them to go on board the schooner. On the quay, close by the captain's yawl, they found a tall young man, attired in a blue frock coat buttoned up to the chin, with a dark complexion, large black, bright eyes, and a frank and intelligent address. From the way in which he carried his shoulders, as well as from his little curled moustache, it was easy to recognise a military man; for, at that epoch, moustaches did not appear in every street, and the National Guard had not yet introduced into every family the costume and the habits of the guard-house.

The young man lifted his cap at the Colonel's approach, and thanked him in proper terms, and without embarrassment, for the service which he was rendering him.

'Delighted to do you a kindness, my lad,' giving him a friendly nod as he stepped into the boat.

'Your Englishman is free and easy,' said the young man to the captain, in Italian, and in a low tone of voice.

The captain put his forefinger under his left eye, and drew down the corners of his mouth. For those who understand the language of signs, it meant to say that the Englishman knew Italian, and that he was an eccentric personage. The young man slightly smiled, touched his forehead in reply to Matei's sign, as much as to say that all the English had bees in their bonnets. He then seated himself beside the captain, and regarded with considerable attention, but without impertinence, the movements of his fair fellow-traveller.

'The French soldiers have a good carriage,' the Colonel remarked to his daughter, in English, 'which renders it easy to make officers of them.' Then addressing the young man in French, he asked, 'What regiment did you belong to, my man?'

The person interrogated slightly touched the elbow of the father of the godson of his second cousin, and suppressing an ironical smile, replied that he had been in the Chasseurs à pied de la Garde, and that he had lately left the 7th Light Infantry.

'Were you at Waterloo? You are too young for that.'

'I beg your pardon, Colonel; it is my only campaign.'

'It counts for two,' replied the Colonel.

The young Corsican bit his lips.

'Papa,' said Miss Lydia, in English, 'ask him if the Corsicans are very fond of their Bonaparte.'

Before the Colonel could translate the question into French, the young man replied, in very good English, although with a decided accent, 'You are aware, mademoiselle, that no one is a prophet in his own country. We, who are compatriots of Napoleon, are, perhaps, not quite so fond of him as the French are. For my own part, although my family was formerly at enmity with his, I both admire him and love him.'

'You speak English,' exclaimed the Colonel.

' Very badly, as you perceive.'

Miss Lydia, although slightly offended at his easy tone, could not help laughing at the idea of a personal enmity between a corporal and an Emperor. It was a sort of foretaste of Corsican singularities, and she resolved to make a note of it in her journal.

' Perhaps you were a prisoner in England ?' asked the Colonel.

' No, Colonel. I learnt English in France, when I was a boy, of a prisoner who belonged to your nation.' Then, addressing Miss Nevill, he added, ' Matei informs me that you have just left Italy. Doubtless, mademoiselle, you speak pure Tuscan; you will have some difficulty, I fear, in understanding our patois.'

' My daughter understands all the Italian dialects ; she has the gift of tongues.   She is not like me.'

' Would mademoiselle understand, for instance, these lines from one of our Corsican songs ? A shepherd says to a shepherdess—

> S'entrassi 'ndru paradisu santu, santu,
> E nun travassi a tia mi n'esciria ?*

Miss Lydia did understand; and as she considered the quotation bold, and still more the look which accompanied it, she answered with a blush, ' *Capisco*.'

' And you are returning home on a leave of absence ?' inquired the Colonel.

' No, Colonel; they have put me on half-pay, pro-

---

* If I were to enter into Paradise holy, holy, and did not find you there, I would walk out again.

bably because I was at Waterloo and am a countryman of Napoleon. I come back, as the song says,
light in hopes and light in money.' And he sighed,
and looked up at the clouds.

The Colonel put his hand in his pocket, and closing
his fingers over a piece of gold, he tried to find a
phrase that would help him to slip it politely into
the hand of his unfortunate enemy.

'That's exactly my case,' he said, good-humouredly,
'they have put me on half-pay. But your half-pay
is not enough to find you in tobacco. Here, corporal.' And he tried to thrust the piece of gold into
the young man's closed hand, which was resting on
the edge of the boat.

The young Corsican blushed, drew himself up, bit
his lips, and seemed on the point of answering angrily,
when suddenly, changing the expression of his countenance, he burst out laughing. The Colonel, with his
piece of money in his hand, was completely aghast.

'Colonel,' said the young man, resuming his serious-
ness, 'allow me to give you a double piece of advice.
The first is, never to offer money to a Corsican, for
some of my countrymen are rude enough to throw it
at your head : the second is, not to give people titles
to which they put no claim. You call me corporal,
and I am a Lieutenant. Doubtless, the difference is
but trifling ; still—'

'Lieutenant !' exclaimed Sir Thomas. 'A lieutenant ! But the captain told me you were a corporal, and your father also, as well as all the males
of your family.'

At these words, the young man, falling backwards, began to laugh so loud and so heartily that the captain and his two sailors burst out in chorus.

'I beg your pardon, Colonel,' he said, at last, 'but the mistake is admirable, and I have only just comprehended it. In fact, my family is proud of reckoning certain corporals amongst our ancestors; but our Corsican corporals have never worn stripes of lace upon their coat-sleeves. About the year of grace 1100, certain parishes, having revolted against the tyranny of the seigneurs of the mountains, elected chiefs whom they named *caporali*. In our island, it is considered an honour to be descended from one of those worthies.'

'Excuse me, sir,' exclaimed the Colonel; 'pray excuse me. Since you understand the cause of my mistake, I really hope that you will forgive it.' And he offered him his hand.

'It is a just punishment for my little spice of pride,' said the young man, laughing again, and cordially shaking the Englishman's hand. 'I have not the slightest right to take offence. Since my friend Matei has introduced me so clumsily, allow me to introduce myself. My name is Orso della Rebbia, Lieutenant on half-pay; and if, as I presume from the presence of these two handsome dogs, you are going to Corsica with the intention of shooting, I shall be very proud to do the honours of our mâquis and our mountains—that is, if I have not forgotten them;' he added, with a sigh.

At that moment, the yawl reached the schooner.

The Lieutenant offered his hand to Miss Lydia, and then aided the Colonel to mount to the deck. On arriving there, Sir Thomas, still excessively annoyed at his blunder, and hardly knowing how to cause his impertinence to be forgotten by a man who dated from the year 1100, did not wait this time for his daughter's consent, but invited his new acquaintance to supper with a renewal of excuses and handshakings. Miss Lydia knitted her brows just a little; but, after all, she was not sorry to have learned what a *caporale* was. Their guest was not displeasing in her eyes; she even began to remark in him a certain aristocratic *je ne sais quoi;* only his manners were too frank and cheerful to suit a hero of romance.

'Lieutenant della Rebbia,' said the Colonel, saluting him in the English style with a glass of Madeira in hand, 'I met with a great many of your countrymen in Spain. They were the famous foot riflemen.'

'Yes, many were killed in Spain,' said the Lieutenant, with a serious air.

'I shall never forget the conduct of a Corsican battalion at the battle of Vittoria,' continued the Colonel. 'I ought to remember it,' he added, rubbing his chest. 'They had been firing at us all day long, out of gardens and from behind hedges, and had killed I don't know how many men and horses. As soon as they had determined to make a retreat, they rallied and made themselves scarce in double-quick time. Out in the open plain, we expected to have our revenge; but the rascals—excuse me, Lieutenant —the brave fellows I mean—had formed into a square and there was no possibility of breaking it. In the middle of the square—I think I see him now—there was an officer mounted on a little black horse; he kept close to the side of the eagle, smoking his cigar just as coolly as if he had been at the café. Now and then, as if to defy us, their band would give us a flourish of trumpets. I charged them with my two first squadrons; but instead of breaking into the square, my dragoons were obliged to pass on one side, make a circuit, and return in great disorder, more than one horse without his rider. And, continually, that infernal band playing! When the smoke which enveloped the battalion cleared away, I again saw the officer by the side of the eagle still smoking his cigar. In a rage, I put myself at the head of a final charge. Their rifles, fouled with constant firing, would hardly go off; but the men were drawn up in six ranks, with their bayonets projecting as far as the horses' muzzles: you would have said it was a wall. I shouted, I urged on my dragoons, I digged my spurs into my horse to make him advance, when the officer whom I have just mentioned, throwing away his cigar at last, pointed me out to one of his men: I heard words that sounded like "*Al capello bianco!*" "Fire at the white hat!" I wore a white feather. I heard no more, for a bullet went through my chest. Ah, that was a fine battalion, Monsieur della Rebbia, the first of the 18th Léger, every one of them Corsicans, as I have afterwards been told.'

'Yes,' said Orso, whose eyes sparkled during the narrative; 'they made good their retreat and saved their eagle ; but two-thirds of those brave fellows are now sleeping on the plain of Vittoria.'

'And do you, by any chance, know the name of their commanding officer?'

'It was my father. He was then major in the 18th, and was promoted to his colonelcy for his conduct on that unfortunate day.'

'Your father! Then, he was a brave fellow! I should be delighted to see him again ; and I should know him again, I am quite certain. Is he still living?'

'No, colonel, he is not,' answered the young man, turning slightly pale.

'Was he at Waterloo?'

'He was; but he had not the good fortune to fall on a field of battle. He died in Corsica, two years since. Ah! how lovely the sea is! It is ten years since I have seen the Mediterranean. Don't you think the Mediterranean more beautiful than the ocean, mademoiselle?'

'I think it too blue—and its waves are deficient in grandeur.'

'You are fond of savage beauty, mademoiselle? In that case I believe you will be pleased with Corsica.'

'My daughter,' said the Colonel, 'is fond of everything that is extraordinary. That is the reason why she found so little to interest her in Italy.'

'All I know of Italy,' said Orso, 'is Pisa, where I spent some time at school; but I cannot think without admiration of the Campo Santo, the Cathedral,

and the Leaning Tower—of the Campo Santo especially.   You remember Orcagna's figure of Death?
I believe I could sketch it, so firmly is it fixed in my
memory.'

Miss Lydia began to fear that Monsieur the Lieutenant was going to give way to a burst of enthu-
siasm.

'It is very pretty,' she said, gaping. 'Excuse me,
papa, I have a slight headache; I will go to my
cabin.'

She kissed her parent on the forehead, made a
majestic bow to Orso, and disappeared. The two
gentlemen were left alone to talk about shooting and
warfare.

They learned that at Waterloo they were posted
face to face, and that they must have exchanged
many a bullet. Their good understanding was redoubled in consequence. They criticised Napoleon,
Wellington, and Blucher, and then they chased in
company the fallow-deer, the wild boar, and the
moufflon. At length, as it was getting very late, and
the last bottle of Bordeaux was finished, the Colonel
again shook the Lieutenant's hand and wished him
good night, expressing the hope of cultivating an acquaintance which had commenced in so ridiculous a
fashion. They parted, and each retired to his sleep-
ing-place.

III.

It was a fine night, the moonbeams played on the
waves, and the vessel glided along under a gentle

breeze. Miss Lydia felt no inclination to sleep; it was only the presence of one person that had prevented her from enjoying those emotions which every human being with half a grain of poetry in his heart experiences by moonlight and out at sea. When she guessed that the young Lieutenant was sound asleep, like the prosaic creature that he was, she rose from her couch, wrapped herself in a pelisse, called up her maid, and went on deck. There was no one there except a sailor at the helm, who was chanting a sort of complaint in the Corse dialect to a wild and monotonous air. In the calm of the night this strange music had its charm, Unfortunately, Miss Lydia could not perfectly comprehend what the sailor was singing. Amongst a great deal of common-place one energetic verse greatly excited her curiosity; but just as a fine passage appeared to be coming, a number of words in patois prevented her from following the meaning. She understood, nevertheless, that there was a murder in question. Imprecations against the assassins, threats of vengeance, and praises of the deceased person, were all mingled pell-mell together. She contrived to retain a few of the lines, which I will endeavour to translate into prose :

' . . . Neither cannons nor bayonets could blanch his forehead—calm on the field of battle—like a summer's sky—He was the falcon, the friend of the eagle, —honey of the heath towards his friends,—for his enemies, the raging sea.—Loftier than the sun,—gentler than the moon.—He whom the enemies of France could never reach,—the assassins of his own country—

smote in the back,—as Vittolo killed Sampieri Corso.*
—Never would they dare to look him in the face.—
. . . Fix on the wall, before my bed,—my Cross of
Honour hardly-earned.—Red is its ribbon.—Redder is
my shirt.—For my son, my son in a distant land,—
keep my cross and my bloody shirt.—He will behold
therein a couple of holes.—For each hole, a hole in
another shirt.—But will vengeance be then complete?—I must have the hand which pulled the
trigger,—the eye which took aim,—the heart which
plotted . . .'

The sailor stopped short abruptly.

'Why don't you go on with your lament, my
good friend?' inquired Miss Nevill.

The sailor,,by a motion of the head, called her attention to a figure which came from behind the schooner's
mainsail. It was Orso come to enjoy the moonlight.

'Finish the chant,' said Miss Lydia; 'it interests
me exceedingly.'

The sailor leaned forward towards her, and said,
almost in a whisper, 'I never give the *rimbecco* to any
one.'

'Give what? the —?'

The sailor, without further reply, began to whistle.

'I find you are admiring our Mediterranean, Miss
Nevill,' said Orso, advancing.' 'You must allow that
such a lovely moon as this is not to be seen elsewhere.'

* See Filipini, liv. xi.—The name of Vittolo is still held in
execration amongst the Corsicans. At the present day, it is
synonymous with the word traitor.

'I was paying no attention to it, being fully occupied in studying Corse. Our helmsman, who was singing a most tragical complaint, broke off abruptly at the most exciting point.'

The sailor stooped, as if to get a better sight at his compass, and gave a rough pull at Miss Nevill's pelisse. It was clear that the complaint could not be sung in Lieutenant Orso's presence.

'What were you singing there, Paolo Francè?' asked Orso. 'Was it a *ballata?* a *vocero?*' * Mademoiselle understands you, and would like to hear the end.'

'I have forgotten it, Ors' Anton,' said the sailor, and immediately he thundered out an ear-splitting canticle to the Virgin.

Miss Lydia carelessly listened to the canticle, and did not press the singer further, resolving to ferret out the secret by-and-by. But her maid, who was a native of Florence, and did not understand the

---

* When a man is dead, especially when he has been assassinated, they place his body on a table, and the women of his family, or, in their default, female friends or even strangers noted for their poetic talents, improvise before a numerous audience complaints in verse in the dialect of the country. These women are called *voceratrici*, or, according to the Corse pronunciation, *buceratrici*, and the complaint is called *vocero*, *buceru*, buceratu, on the eastern side of the island ; *ballata* along the opposite coast. The word *vocero* as also its derivatives *vocerar*, *voceratrice*, comes from the Latin *vociferare*. Sometimes several women improvise by turns, and often the wife or the daughter of the defunct sings herself the funeral complaint.

Corsican dialect better than her mistress, was equally.
curious after information ; and addressing Orso before
Miss Nevill could check her, 'Il Signor Capitano,'
she said, ' what is the meaning of to give the *rimbecco ?'* *

'The *rimbecco!*' said Orso. 'It is the most deadly
insult that a Corsican can receive. It is a reproach
that he has not avenged his injuries. Who has been
talking to you about *rimbecco ?*'

'Yesterday, at Marseilles,' replied Miss Lydia,
hurriedly, ' the captain of the schooner made use of
the word.'

'And of whom was he talking?' inquired Orso,
with vivacity.

' Oh, he was telling us a piece of old history—of
the time of—yes, I believe it was something about
Vannina d'Ornavo.'

'The death of Vannina, I suppose, mademoiselle,
has not made you very fond of our hero, the brave
Sampiero ?'

'But do you think him so very heroic ?'

'His crime finds its excuse in the savage manners
of the times. Moreover, Sampiero was waging a

---

* *Rimbeccare*, in Italian, means to send away, to rebuke,
to reject. In the Corse dialect, it is, to address a public and
offensive reproach. You give the *rimbecco* to the son of a
man who has been murdered, when you tell him that his
father is not avenged. The *rimbecco* is a sort of 'setting
down' for the man who has not washed out an insult in
blood. The Genoese law punished very severely any one
who gave the *rimbecco.*

war to the death with the Genoese. What confidence could his fellow-countrymen have placed in him, if he had not punished her who sought to treat with Genoa?'

'Vannina,' interposed the helmsman, 'departed without her husband's permission. Sampiero was quite in the right to wring her neck.'

'But,' said Miss Lydia, 'she went to save her husband. It was through love for him that she went to implore his pardon of the Genoese.'

'To implore his pardon was to disgrace him!' exclaimed Orso.

'And to kill her himself!' pursued Miss Nevill. 'What a monster he must have been!'

'You know that she begged as a favour to perish by his hand. Do you regard Othello, mademoiselle, as a monster?'

'What a different case! He was jealous: Sampiero was only impelled by vanity.'

'And jealousy,—is not that vanity also? It is the vanity of love: but you will perhaps excuse it in favour of the motive.'

Miss Lydia's eyes shot a glance of dignity, and addressing the sailor, she inquired when the schooner would arrive at port.

'The day after to-morrow,' he replied, 'if the wind continues.'

'I wish I were already at Ajaccio, for this ship wearies me to death.'

She rose, took the arm of her maid, and paced

backwards and forwards on the deck. Orso remained at the helm, not feeling sure whether he ought to accompany her, or drop a conversation which appeared to annoy her.

'A handsome girl, by the Madonna!' said the sailor.

Miss Lydia probably overheard this unsophisticated eulogy of her beauty, for she almost immediately went down to her cabin. Shortly afterwards, Orso likewise retired. As soon as he had left the deck, the waiting-maid came up again, and, after interrogating the sailor, reported the following information to her mistress:—The ballata, interrupted by Orso's presence, had been composed on the occasion of Colonel della Rebbia's death, the father of the aforesaid, assassinated two years ago. The sailor had no doubt that Orso was returning to Corsica *per fare la vendetta*—to do the vengeance, that was his expression—and affirmed that before long there would be 'fresh meat' in the village of Pietranera. Interpretation made of this national term, it resulted that the Signor Orso proposed to assassinate two or three persons suspected of having assassinated his father —persons who, in truth, had received the attentions of justice on account of that event, but who came out of the inquiry as white as snow, seeing that they held under their thumb judges, advocates, préfet, and gendarmes. 'There is no such thing as justice in Corsica,' added the sailor; 'and I put more faith in a good gun than in a counsellor of the royal court.

Wen one has an enemy, the choice lies between the three S's.*'

These interesting details made a notable change in the deportment and disposition of Miss Lydia, with regard to Lieutenant della Rebbia. From that moment; he became a personage in the eyes of the romantic English girl. Now that air of indifference, that frank and good-humoured tone, which at first had impressed her unfavourably, became for her an additional merit, for they were the profound dissimulation of an energetic soul, which will not allow any of its private feelings to appear externally. Not till then had Miss Nevill remarked that the young Lieutenant had very large eyes, white teeth, an elegant figure, a good education, and a certain knowledge of the world. She addressed him frequently during the following day, and his conversation interested her. He was fully questioned respecting his country, and he spoke of it in eloquent terms. Corsica, which he had left at an early age—at first to go to college, and afterwards to the military school,— remained fixed in his mind, adorned with poetic colouring. He became animated as he talked of its mountains, its forests, and the original customs of its inhabitants. As may be imagined, the word vengeance occurred more than once in his narrative; for it is impossible to speak of the Corsicans without either attacking or justifying their proverbial passion. Orso took Miss Nevill a little by surprise, by con-

* A national expression ; that is to say, *schioppetto, stiletto, stradd* ; gun, dagger, or flight.

demning, in general terms the interminable feuds of
his countrymen. With the peasantry, nevertheless,
he sought to praise them, pretending that the vendetta is the duel of the poor. 'This is so true,' he
said, 'that they do not assassinate until after a
regular challenge. "Take care of yourself; I take
care of myself," are the sacramental words exchanged
between enemies before they try to entrap each other.
There are more murders, with us,' he added, 'than
anywhere else; but never will you find an ignoble
cause for those crimes. We have, it is true, many
murderers, but not a single thief.'

When he pronounced the words vengeance and
murder, Miss Lydia regarded him attentively, but
without discovering the slightest trace of emotion
on his countenance. As she had come to the conclusion that he possessed the strength of mind requisite to render himself impenetrable to every eye—
except her own, be it understood,—she continued
in the firm belief that the manes of Colonel della
Rebbia would not have long to wait for the satisfaction which they demanded.

The schooner was already within sight of Corsica.
The captain named the most conspicuous points along
the coast; and, although they were perfectly unknown to Miss Lydia, she still took a pleasure in
learning their names. Nothing is more tiresome
than an anonymous landscape. Now and then, the
Colonel's telescope helped them to discover some
islander, clad in brown cloth, armed with a gun,
mounted on a little horse, and galloping down rapid

slopes. Miss Lydia took every one of them for a bandit, or for a son on the way to avenge his father; but Orso assured her that they were only peaceable inhabitants of the nearest market-town, travelling on business; that they carried guns less from necessity than through 'gallantry,' fashion, exactly as a dandy walks out with an elegant cane in his hand. Although a gun is a less noble and a less poetical weapon than a stiletto, Miss Lydia thought that, for a man, it was more becoming than a cane, and she called to mind the circumstance that all Byron's heroes meet with their death from a bullet, and not from the classical dagger.

After a three-days' voyage, they found themselves in front of the Sanguinaires, and the magnificent panorama of the Gulf of Ajaccio spread itself before the eyes of our travellers. It has been compared to the Bay of Naples, and not without reason; and at the moment when the schooner entered the port, a mâquis on fire, covering the Punta di Girato with smoke, increased the resemblance by suggesting the presence of another Vesuvius. To make it complete, an army of Goths would have to devastate the environs of Naples; for all around Ajaccio is desert and dead. Instead of the elegant buildings which meet the eye in all directions, from Castellamare to the Cape of Misenum, nothing is seen around the Gulf of Ajaccio but sombre brush-wood, and in the back-ground, naked mountains. Not a villa, not a human dwelling. Only, here and there, on the heights around the town, a few white buildings stand out in contrast

with a verdant ground; they are funereal chapels—
family burial-places. In this landscape, every detail
is stamped with a grave and melancholy beauty.

The aspect of the town, especially at that epoch,
still further increased the impression produced by
the solitude of its neighbourhood. No traffic in the
streets, where a few idle faces were all that were to
be seen, and those constantly the same. No women,
except two or three peasants come to sell their wares.
No talking aloud, no laughing nor singing are to be
heard, as in the Italian towns. Sometimes, beneath
the shade of a tree on the public walk, a dozen of
armed country-people play at cards, or watch others
playing.

They do not shout, and never dispute; if the game
becomes exciting, you hear several pistol-shots, which
are the invariable preface to threatening words. The
Corsican is naturally grave and silent. In the evening, a few figures appear, to enjoy the freshness of
the air; but the persons who walk up and down the
Corso are almost always strangers. The islanders
remain in front of their doors; each one seems on the
look out, like a falcon keeping watch over his nest.

IV.

After having visited the house where Napoleon
was born, and obtained by more or less catholic means
a small supply of paper-hangings, Miss Lydia, two
days after landing in Corsica, became oppressed with
profound melancholy, as must happen to every stranger on his arrival in a country whose unsociable

habits condemn him to an utter isolation. She regretted her whim; but to leave the place immediately would be to compromise her reputation as an intrepid traveller; she therefore resigned herself to bear her lot patiently and to kill time as best she might. With this noble determination, she prepared her crayons and her colours, sketched the best points of view on the gulf, and took a portrait of a sunburnt peasant, who was selling melons like any other market-gardener on the Continent, but who had a white beard and the most rascally-ferocious looks you ever beheld. All this did not suffice to keep her amused; so she made up her mind to turn the head of the descendant of the *caporali*, which was not difficult; for, far from being in any hurry to return to his village, Orso seemed very contented to remain at Ajaccio, although he did not visit a creature there. Moreover, Miss Lydia proposed to herself a noble task; namely, to civilize this mountain bear,* and make him renounce the sinister designs which were the motive of his journey. Ever since she had taken the trouble to study him, she said it would be a pity to allow so nice a young man to rush on to his ruin, and that it would be a great credit to her if she could convert a Corsican.

Our travellers spent the day as follows: in the morning, the Colonel and Orso went out shooting; Miss Lydia painted or wrote to her lady friends, for the pleasure of dating her letters from Ajaccio.

* Orso means bear.—Tr.

About six, the gentlemen returned laden with game;
then dinner; Miss Lydia sang, the Colonel went to
sleep, and the young people remained chatting till a
very late hour.

Some formality in respect to his passport, I cannot
say what exactly, obliged Colonel Nevill to pay a
visit to the Préfet; that official personage who, like
the rest of his colleagues, suffered considerably from
the effects of *ennui*, had been delighted to hear of the
arrival of an Englishman who was rich, a man of the
world, and the father of a pretty daughter. Consequently, he received him in most gracious and
friendly style, and overwhelmed him with offers of
service. What is more, a very few days afterwards,
he came to return the visit. The Colonel, who had
not long risen from table, was comfortably reposing
on the sofa and on the point of falling asleep; his
daughter was singing to a cracked piano; Orso was
turning over the leaves of the music-book, and admiring the performer's fair hair and white shoulders.
Monsieur le Préfet was announced; the piano was
silent, the Colonel rose, rubbed his eyes, and introduced the Préfet to his daughter: 'I do not present
Monsieur della Rebbia to you,' he said, 'because you
are doubtless already acquainted with him.'

'Is Monsieur the son of the late Colonel della
Rebbia?' inquired the Préfet with some slight embarrassment.

'I am, monsieur,' Orso replied.

'I had the honour of knowing your father.'

The common-place topics of conversation were soon

exhausted. In spite of himself, the Colonel felt a
great inclination to yawn; Orso, playing the part of
a liberal, did not feel it consistent to talk much with
a satellite of power; Miss Lydia alone sustained the
conversation. The Préfet on his part was not behind-
hand, and it was evident that it gave him great
pleasure to talk about Paris and its society with a
lady who was acquainted with all the notabilities
of Europe. From time to time, as he spoke,
he regarded Orso with singular curiosity.

'Did you know Monsieur della Rebbia on the
Continent?' he inquired.

Miss Lydia replied, with some embarrassment,
that they had made his acquaintance on board the
vessel which brought them to Corsica.

'He is a young man *très comme il faut*,' said the
Préfet in an under tone. 'And has he told you,' he
continued still lower, 'with what intentions he is
come to Corsica?'

Miss Lydia put on her majestic air: 'I have not
asked him, you can put the question.'

The Préfet said no more; but, an instant afterwards, hearing Orso address the Colonel in English,
he observed, 'You have travelled a great deal, it would
seem, monsieur. You must have forgotten Corsica
and its customs.'

'It is true; I was very young when I left it.'

'Do you still belong to the army?'

'I am on half-pay, monsieur.'

'You have been too long in the French army, not
to become a Frenchman altogether; there can be no

doubt of it, monsieur.' He pronounced these last words with marked emphasis.

The Corsicans do not feel prodigiously flattered when they are reminded that they belong to the *Grande Nation*. They wish to be considered a people by themselves ; and they sufficiently justify the pretension to cause it to be granted to them. Orso, a little piqued, replied, 'Do you think, Monsieur le Préfet, that it is necessary for a Corsican to have served in the French army, in order that he should be a man of honour ?'

'Certainly not,' said the Préfet. 'That is not at all what I am thinking about. I only speak of certain customs of this country, some of which are not what an administrator likes to see.' He emphasised the word *customs*, and assumed the most serious expression of which his countenance was capable. Shortly afterwards he rose and departed, after obtaining Miss Lydia's promise that she would call and see his lady at the préfecture.

When he was gone, Miss Lydia remarked, 'I was obliged to come to Corsica, to learn what sort of a person a Préfet is. This one seems tolerably amiable.'

'For my part,' said Orso, 'I cannot quite agree with you; he strikes me as very singular with his mysterious and sententious airs.'

The Colonel was more than half asleep; Miss Lydia cast a glance at him, and dropping her voice, said, 'For my part, I do not find him so mysterious as you pretend, for I fancy I understand what he means.'

'You are, assuredly, extremely clear-sighted, Miss Nevill; and if you can see any wit in what he has just been saying, it is certainly you who feel it there.'

'The speech belongs to the Marquis de Mascarille, I believe; but—will you like me to give you a proof of my penetration. I am a little bit of a sorceress, and I know people's thoughts after I have seen them twice.'

'Mademoiselle! You frighten me. If you are able to read my thoughts, I hardly know whether I ought to be sorry or glad.'

'Monsieur della Rebbia,' continued Miss Lydia, blushing, 'our acquaintance is only a few days old; but at sea, and in a barbarous country,—I hope you will excuse me,—in a barbarous country, people become friends more quickly than they do in society . . . Therefore you will not be surprised if I talk to you as a friend of matters which may be considered private, and with which a stranger has perhaps no right to interfere.'

'Oh, do not say that word, Miss Nevill; the other pleased me a great deal better.'

'Well then, monsieur, I ought to tell you that, without having endeavoured to discover your secrets, I have partially become acquainted with them, and that they give me great anxiety. I am aware of the misfortune which has occurred in your family; a great deal has been said about the vindictive character of your countrymen and of the way in which they avenge themselves—is not that what the Préfet alluded to?'

'Can you possibly think so?' And Orso turned as pale as death.

'No, Monsieur della Rebbia,' she said, interrupting him. 'I know that you are a man of honour. You have told me yourself that the only persons in your country who now practise the *vendetta* are the common people, which you think proper to call a form of duel.'

'Do you believe me capable of becoming an assassin?'

'Since I have mentioned the subject to you, Monsieur Orso, you must clearly see that I entertain no doubts respecting your conduct; and if I have spoken at all,' she continued, dropping her eyes, 'it was because I felt that returning to your native land, and beset, perhaps, by barbarous prejudices, you might be glad to know that there is one who esteems you for your courage in resisting them. Come,' she said, rising; 'let us say no more about these ugly matters, they have given me a headache, and besides it is very late. You are not angry with me? Good night, in the English fashion;' and she offered her hand.

Orso pressed it with a serious and grateful look. 'Mademoiselle, do you know there are moments when the instinct of my country is awakened in me. Sometimes, when I think of my poor father, frightful ideas rise in my soul. Thanks to you, I am for ever delivered from them. Thank you! thank you!'

He was about to add more; but Miss Lydia let a spoon fall, and the noise awoke the Colonel from his slumbers.

' Della Rebbia, we will start to morrow to see what
we can find, at five o'clock precisely.'

'Yes, Colonel ; I will be ready at the time.'

v.

Next day, a little before the sportsmen's return,
Miss Nevill, coming back from a walk on the sea-
side, was proceeding towards the hotel, together with
her maid, when she remarked a young woman dressed
in black, mounted on a small but spirited horse,
entering the town. She was followed by a sort of
peasant, on horseback also, in a brown cloth coat out
at elbows, a calabash slung across his shoulders, and
a pistol hanging from his girdle. In his hand was a
gun whose butt-end rested in a leather pocket attached to the saddle-bow. In short, in the complete
costume of a melodramatic brigand, or of a Corsican
burgess out on his travels. The young woman's remarkable beauty immediately attracted Miss Nevill's
attention. She appeared about twenty years of age.
She was tall, fair-complexioned, with dark blue eyes.
a rosy mouth, and enamelled teeth. In her expression were to be read at once pride, sadness, and
inquietude. On her head she wore the black silk
veil called *mezzaro*, which the Genoese introduced
into Corsica, and which is so becoming. Long braids
of chestnut hair formed a sort of turban around her
head. Her costume was neat, but of the most extreme simplicity.

Miss Nevill had plenty of time to observe her ; for
the lady in the mezzaro had stopped in the street to

question some one with considerable interest, as was evident from the expression of her eyes. At the answer which she received, she gave her steed a touch of the whip, and starting off at full trot, did not stop till she reached the gate of the hotel, where Sir Thomas Nevill and Orso were staying. There, after exchanging a few words with the host, the young lady sprang lightly from her saddle and seated herself on a stone bench by the side of the entrance-gate, whilst her squire led the horses to the stable. Miss Lydia, in her Parisian costume, passed before the stranger without causing her to raise her eyes. A quarter of an hour afterwards, opening the window, she again beheld the lady in the mezzaro seated in the same place, and in the same attitude. The Colonel and Orso soon appeared, returning from the chase. At their approach, the landlord said a few words to the damsel in mourning, pointing to young della Rebbia. She blushed, rose hastily, set a few steps in advance, and then remained motionless, and as it were, in amazement. Orso had come quite close to her, regarding her with curiosity.

'You are,' she said, in trembling accents, 'Orso Antonio della Rebbia? I am Colomba.'

'Colomba!' exclaimed Orso. And taking her in his arms he embraced her tenderly, which rather astonished the Colonel and his daughter; for in England people do not kiss each other in the streets.

'My dear brother,' said Colomba, 'you will excuse me if I have come without your orders; but our friends informed me that you had arrived, and it was such a consolation to see you.'

Orso embraced her once more; then, addressing the Colonel, he said, 'It is my sister, whom I should not have known again if she had not told me who she was. Colomba, Colonel Sir Thomas Nevill. Colonel, you will have the kindness to excuse me, but I cannot have the honour of dining with you to day. My sister—'

'Well, where the deuce do you mean to dine, my dear fellow? You know there is only one dinner in this wretched inn, and that is our dinner. Mademoiselle will greatly oblige my daughter by joining us.'

Colomba looked at her brother, who did not require much pressing, and they entered together the large room of the inn, which served the Colonel both for dining-room and drawing-room. Mademoiselle della Rebbia, presented to Miss Nevill, made a low curtsey, but did not say a word. It was easy to see that she was very wild, and that, perhaps, for the first time in her life she found herself in the presence of people of the world. Nevertheless, there was nothing provincial in her manners. Her very strangeness saved her from awkwardness. She pleased Miss Nevill on that very account; and, as there was no disposable chamber in the hotel, the Colonel and his suite having taken possession of every room, Miss Lydia carried her condescension, or her curiosity, so far as to offer to have a bed for Mademoiselle della Rebbia put up in her own proper chamber.

Colomba stammered a few words of acknowledgment, and hastened to follow Miss Nevill's maid, in order to bestow on her dress those little arrangements which are rendered necessary by a journey on horseback through sunshine and dust.

On returning to the saloon, she made a halt in front of the Colonel's guns, which the sportsmen had just placed in a corner apart. 'What beautiful arms,' she exclaimed. 'Are those yours, brother?'

'No, they are the Colonel's English guns. They are just as good as they are handsome.'

'I should be very glad,' said Colomba, 'if you had a gun like those.'

'There is certainly one amongst the three which belongs to della Rebbia,' exclaimed the Colonel. 'He knows so well how to use it. To-day he fired only fourteen shots, and brought down fourteen head of game.'

Immediately there began a contest of generosity, in which Orso was the vanquished party, to his sister's great satisfaction, as was easy to perceive from the expression of childlike joy which suddenly lighted up her countenance, hitherto so serious. 'Take the one you like best,' said the Colonel. Orso refused. 'Very well, mademoiselle your sister shall choose for you.' Colomba did not wait to be asked twice. She selected the plainest of the guns, but it was an excellent Manton with a large bore. 'This,' she said, 'ought to carry ball.'

Her brother was losing his way in a labyrinth of thankful expressions, when dinner appeared very apropos to help him out of it. Miss Lydia was delighted to observe that Colomba, who made some scruples about taking her place at table, and who only yielded at a look from her brother, made the sign of the cross, like a good Catholic, before she began to eat. 'Capital,' she said to herself; 'that's primitive;' and she awaited further interesting revelations from the young representative of the ancient manners of Corsica. As for Orso, he was evidently somewhat ill at ease, doubtless through the apprehension that his sister might say or do something which might betray village rusticity. But Colomba watched him incessantly, and regulated her own movements by his. Sometimes she looked at him fixedly with a strange expression of melancholy; and then, if Orso's eyes met hers, he was the first to withdraw his gaze, as if he wished to escape from a question which his sister put to him, and which he understood only too well. They spoke French, because the Colonel expressed himself very badly in Italian. Colomba understood French, and even pronounced tolerably well the few words which she was obliged to exchange with her hosts.

After dinner, the Colonel, who had remarked the sort of restraint which reigned between the brother and sister, inquired of Orso, with his usual frankness, whether he would not like to converse alone with Mademoiselle Colomba, offering in that case to step with his daughter into the next room; but Orso made haste to decline the proposition, saying that they would have plenty of time to talk at Pietranera, which was the name of the village where he would have to take up his residence.

The Colonel, therefore, took his accustomed place on the sofa, and Miss Nevill, after trying several subjects of conversation and despairing to get the fair Colomba to talk, begged Orso to read them a canto of Dante, her favourite poet. Orso selected the canto of the Inferno which contains the episode of Francesca da Rimini, and recited it, giving his best emphasis to those sublime verses, which express so well the danger of lovers reading love books in company. As he went on reading Colomba drew nearer to the table and raised her head, which she had kept bowed. Her dilated pupils shone with unwonted fire; she blushed and turned pale alternately, with convulsive shiftings on her chair. Admirable is the Italian organization! To relish poetry it has no need of a pedant to indicate its beauties.

When the reading was finished, 'How beautiful it is!' she exclaimed. ' Who wrote that, brother?'

Orso was a little disconcerted, and Miss Lydia replied with a smile, that it was a Florentine poet, who died several centuries ago.

' I will read Dante with you,' said Orso, ' when we are at Pietranera.'

'Brother, how fine it is!' repeated Colomba; and she repeated three or four stanzas which she had caught, at first in a low voice, afterwards, growing animated, she declaimed them aloud with more expression than her brother had employed in his recitation.

Miss Lydia, exceedingly astonished, said, ' You appear to be very fond of poetry. How I envy the pleasure which awaits you on reading Dante for the first time !'

' You see, Miss Nevill, what must be the power of Dante's verse to stir in this way a little female savage, who only knows her paternoster. But I am mistaken. Now I remember, Colomba is one of the craft. While a mere child she dabbled in versification, and my father wrote me word that she was the greatest *voceratrice* in Pietranera and for five miles round.

Colomba cast a look of entreaty at her brother. Miss Nevill had heard speak of the Corsican improvisatrices, and was dying to hear one, consequently she lost no time in begging Colomba to give her a specimen of her talents. At this Orso interposed, exceedingly annoyed at having so well recollected his sister's poetical propensities. It was in vain that he declared there was nothing more stupid than a Corsican *ballata*, protesting that to recite Corsican verses after those of Dante was betraying the weakness of his own country. He thereby merely excited Miss Nevill's curiosity to a higher pitch, and was obliged at last to say to his sister, ' Well, then, improvise us something, but let it be short.'

Colomba sighed, looked hard for a minute at the table-cloth, and then at the rafters of the ceiling ; at last, putting her hand before her eyes, like the birds which fancy they are not seen when they do not see themselves, she chanted, or rather declaimed with an unsteady voice, the following *serenata :—*

The Girl and the Ringdove.

'In the valley, far behind the mountains—the sun only shines there once a day—in the valley there stands a sombre house; the grass grows rank upon its threshold; its doors and its windows are always closed; from its roof no wreaths of smoke ascend. But at noon when the sunbeams play, a single window is then thrown open, and the orphan sits by her spinning-wheel; she spins and sings to cheer her work, a sad 'and cheerless song of ;woe. No other song responds to hers. But one day, a day of spring, a ringdove perched on a neighbouring tree, and heard the orphan's cheerless song. " Your tears," it said "are shared by me: a cruel hawk has slain my mate." " Ringdove, show me that cruel hawk; were he higher than the clouds of heaven soon will I bring him to the ground. But I, where shall I find my brother—my brother, now in a distant land?" " Say, poor girl, where your brother is, my wings shall waft me to his presence."'

'What a polite and obliging ringdove it was!' exclaimed Orso, embracing his sister with a degree of emotion in contrast with the tone of pleasantry which he affected.

'Your song is charming,' said Miss Lydia. 'You must write it for me in my album. I will translate it into English, and have it set to music.'

The brave Colonel, who had not understood a word joined his compliments to those of his daughter, adding, ' Is the ringdove which you mention, made-

moiselle, the same bird which we have eaten to-day
à la crapaudine ?'

Miss Nevill fetched her album, and was not a little
surprised at beholding the improvisatrice write her
song with a singular economy of paper. Instead of
standing separate the verses followed each other in
the same line as far as the breadth of the leaf would
admit, so that they refused to answer to the well-
known definition of poetical compositions : ' A collection of short lines, of unequal length, with a margin
on either side.' Certain observations might also
have been made on Mademoiselle Colomba's rather
capricious orthography, which more than once made
Miss Nevill smile and sadly tormented Orso's frater-
nal vanity.

The hour of bed-time having arrived, the two
young ladies retired to their chamber. There, whilst
Miss Lydia was unfastening necklace, buckles, and
bracelets, she watched her companion, who drew from
her robe something as long as a busk, but nevertheless of a very different shape. Colomba placed this
carefully, and almost stealthily, beneath her mezzaro,
that was laid on a table ; after which she knelt and
devoutly said her prayers. In two minutes she was in
bed. Naturally very inquisitive, and slow in un-
dressing, as all Englishwomen are, Miss Lydia went
up to the table, and, pretending to look for a pin, she
lifted the mezzaro and perceived a tolerably long
stiletto, curiously mounted in mother-of pearl and
silver. The workmanship was remarkable, and it
was an ancient weapon of great value for an amateur.

'Is it the custom here,' asked Miss Lydia, laughing, 'for young ladies to carry these little instruments in their corset?'

'It cannot be helped,' replied Colomba, with a sigh, 'there are so many wicked people.'

'Would you really have the courage to give such a stab as this?' And Miss Nevill, dagger in hand, performed the action of stabbing as they stab at the theatre, from above downwards.

'Yes, if it were necessary to do so,' said Colomba, in her soft and musical voice, 'in my own defence or that of my friends. But that is not the way you ought to hold it; you might wound yourself if the person whom you wanted to strike were to start suddenly back.' And sitting up in the bed, she added, 'Look, this is the way,' directing the blow upwards; 'so it is mortal, as I am told. Happy those who have no need of such weapons.'

She sighed, dropped her head on the pillow, and closed her eyes. A more lovely, noble, or virginal head, was no where to be seen. Phidias, to sculpture his Minerva, would not have desired a better model.

VI.

At the outset, I plunged *in medias res* into the midst of my story, in conformity with Horace's precept. But now that everybody is fast asleep—fair Colomba, the Colonel, and his daughter—I will take advantage of the moment to acquaint the reader with certain particulars of which he ought not to remain ignorant, if he feels inclined to continue the perusal of this veracious history. He is already aware that Colonel della Rebbia, Orso's father, met his death from the hand of an assassin. Now you are not assassinated in Corsica, as you are in France, by the first escaped convict from the galleys, who knows no better way of robbing you of your plate—you are assassinated by your enemies ; but the reason why you have enemies is very often difficult to state. Many families hate each other merely through inveterate habit, the tradition of the original cause of their hatred being lost past all recovery.

The family to which Colonel della Rebbia belonged hated several other families, but it hated to a singular degree the family of the Barricini. Some said that, in the sixteenth century, a male della Rebbia had seduced a female Barricini, and had afterwards been stabbed by a relation of the outraged damsel. It is true there was a different version of the story, to the effect that it was a female della Rebbia who had been seduced, and a male Barricini who was stabbed. At all events, to make use of a well-tried expression, there was blood between the two houses. Nevertheless, contrary to custom, this murder was not the parent of other murders ; because the della Rebbias and the Barricinis having been alike persecuted by the Genoese government, and the young people on either side having expatriated themselves, the two families were deprived, for several generations, of their energetic representatives. At the close of the last century, a della Rebbia, an

officer in the Neapolitan service, happened to quarrel
with some military men in a low gambling-house,
who, amongst other insults, called him a Corsican
goatherd. He drew his sword; but, as they were
three to one, he might have spent his time unplea-
santly, if a stranger, who was playing in the same
saloon, had not shouted, 'I am a Corsican as well!'
and come to his assistance. This stranger was a
Barricini, who, moreover, did not know his countryman. On coming to an explanation, there was great
politeness on either side, and vows of eternal friendship; for, on the Continent, the Corsicans quickly
make acquaintance, whilst it is exactly the contrary
upon their own island. This very circumstance
afforded an instance: della Rebbia and Barricini
were intimate friends as long as they remained in
Italy; but, after their return to Corsica, they very
rarely saw each other, although they both dwelt in
the same village; and, at their death, it was said
they had not spoken for the last five or six years.
Their sons in like manner lived 'in etiquette,' as
they say in the island. One, Ghilfuccio, Orso's
father, was a soldier; the other, Giudice Barricini,
was an advocate. Being both heads of families, and
separated by their respective professions, they scarcely
ever saw each other, or heard each other mentioned.

Nevertheless, on one occasion, about the year 1809,
Giudice, reading in a journal at Bastia that Captain
Ghilfuccio had been decorated with the Cross of the
Legion of Honour, said, before witnesses, that he
was not surprised at the circumstance, seeing that

General * * * patronised his family. This speech
was reported to Ghilfuccio at Vienna, who remarked
to a compatriot that on his return to Corsica he would
find Giudice very rich, because he earned more
money by the causes he lost than by those he gained.
It was never known whether he meant to insinuate
that the advocate betrayed and sold his clients, or
whether he merely stated the commonplace truth
that a bad case puts more into a lawyer's pocket than
a good case. However that may be, the advocate
Barricini was cognisant of the witticism, and did not
forget it. In 1812 he petitioned to be made mayor
of the commune, and had every reason to expect
success, when General * * * wrote to the Préfet
rcommending a gentleman who was nearly related to
Ghilfuccio's wife. The Préfet did his best to oblige
the General, and Barricini entertained no doubt that
his discomfiture was owing to Ghilfuccio's intrigues.
After the fall of the Emperor, in 1814, the General's
protégé was denounced as a Bonapartist, turned out,
and replaced by Barricini ; who in turn was dismissed during the Hundred Days : but, after that
tempest, he took possession with great pomp of the
mayor's official seal and the registers of the *Etat Civil*.

From that moment his star became more brilliant
than ever. Colonel della Rebbia, who had retired on
half-pay to Pietranera, had to sustain an underhand
war of incessant and never-ending chicanery. Sometimes he was sued for damages for injury committed
by his horse in the Mayor's enclosures ; sometimes
the Mayor, under pretence of mending the pavement

of the church, would carry off a broken slab that bore
the arms of the della Rebbias, and which covered
the grave of some member of that family. If the
Colonel's young plantations were devoured by goats,
the proprietors of those animals were screened and
protected by the Mayor. The grocer who kept the
Pietranera post-office, and the Garde Champêtre, a
sort of rural policeman, an old wounded soldier, both
clients of the della Rebbias, were successively dismissed and replaced by creatures of the Barricinis.

The Colonel's wife before her death expressed a
wish to be buried in the middle of a grove which had
been her favourite walk. The Mayor at once declared that she should be buried in the cemetery of
the commune, seeing that he had received no authorisation to allow of any isolated interment. The
Colonel, in a rage, declared that in the meantime, till
the authorisation came, his wife should be buried in
the spot she had chosen; and he caused a grave to
be dug there. The Mayor in turn had a grave dug
in the cemetery, and summoned the gendarmes, in
order, as he said, that the law might be enforced.
On the day of the funeral the two parties met, and
for a moment it appeared likely that a battle would
be fought to obtain possession of Madame della
Rebbia's remains. Some forty well-armed peasants,
headed by the deceased lady's relations, compelled
the Curé, on leaving the church, to direct his steps
towards the grove; on the other hand, the Mayor
with his two sons, his followers, and the gendarmes
opposed that movement. When he showed himself,

and summoned the funeral procession to turn back, he was received with hootings and threats ; the advantage of numbers was on the side of his adverries, and they seemed determined to make the most of it. As soon as they saw him, many of them cocked their guns: one shepherd went so far as to take aim at him ; but the Colonel raised the gun, saying, ' Let no one fire without orders from me !' The Mayor having, like Panurge, 'a natural fear of blows,' and declining the combat, retired with his escort. Then the funeral procession moved on, purposely taking the longest road, in order to pass in front of the town-hall. As they were defiling, an idiot who had joined the cortège, took it into his head to shout, ' Vive l'Empereur !' Two or three voices responded to him ; and the Rebbianists, growing more and more excited, proposed the slaughter of one of the Mayor's cattle which chanced to block the way. Happily the Colonel prevented that act of violence.

It is easy to conceive that a procès-verbal was drawn up, and that the Mayor addressed to the Préfet a report, written in his sublimest style, in which he painted laws human and divine trodden under foot— the majesty pertaining to himself, the Mayor, and that of the Curé, denied and insulted—Colonel della Rebbia putting himself at the head of a Bonapartist conspiracy to change the order of succession to the throne, and to excite the citizens to civil war, crimes whose punishment is provided for by Articles 86 and 91 of the Penal Code.

The exaggeration of this complaint destroyed its effect. The Colonel wrote to the Préfet and to the Attorney-general. One of his wife's relations was allied to one of the deputies for the island, another was cousin to the President of the Cour Royale. Thanks to their protection, the conspiracy vanished; Madame della Rebbia was left to repose in her grave, and the idiot alone was condemned to a fortnight's imprisonment.

The advocate Barricini, dissatisfied with the result of this affair, turned his batteries in another direction. He raked up an old title-deed, on the strength of which he determined to contest the Colonel's right of property in a certain water-course which turned a mill. A lawsuit began, which went on slowly. At the end of a twelvemonth the Court was on the point of pronouncing judgment, and according to all appearance in the Colonel's favour, when Barricini placed in the Attorney-general's hands a letter signed by a certain Agostini, a celebrated bandit, which threatened him, the Mayor, with fire and bullet if he did not desist from his pretensions. It is well known that in Corsica the protection of bandits is greatly sought after, and that, to oblige their friends, they often interfere in private quarrels. The Mayor 'made capital' of this letter, when a new incident happened to complicate the affair. The bandit Agostini wrote to the Attorney-general to complain that his hand-writing should be counterfeited and doubts thrown on his character by making him pass for a man who made a market of his influence. 'If I discover the forger,' he said, in conclusion, 'he shall suffer exemplary punishment.'

It was clear that Agostini had not written the threatening letter to the Mayor. The della Rebbias accused the Barricinis of having done it, and *vice versâ*. Both parties threatened loudly, and the authorities were unable to say which of the two was the guilty one.

While things were in this state, Colonel Ghilfuccio was assassinated. The facts, as they were proved in evidence, were these:—On the 2nd of August, 181—, towards nightfall, the woman Madeleine Pietri, who was carrying corn to Pietranera, heard two shots, one immediately after the other, that had been fired, as she thought, in a deep lane leading to the village, about a hundred and fifty paces from the spot where she was. Almost at the same time she saw a man running and stooping as he ran, along a path through the vineyards towards the village. This man halted for an instant and turned round, but he was too far off for the woman Pietri to distinguish his features, and moreover he had a vine-leaf in his mouth which concealed nearly the whole of his face. He made a signal with his hand to some companion whom the witness did not see, and then disappeared amongst the vines.

The woman Pietri, having deposited her burthen, ran up the lane, and found Colonel della Rebbia weltering in his blood, pierced with a couple of bullets, but still breathing. His gun was beside him, loaded and cocked, as if he had prepared to defend himself against some person who attacked him in front at the very moment when some one else fired at him behind. He rattled in his throat and struggled against death, but was unable to pronounce a word, which the doctors explained by the nature of his wounds which traversed the lungs. His blood was choking him; it flowed slowly in the shape of red froth. It was in vain that the woman Pietri raised him up and questioned him. She saw evidently that he wished to speak, but he could not make himself understood. Observing that he tried to put his hand into his pocket, she helped him to draw from it a small pocket-book, which she opened and gave him. The wounded man took the pencil belonging to the pocket-book, and tried to write. In fact, the witness saw him form several characters with considerable difficulty; but not being able to read, she could not understand their meaning. Exhausted by the effort, the Colonel left the pocket-book in the woman Pietri's hand, which he squeezed very hard, looking at her all the while with a singular expression, as if he wished to say (they are the words of the witness), ' This is important ; it is the murderer's name !'

The woman Pietri was proceeding to the village when she met Monsieur the Mayor Barricini with his son Vincentello. It was then almost dark. She told what she had seen. The Mayor took the pocket-book, and hastened to the Town Hall to gird on his official sash and to call his secretary and the gendarmes. Madeleine Pietri, when left alone with young Vincentello, proposed that they should go and assist the Colonel, in case he should be still surviving. But Vincentello replied, that if he went near a man who had been the bitter enemy of his family, people would accuse him of having caused his death. Shortly afterwards the Mayor arrived, found the Colonel dead, had the body removed, and drew up a procès-verbal.

In spite of his agitation, which was very natural on such an occasion, M. Barricini lost no time in securing the Colonel's pocket-book under the public seal, and in making every inquiry that lay in his power ; but no discovery of any importance was made. When the public prosecutor, the Juge d'Instruction, came, the pocket-book was opened, and on a page stained with blood they found several letters traced by an unsteady hand, but quite legible nevertheless. He had written *Agosti*—, and the Judge had no doubt that the Colonel intended to denounce Agostini as his murderer. Meanwhile Colomba della Rebbia, called upon by the Judge to give evidence, requested to examine the pocket-book. After searching through it for a considerable time, she stretched out her hand towards the Mayor, and cried, 'There is the murderer!' Then, with a degree of precision and clearness which were surprising in the transport of grief in which she was plunged, she stated that her father, having received a letter from his son a few days previously, had burnt it, but that before doing so he had written in pencil, in his pocket-book, Orso's address, which had just been changed from one garrison town to another. Now this address was no longer to be found in the pocketbook, and Colomba thence concluded that the Mayor had torn out the leaf on which it was written, and which must have been the very same on which her father had traced the assassin's name; and for this name, according to Colomba, the Mayor had substituted that of Agostini. The Judge saw, in fact, that a leaf was missing from the quire of paper on which the name was written; but he soon discovered that other leaves were also missing from other quires in the same pocket-book; and witnesses declared that the Colonel had the habit of thus tearing out the pages of his pocket-book when he wished to light a cigar; nothing, therefore, could be more likely than that he had himself burned the address which he had copied. Besides, it was proved that when the Mayor received the pocket-book from the woman Pietri it was too dark for him possibly to read it; that he had not halted an instant before entering the Town Hall; that the brigadier of the gendarmes had accompanied him, had seen him light a lamp, put the pocket-book in an envelope, and seal it in his presence.

When the Brigadier had ended his deposition, Colomba, in a transport of excitement, threw herself at his knees, and entreated him, by all that he held most sacred, to declare whether he had not left the Mayor alone for an instant. The Brigadier, after hesitating for a while, and visibly affected by this passionate appeal, avowed that he did go into an adjoining room to fetch a large sheet of paper, but that he did not stop there a minute, and that the Mayor never never ceased talking to him while he was searching for the paper in a drawer. Moreover, he affirmed, that on his return the bloody pocket-book was lying in the same place on the table where the Mayor had thrown it on entering.

M. Barricini gave his evidence with perfect calmness. He could excuse, he said, Mademoiselle della Rebbia's excitement, and would condescend to justify himself. He proved that he had remained in the village all that afternoon and evening; that his son, Vincentello was with him in front of the Town Hall at the moment when the crime was committed; finally that his son Orlanduccio, who had been attacked by fever that very day, had not left his bed. He produced all the guns in his house, and not one of them had been fired for some time past. He added that, with respect to the pocket-book, he immediately saw the importance that would be attached to it; that he had put it under seal immediately and had deposited it in the hands of the Deputy Mayor, foreseeing that, in consequence of his enmity with the Colonel, suspicion might fall upon himself. Lastly he reminded them that Agostini had threatened death to whosoever had written a letter in his name: and he insinuated that that wretched man, probably suspecting the Colonel, had murdered him. Such a revenge for a similar motive was not unexampled in the history of bandits.

Five days after Colonel della Rebbia's death, Agostini, surprised by a detachment of voltigeurs, was killed, fighting desperately. They found on him a letter from Colomba, adjuring him to declare whether or not he were guilty of the murder imputed to him.

The bandit having given no reply, it was generally concluded that he had not had the courage to tell a daughter that he had slain her father. Nevertheless, persons who pretended to be well acquainted with Agostini's character, whispered their belief that, if he had really killed the Colonel, he would have boasted of it. Another bandit, known by the name of Brandolaccio, got conveyed to Colomba a declaration in which he attested *upon his honour* his comrade's innocence; but the only proof which he alleged was that Agostini had never told him he suspected the Colonel.

Conclusion: the Barricini were left in quiet; the Juge d' Instruction passed a high eulogium on the Mayor, who gave the finishing touch to his handsome behaviour by withdrawing all further claims on the brook about which he had gone to law with Colonel della Rebbia.

Colomba improvised, according to the usage of the country, a *ballata* before her father's dead body, in presence of his assembled friends. She therein breathed forth all her hatred of the Barricini, and formally accused them of the murder, threatening them with her brother's vengeance. It was this *ballata*, which became very popular, that the sailor sang in Lydia's hearing. Orso, when informed of his father's death, was then in the north of France; he asked for leave of absence, but could not obtain it. At first, in consequence of a letter from his sister, he believed the Barricini to be guilty; but he soon received copies of all the depositions; and a private

letter from the Judge almost convinced him that the
bandit Agostini was alone the guilty party. Once every
three months Colomba wrote to him, reiterating her
suspicions, which she called proofs. In spite of himself these repeated accusations made his Corsican blood
boil, and sometimes he was very near participating in
his sister's prejudices. Nevertheless, every time he
wrote to her he insisted that her allegations rested
on no solid foundation, and were unworthy of credence.
He even forbade her, but in vain, to make further
mention of the subject. Two years passed in this way,
at the end of which he was put on half-pay ; he then
thought of revisiting his native land, not to be avenged
on people whom he believed innocent, but to find a
husband for his sister, and to sell his little property,
if it should prove sufficiently valuable to allow him to
live on the Continent.

VII.

Whether the arrival of his sister reminded Orso
more forcibly of his paternal roof, or whether the
presence of his civilized friends made him blush for
Colomba's costume and insular manners, he next day
announced his intention of leaving Ajaccio and returning to Pietranera. Nevertheless he made the
Colonel promise to come and stay in his humble
mansion when he went to Bastia, and in return he
engaged to procure him excellent sport with deer,
pheasants, wild boar, and the rest.

The day before his departure, instead of going out
shooting, Orso proposed a walk along the shores of

the gulf.   Offering his arm to Miss Lydia, they were able to converse at liberty; for Colomba remained in town to complete her purchases, and the Colonel left them every now and then to fire at terns and gulls, to the great surprise of the passers by, who could not comprehend why powder should be wasted on such ignoble game.

They followed the path which leads to the Greek chapel, from whence you have the finest view of the bay; but they paid no attention to it.

' Miss Lydia,' said Orso, after a silence which was long enough to become embarrassing ; ' frankly, what do you think of my sister ?'

' I like her very much,' replied Miss Nevill. ' Much better than I like you,' she added, smiling, ' for she is really Corsican, whilst you are a savage spoiled by civilization.'

' A savage spoiled!   Well—and I cannot help it— I feel that I have become again a savage, ever since I have set foot on the island.   I am agitated and tormented by a thousand frightful thoughts, and I had need have a little conversation with you before I take my final plunge into the wilderness.'

' You must take courage, monsieur ; notice your sister's resignation ; she sets you the example.'

' Ah, undeceive yourself!   Put no faith in her resignation.   She has not yet spoken a single word, but in her every look I can read what she expects of me.'

' And what can she expect ?'

' Oh ! nothing—Only she would like me to try if

your father's gun is as effectual with human game as
it is with partridges.'

'What an idea! How can you imagine that? You
have just confessed that she has not yet breathed a syllable of the kind. It is frightful conduct on your part.'

'If she thought no more of vengeance, she would
at once have talked to me about our father: she has
not done so. She would have mentioned the names
of those whom she regards—I know unjustly—as his
murderers. Well! Not a word. The reason is, you
see, that we Corsicans are a crafty race. My sister
understands that she does not completely hold me in
her power, and does not choose to alarm me while I
am still able to make my escape. When once she
has led me to the edge of the precipice, and my head
turns giddy, she will then push me into the abyss.'
Orso then related to Miss Nevill a few details respecting his father's death, and summed up the principal proofs which, to his mind, combined to fix the
guilt on Agostini. 'Nothing,' he added, 'could convince Columba. I saw it by her last letter. She
has sworn the death of the Barricini; and—Miss
Nevill, you see what confidence I place in you—perhaps they would no longer belong to this world, if,
by one of those prejudices which are excused by her
savage education, she had not persuaded herself that
the execution of the vengeance belongs to me officially,
as the head of the family, and that my honour is
therein implicated.'

'Really, Monsieur della Rebbia,' said Miss Nevill,
'you calumniate your sister.'

'No ; they are your own words—she is Corsican ; she thinks exactly as everybody here thinks. Do you know why I was so out of spirits yesterday?'

'No ; but for some time past you have been subject to fits of melancholy. You were more amiable at the beginning of our acquaintance.'

'Yesterday, on the contrary, I was more gay, more cheerful than ordinary. You were so kind, so indulgent towards my sister ! We were coming back, the Colonel and myself, in a boat. Can you guess what one of the boatmen said in his wretched patois ?— " You have killed plenty of game, Ors' Anton,' but you will find Orlanduccio Barricini a better sportsman than you are." '

'Well ! what is there so very terrible in that ? Are your pretensions to sportsmanship so incomparably higher than everybody else's ?'

'But don't you see that the wretch meant to insinuate that I had not the courage to kill Orlanduccio ?'

'Do you know, Monsieur della Rebbia, you make me shudder. It seems that the air of your island not only gives people the fever, but drives them mad. Fortunately, we shall shortly take our departure.'

'Not before you have been to Pietranera? My sister has your promise.'

'And if we fail to keep our promise, we may doubtless expect the weight of your vengeance.'

'You remember what your father told us the other day about the Indians, who threatened the governors of the Company to starve themselves to death if their requests were not complied with?'

'That is to say, you would starve yourself to death? I doubt it. You would remain one day without eating; and then Mademoiselle Colomba would bring you a *bruccio*,* so tempting as to make you renounce your project.'

'Your railleries are cruel, Miss Nevill. You ought to treat me with more consideration. You see that here I am quite alone in the world. I have only you to prevent me from going mad, as you say; you are my guardian-angel; and now—'

'Now,' said Miss Lydia, seriously, 'you have, to sustain your tottering reason,—your honour as a soldier and a gentleman, and,' she added, turning on one side to gather a flower, 'if that can be of any use to you—the remembrance of your guardian angel.'

'Ah! Miss Nevill, if I could only think that you really take any interest—'

'Listen, Monsieur della Rebbia,' said Miss Nevill, with slight emotion, 'since you are a child, I will treat you like a child. When I was a little girl, my mother gave me a handsome necklace which I ardently desired; but she said, "every time you put on the necklace, remember that you don't yet know French." The necklace lost a little of its merit in my eyes. It was converted into a sort of remorse:— but I wore it, and I learnt French. You see this ring. It is an Egyptian scarabæus, found, with your

---

* A sort of cheese made of clotted cream; a national Corsican dish.

leave, in a pyramid. This curious figure, which you might take perhaps for a bottle, means *human life.* There are people in my country who would consider the hieroglyphic very appropriate. This, which follows it, is a shield with an arm holding a spear, and means *combat, battle.* The two characters, therefore, put together, form the device, which I think not bad, *Life is a battle.* Do not suppose that I am able to read hieroglyphics fluently; the explanation was given me by a most learned linguist. Here then, I present you with my scarabæus. When you feel any bad Corsican thought arise, look at my talisman, and say to yourself that you must come off victorious from the battle which we have to wage with our evil passions. Really, I think I don't preach badly.'

'I will think of you, Miss Nevill, and will say to myself—'

'Say to yourself that you have a friend who would be exceedingly sorry—to—hear that you were hung; which would also give considerable pain to the *Caporali,* your ancestors.' With these words, she left Orso's arm, laughing and calling to her father, 'Papa, let those poor birds be at peace, and come with us to make a little poetry in Napoleon's grotto.'

VIII.

There is always something solemn in a departure, even when people separate only for a short absence. Orso was to start with his sister very early in the morning, and took leave of Miss Lydia the previous evening ; for he did not expect that she would make

any change in her usual habits in his favour. Their
adieux were cold and formal. Ever since their conversation on the beach, Miss Lydia feared that she
had perhaps displayed too lively an interest in Orso's
welfare; and Orso, on his part, was vexed at her
railleries and her tone of levity. At one moment, he
thought he could trace a sentiment of nascent affection in the young Englishwoman's manners; now,
disconcerted by her pleasantries, he said to himself
that he was no more than a simple acquaintance in
her eyes, who would soon be forgotten. Great, therefore, was his surprise next morning when, as he sat
taking his coffee with the Colonel, Lydia entered,
followed by his sister. She had risen at five; and,
for an Englishwoman—for Miss Nevill especially
—the effort was great enough to afford a little grati-
fication to his vanity.

'I am sorry you disturbed yourself so early,' said
Orso. 'No doubt my sister woke you up, in spite of
my recommendations to the contrary, and you have a
right to be angry with us. Perhaps you wish me
hanged already?'

'No,' said Miss Lydia, very low and in Italian,
evidently that her father might not hear. 'But you
were cross with me yesterday for my innocent jokes,
and I should not wish you to carry away an unfavourable recollection of your humble servant. What
terrible folks you are, you Corsicans! Adieu, then;
we shall soon meet again, I hope.' And she offered
her hand.

Orso could only answer with a sigh. Colomba

F 2

stepped up to him, led him to the embrasure of a window, and showing him something which she held concealed beneath her mezzaro, addressed him in a low tone of voice.

'My sister,' Orso said to Miss Nevill, 'wishes to offer you a singular present; but we Corsicans have no great things to give—except our affection—which is not effaced by lapse of time. My sister tells me that you have inspected this stiletto with curiosity. It is a family antique. In all probability, it was once suspended from the girdle of one of those Caporali to whom I owe the honour of your acquaintance. Colomba believes it so valuable, that she has asked my permission to give it to you; and I hardly know whether I ought to allow it, because I fear that you will laugh at us.'

'The stiletto is charming,' replied Miss Lydia; 'but it is a family weapon, and I cannot accept it.'

'It is not my father's stiletto,' exclaimed Colomba, earnestly. 'It was given by King Theodore to one of my mother's ancestors. If mademoiselle will accept it, she will oblige us greatly.'

'Pray, Miss Lydia,' said Orso, 'do not disdain the stiletto of a king.'

For a curiosity-collector, King Theodore's relics are far more precious than those of the most powerful living monarch. The temptation was great, and Miss Neville already foresaw the effect this weapon would produce lying on a lac table in St. James's Square. 'But,' she said, taking the stiletto with the hesitation of a person who wishes to accept, and

directing one of her most amiable smiles to Colomba,
'dear Mademoiselle Colomba—I cannot—I dare not
allow you to depart thus disarmed.'

'My brother is with me,' said Colomba, proudly;
'and we have the good gun which your father gave
us. Orso, have you loaded it with ball?'

Miss Nevill kept the stiletto; and Colomba, to avert
the danger incurred by *giving* any cutting or piercing
instrument to one's friends, exacted a sou in payment
for it.

They were obliged to take their departure at last.
Orso once more pressed Miss Nevill's hand; Colomba
embraced her, and then offered her rosy lips to the
Colonel, who was quite astonished at Corsican politeness. From the window of the saloon, Miss Lydia
saw the brother and sister mount on horseback. Colomba's eyes sparkled with a malignant joy which she
had never observed before. This tall and powerful
young woman, fanatically devoted to her notions of
savage honour, with her proud forehead, and her lips
curved by a sardonic smile, leading away her brother
ready armed as if for some sinister expedition, recalled
all Orso's apprehensions; she seemed to be his evil
genius dragging him to his ruin. Orso, already on
horseback, raised his head, and saw Miss Nevill.
Whether he had guessed her thoughts, or whether to
bid a final adieu, he took the Egyptian ring, which
he had suspended by a silken cord, and raised it to
his lips. Miss Lydia retired from the window,
blushing; but returning almost immediately, she
beheld the two Corsicans rapidly galloping away on

their little ponies, in the direction of the mountains. Half an hour afterwards, the Colonel showed them to her through his telescope, skirting the further end of the gulf; and she noticed that Orso frequently turned his head in the direction of the town. He finally disappeared behind the marshes, which are now replaced by a flourishing nursery-ground.

Miss Lydia, looking in the glass, remarked that she was very pale.

'What must this young man think of me?' she said; 'and I, what do I think of him?—and why do I think of him?—a travelling acquaintance! What was my object in coming to Corsica? Oh, I do not love him! No, no; besides that is quite impossible. And Colomba. Me the sister-in-law of a voceratrice, who wears a long stiletto!' And she perceived that she had clutched King Thedore's stiletto in her hand. She threw it on her dressing-table. 'Colomba at London, dancing at Almack's! What a lion to produce! Very likely she would become the rage! He loves me, I am certain of it. He is a hero of romance, whose adventurous career I have interrupted. But had he any real intention of avenging his father in the Corsican style? He was something between a Conrad and a dandy. I have made a pure dandy of him, a dandy with a Corsican tailor.'

She threw herself on her bed and tried to sleep, but that was impossible; and I shall make no attempt to continue her monologue, in which she repeated a hundred times that M. della Rebbia never was, was not, and never would be, anything to her.

IX.

Meanwhile Orso rode on with his sister. The rapid pace at which they travelled prevented their conversing at first; but when the steep hills obliged their horses to walk, they exchanged a few words touching the friends whom they had just left. Colomba was enthusiastic in her praises of Miss Nevill's beauty, her fair hair, and her graceful manners. Then she inquired whether the Colonel were as rich as he appeared to be, and whether Mademoiselle Lydia were an only child. 'It would be an excellent match,' she said. 'Her father seems to be very friendly disposed towards you—' And as Orso made no reply, she continued, 'Our family was rich in former times, and is still one of the highest consideration in the island. All these *Signori* * are nothing. There is no noblesse except in the *Caporali* families; and you know, Orso, that you are descended from the first *Caporali* of the island. You know that our family originated beyond the mountains,† and that the civil wars obliged us to cross over to this side. If I were in your place, Orso, I should not hesitate, I would demand Miss Nevill's hand of her father. [Orso shrugged his shoulders.] With her portion I would buy the wood of La Falsetta

* The descendants of the feudal seigneurs of Corsica are called *Signori*. There is a rivalry of nobility between the families of the *Signori* and those of the *Caporali*.

† That is to say, on the eastern side. The very common expression, *di la dei monti*, changes its meaning according to the position of the person who employs it. Corsica is divided by a chain of mountains running from north to south.

and the vineyards below our house. I would build a handsome mansion of hewn stone, and I would add another storey to the old tower where Sambucuccio killed such a number of Moors in the time of Count Henri the *bel Missere*.'*

'Colomba, you are crazy,' replied Orso, putting his horse to a gallop.

'You are a man, Ors' Anton', and you doubtless understand what to do better than a woman can. But I should like to know what objection this Englishman can make to our alliance. Are there any Caporali in England?'

After a tolerably long stage, and chatting in this way, the brother and sister reached a little village, not far from Bocognano, where they halted to dine and pass the night at the house of a friend of their family. They were received with that Corsican hospitality which must be known to be appreciated. Next day their host, who had been *Compère* * with Madame della Rebbia, accompanied them till they were within a league of their residence.

'Observe these woods and these *máquis*,' he said to Orso, when they were about to separate. 'A man

---

* See Filippini, lib. ii.—The Count *Arrigo bel Missere* died about the year 1000; it is said that at his death a voice was heard in the air, which chanted these prophetic words:—

"E morto il Conte Arrigo bel Missere :

E Corsica sarà di male in peggio.

† *Compère and commère*, the two parties who act together as godfather and godmother to the same infant, which implies, or leads to, greater intimacy in Roman Catholic than in Protestant countries.—Tr.

who has *had a misfortune* might live there ten years in peace without the gendarmes or the voltigeurs coming to look after him. This wood joins the forest of Vizzavona, and when one has friends at Bocognano or the neighbourhood, one need want for nothing. You have a handsome gun there, it ought to carry far. By the Madonna! what a calibre! You can kill with that something better than wild boar.'

Orso coldly replied that his gun was English, and that it carried *shot* to a considerable distance. The friends embraced, and each went his way.

Our travellers were already within a short distance of Pietranera, when, at the entrance of a gorge they would have to traverse, they discovered seven or eight men armed with muskets, some sitting on stones, some lying on the grass, and others standing upright, apparently on the look out. Their horses were grazing a little way off. Colomba examined them for a moment with a spyglass, which she drew out of one of those large leather pockets which every Corsican wears when out on a journey.

'They are our people,' she joyfully exclaimed. 'Pieruccio has done his errand well.'

'What people?' inquired Orso.

'Our shepherds,' she replied. 'The day before yesterday I sent off Pieruccio in the evening, in order to summon these brave fellows to conduct you to your residence. It is not proper that you should make your entry into Pietranera without an escort, and you must besides be aware that the Barricini are capable of anything.'

'Colomba,' said Orso severely, 'I have often requested you never to mention either the Barricini nor your unfounded suspicions. I shall certainly not expose myself to the ridicule of returning home in company with this gang of idle vagabonds, and I am very dissatisfied that you assembled them without consulting me.'

'Brother, you have forgotten your native land. It is my business to prevent you from exposing yourself imprudently. It was my duty to do what I have done.'

At that moment the shepherds perceiving them, seized their horses and rushed to meet them at full gallop.

'Long live Ors' Anton'!' shouted a robust old man with a white beard, covered, in spite of the heat, with a hooded greatcoat of Corsican cloth thicker than the fleece of one of his goats. 'He is the very picture of his father, only taller and stronger. What a beautiful gun! There will be talk about that gun, Ors' Anton'.'

'Long live Ors' Anton',' repeated all the shepherds, in chorus. 'We knew that he would come back again at last.'

'Ah! Ors' Anton',' said a tall fellow, with a brick-red complexion, 'how overjoyed your father would be, if he were only here to receive you! Poor dear man! You might have seen him if he had believed what I told him—if he had allowed me to settle Giudice's business. Poor man! He wouldn't believe me. He knows now that I was right.'

'Good,' resumed the old man; 'Giudice will lose nothing by waiting.'

'Long live Ors' Anton'!' And a dozen gunshots accompanied this acclamation.

Orso, very much out of humour, in the middle of this group of men on horseback, all talking at once, and crowding round him to take his hand, was some time before he could make himself heard. Finally, assuming the look which he put on at the head of his platoon when he distributed reprimands and days of imprisonment. 'My friends,' he said, 'I thank you for the affection which you manifest towards myself, and which you bore to my father; but I expect, and I insist, that no one presumes to give me advice. I know my own business.'

'He is right! He is right!' shouted the shepherds. 'You well know you can reckon upon us.'

'Yes, I reckon upon you; but I have no need of any one now; my house is in no danger of being attacked. Please to wheel right-about-face, and be off to your goats. I know the way to Pietranera, and don't want any one to show it me.'

'Fear nothing, Ors' Anton',' said the old man; '*they* dare not show themselves to-day. The mouse creeps into its hole when the tom-cat comes back.'

'Tom-cat yourself, old greybeard,' said Orso. 'What is your name?'

'What! you don't know me, Ors' Anton', me who have so often let you ride behind me on my vicious mule. Don't you know Polo Griffo? A brave fellow, look you, who belongs to the della Rebbias body and soul. Only say the word, and when your great gun begins to speak, this old musket, as old as its master, will not hold its tongue. Reckon upon that, Ors' Anton'.'

'Well, well! take yourselves off and let us proceed on our journey.'

The shepherds at last withdrew, trotting off towards the village; but they halted from time to time on all the elevated points of the road, as if to make sure that there was no secret ambuscade, and always keeping sufficiently close to Orso and his sister to be able to protect them in case of need. Old Polo Griffo said to his companions, 'I understand, I understand! He does not say what he means to do, but he does it. He is the very picture of his father. Good, that! You bear no malice against any one! You have made a vow to Saint Nega.* Bravo! I wouldn't give a fig for the Mayor's skin. Before a month is out it won't even serve for a leather bottle.'

Preceded by this troop of harbingers, the descendant of the della Rebbias reached his village, and arrived at the old mansion of the Caporali, his ancestors. The Rebbianists, so long deprived of their chief, came in a body to meet him, and the inhabitants of the village, who observed neutrality, were all on their doorsteps to see him pass. The Barricinists kept within doors, and peeped through the cracks in their window shutters.

---

* Which may be Englished as Saint Negative or Saint Denial, a saint not found in the calendar. To make a vow to Saint Nega is to deny everything through thick and thin.

The bourg or market-town of Pietranera is very irregularly built, like all the villages in Corsica; for, in order to find a street you must go to Cargese, built by M. de Marbœuf. The houses, dispersed at hazard, and without the slightest attempt to form a straight line, occupy the summit of a small piece of table-land, or rather a shelf on the mountain-side. Near the middle of the town stands a tall evergreen oak, and close to it is a granite cistern into which a wooden tube conveys the water from a neighbouring spring. This monument of public utility was constructed at the common expense of the della Rebbias and the Barricinis; but you would be greatly mistaken if you took it for an indication of the former concord of the two families. On the contrary, it is the work of their jealousy. Colonel della Rebbia having sent a small sum to the Town Council as his contribution towards a fountain, the Advocate Barricini lost no time in offering a similar donation, and to this contest of generosity Pietranera owes its supply of water. Around the evergreen oak and the fountain is an open space which is called the Piazza, and where leisure folk assemble in the evening. Sometimes they play cards there, and once a year, at the carnival, they dance. At each end of the Piazza there rises a building, taller than it is broad, of granite and schist. These are the hostile *towers* of the della Rebbias and the Barricinis. Their architecture is uniform, their height is the same, and you observe that the rivalry of the two families always continued without coming to any decisive conclusion.

It will, perhaps, be right to explain what is to be understood by the word *tower*. It is a square building, about forty feet high, which in any other country would simply be styled a dovecote. The narrow door, eight feet above the level of the ground, is reached by a very steep staircase. Over the door is a window with a sort of balcony with openings in its floor, like a mâchecoulis, which allow you without the slightest risk to knock any indiscreet visitor on the head. Between the window and the door are two shields rudely sculptured; one formerly bore the Genoese Cross, but, battered all over at the present day, it is only intelligible to antiquaries. On the other shield are engraved the arms of the family, the proprietor of the tower. Add, to complete the decoration, several marks of bullets on the shields and the window-jambs, and you will have some idea of a Corsican mansion of the middle ages. I forgot to mention that the buildings inhabited by the family are contiguous to the tower, and are often connected with it by an interior communication.

The tower and the mansion of the della Rebbias occupy the north side of the Piazza of Pietranera, the tower and the mansion of the Barricinis the south side. From the north tower, as far as the fountain, is the della Rebbias' walk. The Barricinis' is on the opposite side. Ever since the funeral of the Colonel's wife, no member of either family has been seen to show himself on the Piazza, except on the side assigned to him by a sort of tacit convention. In order to avoid a roundabout course, Orso was going to pass in front of the Mayor's house, when his sister warned him, and urged him to take a lane which would lead them to their own house without traversing the Piazza.

'Why should we put ourselves out of our way?' said Orso. 'Does not the Piazza belong to everybody?' And he urged on his horse.

'A brave heart,' whispered Colomba to herself. 'Father you will be avenged!'

On arriving at the Piazza, Colomba placed herself between her brother and the Barricinis' mansion, and kept her eyes constantly fixed on the enemy's windows. She remarked that they had been lately barricaded, and that *archere* had been pierced. They call *archere* certain narrow loopholes left open between large blocks of wood with which the lower part of a window is filled up. When an attack is apprehended they barricade themselves in this way, and are thus able, under the shelter of the faggots, to fire in safety upon their assailants.

'The cowards,' said Colomba; 'look, brother, they are already upon their guard; they have barricaded themselves; but they must leave the house some day or another.'

Orso's presence on the south side of the Piazza produced a great sensation in Pietranera, and was considered as a proof of audacity bordering on rashness. For the neutral parties who met in the evening under the evergreen oak, it was the text of endless commentaries. 'It is lucky,' they said, 'that Barricini's sons are not yet come home, for they are

not so patient as the advocate; and perhaps they
would not have allowed their enemy to pass over
their ground without paying for his bravado. Remember what I say, neighbour,' added an old man,
who was the oracle of the place—'I noticed La
Colomba's countenance to day, she has something in
her head. I smell powder in the air; before long,
butcher's meat will be cheap in Pietranera.'

X.

Sent from home in early youth, Orso had scarcely
the time to know his father. At the age of fifteen
he had left Pietranera to pursue his studies at Pisa,
after which he entered the Ecole Militaire, whilst
Ghilfuccio was parading the imperial eagles all over
Europe. On the Continent Orso saw him only at
rare intervals, and it was not till 1815 that he joined
the regiment which his father commanded. But the
Colonel, inflexible in respect to discipline, treated
his son, as he did all the other young lieutenants,
with great severity. Orso's recollections of his
father were of two kinds. He remembered him at
Pietranera, allowing him to carry his sabre, and to
fire off his gun when he returned from the chase, or
ordering him as a child to take his seat for the first
time at the family table. Then his memory presented him with the Colonel della Rebbia, who put
him under arrest for some heedless act, and never
addressed him otherwise than as Lieutenant della
Rebbia. 'Lieutenant della Rebbia, you are not in
your proper place of battle array—three days' arrest.

Your sharpshooters are six yards too far from the reserve—five days' arrest. You are wearing your foraging cap at five minutes past noon—eight days' arrest.' On one single occasion, at Quatre Bras, he said to him, 'Very well, Orso; but prudence, if you please.' Besides, these last recollections were in no way connected with Pietranera. The sight of the spots familiar to his childhood, the furniture which had been used by his mother, whom he tenderly loved, excited in his heart a crowd of sweet and painful emotions; and then, the sombre future which awaited him, the vague uneasiness with which his sister inspired him, and above all, Miss Nevill's expected visit to his house, which now appeared to him so small, so poor, so unfitted to receive a person accustomed to luxurious habits—the contempt with which it might perhaps inspire her. All these thoughts formed a chaos in his head, and depressed him with deep discouragement.

At supper he took his seat in a large oak arm-chair, black with age, in which his father used to preside over the family repasts, and he smiled on observing that Colomba hesitated to take her place at table with him. He was very thankful for the silence which she observed during supper, and for her speedy retirement afterwards, for he felt himself too much affected to offer any resistance to the attacks whih she was doubtless preparing; but Colomba husbanded her influence, and wished to give him time to come to himself. With his head resting in his hand he sat motionless, recalling in imagination the scenes of the last fortnight of his life. He was terrified at the expectations which everybody seemed to entertain with regard to his conduct towards the Barricini. He already felt that the opinion of Pietranera began to be, for him, the opinion of the world. He must execute vengeance, under pain of passing for a coward. But vengeance on whom? He could not believe the Barricini guilty of murder. Certainly they were the enemies of his family; but it required the coarse prejudices of his countrymen to accuse them of assassination. Sometimes he gazed at Miss Nevill's talisman, repeating low the device, 'Life is a battle.' At last he firmly said to himself, 'I will come off victorious.' With this good thought he rose, and, taking the lamp, was about to mount to his chamber when some one knocked at the house-door. The hour was unusual for receiving a visit. Colomba immediately made her appearance, followed by the woman who waited on them. 'It is nothing,' she said, running to the door. Nevertheless, before opening, she inquired who was there. A soft voice answered, 'It is I.' Instantly the wooden bar placed across the door was raised, and Colomba reappeared in the dining-room, followed by a little girl scarcely ten years of age, barefoot, in rags, with her head covered with an old handkerchief, from beneath which streamed long locks of hair as black as the raven's wing. The child was thin, pale, and sunburnt; but her eyes sparkled with the fire of intelligence. On beholding Orso she timidly stopped short and made him a rustic reverence. She then spoke to Colomba in an undertone, and placed in her hands a fresh-killed pheasant.

'Thank you, Chili,'* said Colomba; 'thank your uncle. Is he quite well?'

'Quite well, mademoiselle, at your service. I could not come sooner, because he was very late. I waited three hours for him in the mâquis.'

'And you have had no supper?

'No, indeed, mademoiselle; I had not the time.'

'You shall have some. Has your uncle still any bread?'

'A little, mademoiselle; but he is most in want of powder.'

'I will give you a loaf for him and some powder. Tell him to use it sparingly, for it is very dear.'

'Colomba,' said Orso, in French, 'who is the object of your charity?'

'A poor bandit belonging to the village,' replied Colomba, in the same language. 'This little girl is his niece.'

'It seems to me that you might bestow your gifts better. Why should you send gunpowder to a rascal who will make use of it to commit some crime or other? If it were not for this deplorable weakness which everybody here seems to have for bandits, they would long have disappeared from Corsica.'

'The worst people in the island are not those who are out in the country.'†

* Pronounced *Keelee*, short for Chilina, which is short for Michelina.—TR.

† To be *alla campagna* is to be a bandit. Bandit is not a

G 2

'Give them bread if you like, we ought not to refuse it to any one; but I do not approve of your supplying them with ammunition.'

'Brother,' said Colomba, gravely, 'you are master here, and everything in the house belongs to you; but, I give you warning, I will hand my mezzaro to this little girl to sell rather than refuse powder to a bandit. Refuse him powder! you might as well deliver him to the gendarmes at once. What is to protect him from them, except his cartridges?'

The little girl meanwhile greedily devoured a morsel of bread, and gazed attentively at Colomba and her brother by turns, trying to discover by their looks the meaning of what they were saying.

'And what has your bandit done? For what crime did he take to the mâquis?'

'Brandolaccio has committed no crime at all,' exclaimed Colomba. 'He killed Giovan Opizzo, who had assassinated his father whilst he was serving in the army.'

Orso turned his head aside, took the lamp, and went to his room without reply. Colomba then gave powder and provisions to the child, and accompanied her to the door, repeating, 'Above all, tell your uncle to keep strict watch over Orso.'

XI.

It was late before Orso could go to sleep, consequently he awoke very late in the morning, at least

---

term of odium; it is received in the sense of banished—it is the *outlaw* of the English ballads.

for a Corsican. He was scarcely out of bed, when the first object which met his view was the mansion of his enemies, and the *archere* which they had lately made. He went downstairs and inquired for his sister. 'She is in the kitchen casting bullets,' replied the servant Saveria. Thus, he could not set a step without being pursued by the image of war.

He found Colomba sitting on a camp-stool, surrounded by fresh-cast bullets, and in the act of cutting off their tails.

'Colomba, what are you about there?' asked her brother.

'You had no bullets which would fit the Colonel's gun,' she answered in her sweet and gentle voice. 'I have found a mould which suits the size of your barrel, and you shall have a couple of dozen cartridges this very day, brother.'

'I am in no want of them.'

'You ought not to be caught unprovided, Ors' Anton'. You have forgotten your country and the people by whom you are surrounded.'

'If I were to forget, you would soon refresh my memory. But tell me, did not a large trunk arrive a few days since?'

'Yes, brother. Shall I take it up to your room?'

'You take it! Why you have not the strength to lift it. Is there no man here to do it?'

'I am not so weak as you think,' said Colomba, tucking up her sleeves and displaying a white round arm of perfect shape, but announcing uncommon strength. 'Come, Saveria,' she said to the servant, 'give me a helping hand.' She had already raised the heavy trunk by herself, when Orso hastened to her assistance.

'In this trunk, my dear Colomba,' he said, 'there is something for you. You will excuse the trifling value of the present, for a half-pay lieutenant's purse is never very heavily lined.' So saying, he opened the trunk and took out several dresses, a shawl, and other articles suitable for a young lady's use.

'What beautiful things,' exclaimed Colomba. 'I will lock them up directly, for fear they should get spoiled. I will keep them for my wedding,' she added, with a melancholy smile, 'for I am in mourning now;' and she kissed her brother's hand.

'It is very like affectation, sister, to wear mourning for such a length of time.'

'I have made a vow to do it,' said Colomba, firmly. 'I will not put off mourning till—.' She looked through the window at the Barricini's mansion.

'Till your wedding day,' said Orso, trying to avoid the conclusion of the sentence.

'The man whom I marry,' said Colomba, 'must do three things.' She constantly regarded the house of the enemy with sinister looks.

'Handsome as you are, Colomba, I am surprised that you are not already married. Come, tell me who pays court to you. At any rate, I shall have plenty of serenades to listen to. They ought to be something out of the common way to please a great *voceratrice* like you.'

'Who would have a poor orphan like me? And

besides, the man who makes me go out of mourning, must put the women there into mourning.'

'This is madness,' said Orso to himself; but he made no reply, to avoid any kind of discussion.

'Brother,' said Colomba, coaxingly, 'I have also something to offer you. The clothes you are wearing are much too good for this place. Your handsome frock-coat would be torn to tatters in a couple of days if you went with it into the mâquis. You had better reserve it for Miss Nevill's arrival.' And then, opening a closet, she produced a shooting-dress complete. 'I have made you a velvet coat; and here is a cap like those worn by our *élégants;* I embroidered it for you a long while ago. Will you try it on?'

She made him fit on a large vest of green velvet, having an enormous hind-pocket. She put on his head a pointed black velvet cap, embroidered with jet, and silk of the same colour, and finished off with a sort of crest.

'Here is our father's cartridge-box;* his stiletto is in the pocket of the vest; I will go and fetch the pistol.'

'I look like a regular stage brigand of the Ambigu Comique,' said Orso, looking at himself in a small mirror which Saveria presented.

'That is to say, you look exceedingly well, Ors' Anton,' said the old servant. 'The finest *Pinsuto* †

---

* *Carchera*, the girdle to put cartridges in. A pistol is hung to the left of it.

† Any young man who wears the pointed cap, *barretta pinsuta*.

of Bocognano or Bastelica is not more bravely clad and accoutred!'

Orso breakfasted in his new costume, and during the repast he told his sister that his trunk contained a certain number of books; that his intention was to procure others from France and Italy, and to make her study closely. 'For it is not creditable, Colomba,' he added, 'that a tall young woman like you should still be ignorant of things which, on the Continent, children are taught in the nursery.

'You are right, brother,' said Colomba; 'I am aware of my deficiencies, and there is nothing I should like better than to improve my education, especially if you will kindly give me lessons.'

Several days passed without Colomba's pronouncing the name of the Barricini. She was continually paying little attentions to her brother, and often spoke of Miss Nevill. Orso made her read both French and Italian authors; and he was surprised sometimes at the justice and the good sense of her observations, and sometimes at her profound ignorance of the most common things.

One morning, after breakfast, Colomba left the room for an instant, and, instead of returning with books and paper, she appeared with her mezzaro on her head. Her manner was still more serious than usual. 'Brother,' she said, 'I have to ask you to go out with me.'

'Where do you wish me to escort you?' inquired Orso, offering his arm.

'I have no occasion for your arm, brother; but

take your gun and your cartridge-box. A man ought
never to leave the house without his arms.'

'As you please! I find that I must follow the
fashion. Where are we going?'

Colomba, without making any reply, drew the
mezzaro tight around her head, called the watch-dog,
and went out, followed by her brother. Leaving the
village with hasty steps, she followed a winding path
through the vineyards, after sending the dog in advance by a sign which he appeared to understand
perfectly; for he immediately commenced a zig-zag
course, beating amongst the vines right and left
always fifty paces in front of his mistress, and sometimes halting in the middle of the pathway. looking
back and wagging his tail. He fulfilled his office of
avant-garde to perfection.

'If Muschetto barks,' said Colomba, 'cock your
gun, brother, and stand stock-still.'

About half a mile from the village, after many
windings, Columba all at once halted at a spot where
the lane took a sudden turn. At the corner stood a
small pyramid of boughs and twigs, some green,
others withered, heaped up to the height of about
three feet. From its top protruded the end of a
wooden cross painted black. In many cantons of
Corsica, especially amongst the mountains, an extremely ancient custom, which is perhaps connected
with the superstitions of paganism, obliges the
passers-by to throw a stone or the bough of a tree,
on the spot where a man has met with a violent
death. For long years, as long as the remembrance

of his tragical end remains in the memory of men, this singular offering is thus accumulated from day to day. It is called such-a-one's *mucchio* or *heap*.

Colomba stood still before this heap of foliage, and plucking a branch of arbutus, added it to the pyramid. 'Orso,' she said, 'this is where our father died. Let us pray for his soul, brother!' She knelt; Orso immediately followed her example. At that moment the village bell tolled mournfully; some one had died in the course of the night. Orso melted into tears.

After the lapse of several minutes, Colomba rose with dry eyes, but with an excited countenance. She hastily made with her thumb the sign of the cross, familiar to her countrymen, and which ordinarily accompanies their solemn vows; then dragging her brother away, she returned to the village. They re-entered their house in silence. Orso went upstairs to his room. An instant afterwards Colomba followed him, bringing a little box, which she placed on the table. She opened it, and took out a shirt covered with large stains of blood. 'This is your father's shirt, Orso,' and she threw it on his lap; 'these are the bullets which struck him,' and she laid on the shirt a couple of oxidized balls. 'Orso, my brother!' she exclaimed, throwing herself into his arms, and holding him in a tight embrace. 'Orso! you will avenge him!" She kissed him with the fury of a maniac—kissed the bullets and the bloody shirt, and rushed out of the chamber, leaving her brother, as it were, petrified on his seat.

Orso remained for a considerable time perfectly motionless, not daring to divest himself of those horrible relics. At last, with a strong effort, he replaced them in their box, ran to the other end of the room, and threw himself upon his bed, turning his face towards the wall, and burying his head in the pillow, as if to avoid the sight of a spectre. His sister's last words kept incessantly ringing in his ears, and he seemed to be listening to a fatal, inevitable oracle, which required of him blood, and innocent blood. I will make no attempt to describe the wretched young man's feelings, which were as confused as those which boil in the brain of a madman. Long he remained in the same position, not daring to turn his head. At last he rose, closed the box, and precipitately left the house, scouring the country, and walking straight on, without knowing whither he went.

Little by little the open air relieved him; he became more calm, and examined with some degree of coolness his present position and the means of escaping from it. He did not in the least suspect the Barricini of murder, as the reader already knows; but he accused them of having fabricated the counterfeit letter from the bandit Agostini; and that letter, according to his belief, had been the cause of his father's death. To proceed against them for forgery he felt to be impossible. Sometimes, when the prejudices or the instincts of his country assailed him, pointing to an easy vengeance at the corner of a by-path, he repulsed them

with horror, and turned his thoughts to his military
friends, to Parisian society, and, above all, to Miss
Nevill. Then he thought of his sister's reproaches;
and the Corsican element still subsisting in his character justified those reproaches, and rendered them
more poignant. One single hope was left him in this
struggle between his conscience and his prejudice,
namely, to pick, under any pretext, a quarrel with
one of the Advocate's sons, and to fight a duel with
him. To kill him thus, with sword or bullet, recon-
ciled his Corsican with his French ideas. The expe-
dient once accepted, and meditating the means of
execution, he already felt relieved of a heavy weight,
whilst other gentler thoughts contributed further to
calm his febrile agitation. Cicero, in despair at the
death of his daughter Tullia, forgot his grief while
turning over in his mind the numerous fine things he
might say on the subject; Mr. Shandy consoled himself for the loss of his son by discoursing in like
manner on life and death. Orso cooled his blood by
thinking that he might confide to Miss Nevill a picture of the state of his mind, which picture could not
fail to be highly interesting to that very pretty personage.

He was approaching the village, which he had left
far behind him without being aware of the circumstance, when he heard the voice of a little girl who
was singing, doubtless fancying herself alone, in a
footpath leading to the skirt of the mâquis. It was
the slow and monotonous air consecrated to funeral
aments, and the child sang, 'For my son, my son in

a distant land,—keep my cross of honour and my bloody shirt'—

'What are you singing there, my girl?' said Orso, angrily, as he suddenly made his appearance.

'It is you, Ors' Anton'!' cried the child, a little frightened. 'It is one of Mademoiselle Colomba's songs—'

'I forbid your singing it,' said Orso, in a stern voice.

The child, turning her head to the right and the left, seemed to be looking in which direction she could best make her escape; and doubtless she would have taken to flight had she not been prevented by the responsibility of having in charge a large parcel which lay on the grass at her feet.

Orso was ashamed of his violence.

'What have you got there, my child?' he asked her as gently as he could.

And as Chilina hesitated to answer, he lifted the cloth in which the parcel was wrapped, and saw that it contained a loaf and other provisions.

'To whom are you carrying this loaf, my dear?' he inquired.

'You know quite well, monsieur; to my uncle.'

'Is not your uncle a bandit?'

'At your service, Monsieur Ors' Anton."

'If the gendarmes meet you, they will ask where you are going.'

'I should tell them,' replied the child, without hesitation, 'that I am carrying their dinner to the men from Lucca who are felling the mâquis.'

'And if you met with any hungry sportsman who wanted to dine at your expense, and took away your provisions ?'

'They dare not. I should say it was for my uncle.'

'In fact, he is not the sort of man to let his dinner be stolen. Is your uncle very fond of you ?'

'Oh, yes! Ors' Anton'. Ever since papa's death he takes care of the family ; of my mother, of me, and my little sister. Before mamma was ill, he recommended her to the rich people, to give her work. The Mayor gives me a frock once a year, and the Curé teaches me to read, and the Catechism, ever since my uncle spoke to them. But your sister is the kindest of all.'

At that moment a dog appeared in the path. The little girl, putting two fingers into her mouth, gave a shrill whistle ; the dog immediately ran up to her, and caressed her, and then abruptly darted into the wood. Shortly, a couple of ill-clad men, but well armed, started up from behind the stump of a tree a few paces distant from where Orso was standing. You would have said that they had advanced by creeping like snakes through the brushwood of myrtles and cistuses which covered the ground.

'Oh! Ors' Anton', welcome to you,' said the elder of the two men. 'What! don't you remember me ?'

'No,' said Orso, looking at him fixedly.

' ''Tis curious how completely a beard and a pointed cap alter a man ! Come, Lieutenant, take a good look at me. Have you forgotten your old Waterloo friends? Don't you recollect Borando Savelli, who

tore more than one cartridge by your side on that
unfortunate day ?'

'What! it's you?' said Orso.   'And you deserted
in 1816!'

'Exactly as you say, Lieutenant.   Forsooth, the
service is wearisome ; and besides, I had an account
to settle here.   Ha, ha! Chili, you are a capital girl.
Serve our dinner quickly, for we are hungry.   You
have no idea, Lieutenant, what an appetite the mâquis gives.   Who sends us this, Mademoiselle Colomba
or the Mayor ?'

'Neither of them, uncle.   The miller's wife gave
me this for you, and a blanket for mamma.'

'What does she want of me ?'

'She says that her Lucca people, whom she
engaged to clear a piece of forest ground, now ask
thirty-five sous and the chestnuts, in consequence of
the fever in the lowlands of Pietranera.'

'The idle rascals ! I will soon settle that.   Will
you partake of our dinner, Lieutenant, without ceremony?   We have eaten worse meals together in the
time of our poor countryman who has got his discharge.'*

'Much obliged to you.   I have got my discharge
too.'

'Yes; so I hear.   But you are not particularly
sorry, I guess; 'tis a good opportunity for you to
settle your accounts also.   Come, Curé,' said the
bandit to his comrade, 'sit down to table.   Monsieur
Orso, I beg to introduce Monsieur le Curé ; I am

* Probably Napoleon I., then at St. Helena.—Tr.

not quite sure whether he is a curé, but he has all the learning to make him one.'

'A poor theological student, monsieur,' said the second bandit, 'who was prevented from following his vocation. Who knows? I might have been pope, Brandolaccio.'

'What cause deprived the church of your talents?' Orso inquired.

'A mere nothing—an account to settle, as my friend Brandolaccio says—a sister of mine who played the fool whilst I was cramming Latin and Greek at the University of Pisa. I was obliged to come home to get her married; but the bridegroom was in so much of a hurry that he died of the fever three days before my arrival. I therefore applied, as you would have done in my case, to the dead man's brother. They told me he was married. What could I do?'

'In fact, it was very embarrassing. What did you do?'

'These are cases in which you cannot help coming to the gunflint.'*

'That is to say, you—'

'I put a bullet into his head,' said the bandit, coolly.

Orso started with horror; nevertheless, curiosity, and perhaps also the desire of retarding the moment of returning home, caused him to remain and continue his conversation with these two men, each of whom had at least one murder on his conscience.

Whilst his comrade was speaking, Brandolaccio

La scaglia—a very common expression.

placed before him some bread and meat. He helped himself, and then gave a portion to his dog, whom he presented to Orso by the name of Brusco, as endowed with the marvellous instinct of recognising a voltigeur under any possible disguise. Lastly he cut a piece of bread and a slice of raw ham, which he gave to his niece.

'What a famous life a bandit leads,' exclaimed the student of theology, after swallowing a few mouthfuls. 'You will perhaps one day try it, Monsieur della Rebbia, and you will find how pleasant it is to have no other master than your own caprice.' Thus far the bandit expressed himself in Italian, he continued in French, ' Corsica is not a very amusing country for a single man; but for a bandit, what a difference! The men fear us and the women are crazy after us. I am at home everywhere.'

'You are a learned linguist, monsieur,' said Orso, gravely.

'I speak French, because, look you, *maxima debetur pueris reverentia*, the greatest respect is due to boys and girls. Brandolaccio and I intend the little one to turn out well and to walk straight.'

'As soon as she is fifteen,' said Chilina's uncle, 'I will marry her well. I have already a party in view.'

'Will *you* ask the young man's hand?'

'Certainly. Do you suppose that if I say to any rich man in the neighbourhood, "I, Brando Savelli, shall be pleased to see your son espouse Michelina Savelli," do you suppose he will take long asking?'

'I should advise him not,' said the other bandit. 'My comrade has rather a heavy hand.'

'If I were a rascal,' continued Brandolaccio, 'a canaille, a scamp, I should only have to open my wallet to make five-franc pieces rain into it.'

'Does your wallet,' said Orso, 'contain anything so particularly to attract them?'

'Nothing of the kind; but if I were to write, as there are men who do write, to a rich man, "I want a hundred francs," he would lose no time in sending me them. But, Lieutenant, I am a man of honour.'

'Do you know, Monsieur della Rebbia,' said the bandit whom his companion called the Curé, 'do you know, that in this simple-mannered country, there are, nevertheless, a few wretches who take advantage of the esteem we inspire by means of our passports (pointing to his gun) to extort letters of exchange by forging our handwriting?'

'I do know it,' answered Orso; 'but what letters of exchange?'

'Six months ago,' continued the bandit, 'I was taking a walk in the direction of Orezza, when a clown accosted me, taking off his cap half a mile off, with "Ah! Monsieur le Curé (they all call me so), pray excuse me, and give time. I have only been able to make up fifty-five francs, but 'tis all I could scrape together, and that's the real truth." I, completely astonished, said, "What do you mean, you booby, by fifty-five francs?" "I mean sixty-five," he said; "but as for the hundred you require, it's quite impossible and out of the question !" "How, you nincompoop! *I* ask you for a hundred francs? I don't even know you." Thereupon he handed me a letter, or rather a filthy scrap of paper, in virtue of which he was invited to deposit a hundred francs in a certain spot, under penalty of having his house burnt and his cows killed by Giocanto Castriconi, which is my name. And they had the rascality to counterfeit my signature! What enraged me most was that the letter was written in patois, and full of bad spelling. *I* commit blunders in orthography! I, who had carried off all the prizes at the university! I began by giving the clown a blow which made him spin round twice. "Ah! you take me for a thief, rogue that you are!" I said, and I gave him a good kick. A little relieved, I said, " When ought you to carry this money to the appointed place ?" "This very day." "Good! carry it then." It was at the foot of a fir-tree, and the spot was indicated with perfect clearness. He carried the money, buried it at the foot of the tree, and returned to fetch me. I hid myself close by. I remained there with my man six mortal hours, Monsieur della Rebbia,—I would have waited there three days had it been necessary. At the end of the six hours there came a *Bastiaccio,** an infamous usurer. He stooped to get the money—I fired, and I took

* The Corsican mountaineers detest the inhabitants of Bastia, whom they do not regard as countrymen. Never do they say *Bastiese*, but *Bastiaccio*. It is well known that terminations in *accio* are ordinarily employed in a contemptuous sense.

such good aim that his head as it dropped fell amongst the five-franc pieces he was disinterring. "Now, stupid," I said to the peasant, "take back your money, and never presume to suspect Giocanto Castriconi of baseness like this." The poor fellow trembling from head to foot, picked up his sixty-five francs without taking the trouble to wipe them. He said, "Thank you." I gave him a good kick by way of adieu, and he has not yet done running away.'

'Ah, Curé!' said Brandolaccio, 'I envy you that shot. You must have laughed heartily.'

'I hit the Bastiaccio in the temple,' continued the bandit, 'and that reminds me of Virgil's lines—

———liquefacto tempora plumbo
Diffidit, ac multâ porrectum extendit arenâ.

Liquefacto! Do you believe Monsieur Orso, that a leaden bullet can be melted by the rapidity of its passage through the air? You, who have studied the theory of projectiles, ought to be able to tell me whether it is an error or a truth.'

Orso preferred discussing the question of physics to arguing with the licentiate about the morality of his exploit. Brandolaccio, who saw nothing amusing in this scientific dissertation, interrupted it to remark that the sun was on the point of setting. 'Since you did not choose to dine with us, Ors' Anton',' he said. 'I advise you not to keep Mademoiselle Colomba too long waiting. And, besides, it is not always a healthy practice to wander on the road after sunset. Why do you go out without your

gun? There are dangerous folk in this neighbourhood: be on your guard. To-day you have nothing
to fear; the Barricini are busy receiving the Préfet:
they went to meet him on the road, and he is to stop
a day at Pietranera before he goes to Corte to lay
the first stone of something—a piece of stupid nonsense. He sleeps to-night at the Barricini's, but to-
morrow they are free. There is Vincentello, who is
a bad sort of fellow, and Orlanduccio, who is not a
bit better. Try and catch them separately, this day
one, the next day the other; but take care what you
are about; that is all I have to say to you.'

'Much obliged for the advice.' said Orso, 'but I
have no dispute to settle with them. Unless they
come to look after me I have nothing to say to
them.'

The bandit drew his tongue against his cheek and
made it click in an ironical way, but made no other
answer. Orso rose to take his departure. 'Apropos,'
said Brandolaccio, 'I have not thanked you for the
powder; it came exactly at the nick of time. Now
I myself am in want for nothing—that is to say I am
still in want of shoes, but I will make myself a
pair out of a mouflon's hide one of these days.'

Orso slipped a couple of five franc pieces into the
bandit's hand, 'It was Colomba who sent you the
powder; here is something to help you to buy shoes.'

'No nonsense, Lieutenant,' exclaimed Brandolaccio, returning the money. 'Do you take me for a
mendicant? I accept the bread and the gunpowder,
but I will have nothing to do with anything else.'

'I thought old brother soldiers might help each other. Well then, adieu!' But before leaving he slipped the money into the bandit's wallet without his perceiving it.

'Adieu, Ors' Anton'!' said the theologian. 'Perhaps we shall meet again in the mâquis one of these days, when we will continue our Virgilian studies.'

Orso had left his honest companions a quarter of an hour when he heard a man running after him at the top of his speed: it was Brandolaccio.

'It is a little too bad, Lieutenant,' he exclaimed, out of breath, 'a little too bad! Here are your ten francs. If it had been any one else I would not so easily have excused the trick. My best compliments to Mademoiselle Colomba. You have completely winded me. Good night.'

XII.

Orso found Colomba a little alarmed at his long absence; but when she saw him she resumed the air of sad serenity which was the habitual expression of her countenance. During their evening repast they only conversed on indifferent subjects, and Orso, emboldened by his sister's calm behaviour, told her his encounter with the bandits, and even hazarded a few pleasantries on the moral and religious education which little Chilina received through the attentions of her uncle and his honourable colleague the Sieur Castriconi.

'Brandolaccio is an honest man,' said Colomba; 'but, as for Castriconi, I have been told that he is a man without principles.'

' I believe,' said Orso, 'that he is just as good as Brandolaccio, and Brandolaccio as good as he. Both are at open war with society. Their first crime drags them every day into fresh crimes; and still they are not perhaps so culpable as many people who have not taken refuge in the mâquis.'

A flash of joy beamed on his sister's countenance.

'Yes,' continued Orso; 'these wretched men are not without honour in their way. It is a cruel preju- dice, and not base cupidity, which has driven them to the life they are leading now.'

There was a moment's silence.

' Do you happen to know, brother,' said Colomba, as she poured out his coffee, 'that Carlo Battista Pietri died last night? Yes, he died of the marsh fever.'

' Who is this Pietri ?'

' He is a man belonging to the town, the husband of Madeleine, who received our father's pocket-book as he was dying. The widow has asked me to go to the wake, and to chant something. It will be right for you to go also. They are our neighbours, and it is an act of civility which we can hardly refuse in a small town like this.'

' Do not concern yourself with the wake, Colomba! I don't like to see a sister of mine exhibit herself in that way before the public.'

' Orso,' replied Colomba, 'every one honours their dead according to their own fashion. The *ballata* comes from our ancestors, and we ought to respect it as an ancient custom. Madeleine has not the *gift*, and old Fiordispina, who is the best *voceratrice* in the town, is ill. There must be some one to sing the *ballata.'*

'And do you fancy that Carlo Battista will not be able to find his way to the other world unless somebody sings wretched verses over his bier? Go to the wake if you will, Colomba; I will accompany you if you think I ought to go; but don't improvise. At your age it is highly improper; and—sister—I beg you not.'

'I have given my promise, brother. It is the custom here, you know; and, as I told you before, there is only me to improvise.'

'A stupid custom!'

'It pains me severely to perform these kind of songs. It recalls all our misfortunes to mind. To-morrow I shall be ill in consequence; but I must do it. Give me your permission, brother. Remember that at Ajaccio you told me to improvise for the amusement of that English girl who despises and laughs at our ancient customs. Must not I, then, improvise to-day for poor people who will be obliged by it, and who will be thereby aided to bear their affliction?'

'You must do as you please. I suppose that you have already composed your *ballata,* and do not choose it to be lost.'

'No, brother; I could not compose a thing of that kind beforehand. I place myself in front of the dead person, and I think of those who remain. The tears come into my eyes, and then I chant whatever presents itself to my mind.'

All this was spoken in such a simple way that it was impossible to suppose that the Signora Colomba entertained the slightest poetical vanity. Orso allowed himself to be persuaded, and went with his sister to Pietri's dwelling. The dead man was lying on a table, with his face uncovered, in the largest room in the house. All the doors and windows were open, and several wax candles were burning round the table. The widow stood at the head of the corpse, and, behind her, a great number of women completely occupied one side of the room; the men were ranged on the other side, standing and uncovered, their eyes fixed upon the corpse, and observing a profound silence. As each fresh visitor came in he went up to the table and kissed the corpse,* nodded to the widow and her son, and then took his place in the circle without uttering a word. From time to time, nevertheless, one of the company broke the silence to address a few words to the deceased. 'Why did you leave your good wife?' said one of the gossips. 'Did she not take good care of you? Did you want for anything? Why not wait another month? Your daughter-in-law would have presented you with a grandson.'

A tall young man, Pietri's son, squeezing his father's cold hand, exclaimed, 'Oh! why did you not die of the *evil death*?† We would have avenged you!'

These were the first words that Orso heard on

* This custom still subsisted at Bocognano (1840).
* *La mala morte*—a violent death.

entering the room. The circle opened, and a faint murmur of curiosity betrayed the interest which the assembly took in the *voceratrice's* arrival. Colomba embraced the widow, took one of her hands, and remained several minutes absorbed in herself, with her eyes cast down. Then she threw back her mezzaro, looked steadily at the corpse, and leaning over the dead man, almost as pale as he was, she began as follows:—

'Carlo Battista, may Christ receive your soul!— Life is a long suffering.—You have gone to a place— where there is neither heat nor cold.—You want no more your pruning knife,—nor your heavy mattock.— For you, labour is at an end.—Henceforth, all your days are sabbaths.—Carlo Battista, may Christ keep your soul!—Your son now rules the household.—I have seen the oak fall,—blasted by the storm.—I believed it to be dead.—I passed by again,—and its root had sent forth a shoot.—The shoot is now become an oak,—with a wide-spreading shade.— Beneath its strong branches, Maddelé, take your repose, and think of the oak which is no more.'

Here Madeleine began to sob aloud; and two or three men who, if occasion required, would have fired at Christians with as little scruple as they would at partridges, wiped away the big tears that ran down their tawny cheeks.

Colomba went on in this style for a considerable time, addressing herself sometimes to the deceased, sometimes to his family, and sometimes by a prosopopœia of frequent occurrence in *ballate*, making the dead man himself speak to console his friends or give them counsel. In proportion as her improvisation continued her countenance assumed a sublime expression; her complexion became suffused with a rosy blush which brought out the brilliant whiteness of her teeth and the fire of her dilated pupils. She was the Pythoness on her oracular tripod. Except a few sighs, a few suppressed sobs, not the slightest sound was heard to proceed from the crowd who pressed around her. Although less accessible than any one present to the influence of this wild poetry, Orso soon felt himself sharing the general emotion. Retreating to a dark corner of the room he wept as Pietri's own son was weeping.

All at once a slight movement was observed amongst the audience: the circle opened, and several strangers entered. From the respect shown to them and the eagerness displayed to make room for them, it was evident that they were persons of importance whose visit conferred an unusual honour on the house. Nevertheless, out of respect for the *ballata,* no one spoke to them. The first who entered appeared to be about forty years of age; his black coat, his rosette of red ribbon, and the air of confidence and authority which distinguished his countenance, left no doubt about his being the Préfet. Behind him came a man stooping with age, with a bilious complexion, who tried to hide his timid and uneasy glances behind a pair of green spectacles. He wore a black coat that was too large for him, and which, although still quite fresh, had evidently been made several years ago. Constantly at the Préfet's side,

he seemed to be hiding in his shadow. Lastly, after
him, there entered two tall young men, with sunburnt
complexions and cheeks buried in bushy whiskers,
casting proud and arrogant glances around, and displaying an impertinent curiosity. Time had made
Orso forget the features of his fellow-villagers;
but the sight of that old man in green spectacles
immediately revived old recollections. His presence
in the Préfet's suite sufficed to designate him. It
was the advocate Barricini, the Mayor of Pietranera,
who came with his two sons to treat the Préfet to the
performance of a *ballata*. It would be difficult to define
exactly what was passing at that moment in Orso's
mind; but the presence of his father's enemy made
him feel a sort of horror, and he was conscious of
being more accessible than ever to the suspicions
against which he had so long struggled.

As for Colomba, at the sight of the man to whom
she had vowed a mortal hatred, her expressive
physiognomy immediately assumed a sinister expression. She turned pale; her voice became hoarse;
the verse begun expired on her lips. But soon,
resuming her *ballata,* she continued with fresh
vehemence:—

'When the hawk is mourning—over her empty
nest—the starlings dare to flutter around—offering
insult to her sorrows.'

Here a stifled laugh was heard; it came from the
two young men who had just arrived, and who doubt
less considered the metaphor too bold.

'The hawk will awake, and spread her wings,—she

will wash her beak in blood! And you, Carlo Battista, to whom your friends now address their last adieu. For you, abundant tears are shed. The poor orphan only will not lament you. For why should she weep for you?—You went to sleep full of days—surrounded by your family—well prepared to appear—before the Almighty. The poor orphan weeps for her father—surprised by vile assassins—smitten in the back;—her father whose blood still is red—under the heap of verdant leaves. But she has collected his blood—that innocent and noble blood;—she has scattered it over Pietranera,—to make it turn to a mortal poison. And a mark shall be set on Pietranera—until the day when the blood of the guilty—shall obliterate the stains of innocent blood.'

When she had uttered these words, Colomba dropped on a chair, drew her mezzaro over her face, and was heard to sob. The women in tears crowded around the improvisatrice; several of the men cast fierce looks at the Mayor and his sons; some of the old men murmured at the scandal which their presence had occasioned. The son of the deceased made his way through the crowd, and was about to request the Mayor to leave the house instantly; but that personage did not give him time to do so. He made for the door, and his two sons were already in the street. The Préfet addressed a few words of sympathy to young Pietri, and followed them almost immediately. As for Orso, he went up to his sister, took her arm, and dragged her out of the room.

'Go with them,' said young Pietri, to several of his

friends. 'Take care that nothing happen to them!' Two or three young men hurriedly put their stiletti into the left sleeve of their coats, and escorted Orso and his sister as far as the door of their house.

XIII.

Colomba, panting and exhausted, had not strength to utter a word. Her head was resting on her brother's shoulder, and she held one of his hands clasped in hers. Although Orso, in his own mind, was angry with his sister for her peroration, he was too much alarmed on her account to give expression to the slightest reproach. He awaited in silence the end of the nervous crisis under which she seemed to be suffering; when a knocking was heard at the door, and Saveria entered the room in great alarm, announcing, 'Monsieur le Préfet!' On hearing that name, Colomba raised her head, as if ashamed of her weakness, and remained standing, supporting herself on a chair which trembled visibly beneath her hand.

The Préfet began by a few common-place excuses touching the unusual hour of his visit; was sorry for Mademoiselle Colomba's indisposition, spoke of the danger of violent emotions, blamed the custom of funereal laments, which the very talents of the *voceratrice* rendered still more painful to the parties present; and adroitly introduced a gentle rebuke as to the spirit of the final improvisation. Then, changing his tone, he said,

'Monsieur della Rebbia, I am charged to give you the best compliments of your English friends: Miss

Nevill desires to be most kindly remembered to mademoiselle your sister. I have a letter from her to deliver to you.'

' A letter from Miss Nevill ?' Orso exclaimed.

'Unfortunately I have not brought it with me; but you shall have it in five minutes. Her father has been very ill. For a while we were afraid that he had caught one of our terrible fevers. Happily, he is all right now, and you will be able to judge for yourself, for you will see him shortly, I imagine.'

' Miss Nevill must have been very anxious?'

' By good luck, she was not aware of the danger till after it was past. Miss Nevill spoke much, both of yourself, Monsieur della Rebbia, and of mademoiselle your sister.' Orso bowed. ' She has a great friendship for you both. Beneath a graceful exterior, and an appearance of outward levity, she conceals a solid understanding.'

' She is a charming person,' Orso observed.

'It is almost at her prayer that I have come here, monsieur. No one is better acquainted than I am with the fatal history, which I should be very glad to be spared having to recall to your memory. Since M. Barricini is still the Mayor of Pietranera, and I the Préfet of this department, I have no need to inform you what is my opinion of certain suspicions, which, if I am rightly informed, certain imprudent persons have communicated to you, and which you have repulsed, I am aware, with the indignation which ought to be expected from your position and character.'

'Colomba,' said Orso, restlessly swaying himself on his chair, 'you are very fatigued. You had better go to bed.'

Colomba shook her head in denial. She had recovered her habitual calmness, and her eager gaze was fixed on the Préfet.

'M. Barricini,' continued the Préfet, 'earnestly desires that an end should be put to this sort of hostility—that is to say, this state of uncertainty in which you find yourselves in regard to each other. For my own part, I should be delighted to see you establish with him those relations which ought to exist between persons made to esteem each other.'·

'Monsieur,' interrupted Orso, in a trembling voice, 'I have never accused the Advocate Barricini of having assassinated my father; but he has committed an action which must always prevent my holding any communication with him. He counterfeited a threatening letter, in the name of a certain bandit—at least he insinuated that my father was the author of it. This letter, in short, monsieur, was probably the indirect cause of his death.'

The Préfet collected his thoughts for an instant.

'That your father should have believed it, at the time when, carried away by the warmth of his temper, he was at law with M. Barricini, was excusable; but a similar blindness on your part, now, is no longer permissible. Consider that Barricini had no interest whatever in counterfeiting the letter—I say nothing about his character—you do not know him; you are prejudiced against him; but you cannot suppose that a man acquainted with the law—'

'But, monsieur,' said Orso, rising, 'have the goodness to remember that, when you tell me that that letter was not the production of M. Barricini, you attribute it to my father. His honour, monsieur, is mine.'

'No one,' continued the Préfet, 'is more convinced than I am that Colonel della Rebbia was a man of honour—but—the author of that letter is now discovered.'

'Who is it?' exclaimed Colomba, advancing towards the Préfet.

'A wretch, who is guilty of numerous crimes—such crimes as you Corsicans will not pardon,—a thief; a certain Tomaso Bianchi, now confined in the prison of Bastia, has revealed that he was the author of that fatal letter.'

'I do not know the man,' said Orso. 'What could be his object?'

'He belongs to the town,' said Colomba. 'He is the brother of one of our former millers. He is a bad fellow and a liar, unworthy of belief.'

'You shall see,' continued the Préfet, 'the interest which he had in the business. The miller whom mademoiselle your sister mentions—his name, I believe, was Theodore—rented from the Colonel a mill standing on the water-course, whose possession M. Barricini contested with your father. The Colonel, generous according to his way, derived scarcely any profit from the mill. Now, Tomaso

believed that if M. Barricini obtained the water-
course, he should have a considerable rent to pay,—
for every one knows that M. Barricini is fond of
money.   In short, to oblige his brother, Tomaso
forged the bandit's letter; and that is the whole of
the history.   You are aware that family-ties in Corsica are so powerful as sometimes to incite to crime.
Have the goodness to peruse this letter which I have
received from the Procureur-Général.   It will con-
firm what I have just been stating.'

Orso ran through the letter, which gave a detailed
account of Tomaso's confession, and Colomba read it
at the same time over her brother's shoulder.

When she had finished she exclaimed, 'Orlanduccio Barricini went to Bastia a month ago, when
he knew that my brother was about to return.   He
must have seen Tomaso, and bribed him to utter this
falsehood.'

'Mademoiselle,' said the Préfet, impatiently, ' you
explain everything by odious suppositions; is that
the way to discover the truth ?   You, monsieur, are
in your sober senses: tell me what you think now ?
Do you believe, with mademoiselle, that a man who
has only a comparatively light sentence to fear, would
be so ready to accuse himself of the crime of forgery
to oblige a person with whom he is not acquainted ?'

Orso read the Procureur-Général's letter over again,
weighing every word with special attention ; for,
since he had seen the Advocate Barricini, he found
greater difficulty in convincing himself than he would
have done a day or two ago.   Finally, he was obliged

to avow that the explanation appeared satisfactory. But Colomba exclaimed violently, 'Tomaso Bianchi is a cheat. He will not be condemned, or he will escape from prison, I am certain of it!'

The Préfet shrugged his shoulders.

'I have communicated to you, monsieur,' he said, 'the information which I have received. I will take my departure, and leave you to your own reflections. I trust that you will listen to reason; and I hope that it may have more influence with you than—than your sister's suppositions.'

Orso, after a few words in excuse of Colomba, repeated that he now believed Tomaso to be the only guilty party.

The Préfet, rising to take his leave, said, 'If it were not so late, I should propose your accompanying me to fetch Miss Nevill's letter. At the same time, you might repeat to M. Barricini what you have just said to me, and there would be an end of everything.'

'Never shall Orso della Rebbia enter the house of a Barricini!' exclaimed Colomba, impetuously.

'It seems that mademoiselle is the *tintinajo** of the family,' said the Préfet, with an air of raillery.

'Monsieur,' said Colomba, with a steady voice, 'you have been deceived. You do not know the Advocate. He is the greatest cheat, the most cunning of

---

* The bell-wether, or rather the ram that carries a bell and leads the flock, is so called; metaphorically, the same name is given to the member of a family who takes the lead in all affairs of importance.

men. I conjure you, do not induce Orso to commit an action which would cover him with disgrace.'

'Colomba!' exclaimed Orso, 'passion has deprived you of your senses.'

'Orso! Orso! by the box which I put into your hands, I entreat you, listen to me. There is blood between you and the Barricini; you will not go near them!'

'Sister!'

'No, brother, you will not go; or, if you do, I will leave this house, and you shall never see me more. Orso, have pity on me!'

She fell on her knees.

'I am grieved,' said the Préfet, 'to find Mademoiselle della Rebbia so unreasonable. You will convince her I am certain.' He half opened the door and stopped, apparently waiting for Orso to follow him.

'I cannot leave her now,' said Orso. 'To-morrow, if—'

'I start early in the morning,' said the Préfet.

'At least, brother,' exclaimed Colomba, putting her hands together in entreaty, 'wait till to-morrow morning. Let me look over my father's papers. You cannot refuse me that.'

'Very well; you can look over them this evening: it will at least prevent your tormenting me afterwards by the display of this extravagant hatred. I beg a thousand pardons, Monsieur le Préfet. I feel myself so ill at ease, it is better that it should be to-morrow.'

'Night brings counsel,' said the Préfet, retiring; 'I hope that to-morrow your irresolution will have completely vanished.'

'Saveria,' cried Colomba, 'take the lantern and accompany Monsieur le Préfet. He will give you a letter for my brother.'

She added a few words which were heard by Saveria alone.

Colomba,' said Orso, when the Préfet was gone, 'you have given me great pain. Will you persist in refusing to believe evidence?'

'You have given me until to-morrow,' she replied. 'I have very little time, but I still have hopes.'

She then took a bundle of keys and hastened to a room in the upper storey. There she was heard to be hurriedly opening drawers and searching a secretary in which Colonel della Rebbia formerly kept his most important papers.

XIV.

Saveria was a long time gone on her errand, and Orso's impatience was at its height, when at last she made her appearance, holding a letter, and followed by little Chilina, who was rubbing her eyes, for she had been awakened out of her first sleep.

'My child,' said Orso, 'what are you come here for at this time of night?'

'Mademoiselle wants me,' Chilina replied.

'What can she want with her?' Orso thought; but he hastened to open Miss Lydia's letter, and, whilst he was reading it, Chilina went upstairs to his sister.

'My father has been unwell, monsieur,' wrote Miss Nevill, 'and, moreover, he has such a dislike to writing, that I am obliged to act as his secretary. The other day, as you may remember, he got his feet wet on the beach instead of admiring the scenery with us, and that is quite sufficient to give the fever, in your charming island. I can see here the grimace you make; doubtless, you are feeling for your stiletto, but I hope that you have got rid of it. So my father has had a slight fever, and I a great fright. The Préfet, whom I persist in considering very amiable, gave us some medicine which also was particularly amiable, for it set him all right in a couple of days. The fit has not returned since, and my father wants to go a-shooting again; but I will not allow him quite yet. How did you find your mountain castle? Does your north tower still stand where it did? Are there plenty of ghosts in it? I make all these inquiries because my father has not forgotten that you promised him fallow-deer, wild-boar, mouflon— is that the correct name of the wonderful creature? As we are going to embark at Bastia, we intend to beg your hospitality; and I hope that the Chateau della Rebbia, which you say is so old and ruinous, will not tumble about our ears. Although the Préfet is so amiable that he is never at a loss for conversation—I fancy, by-the-by, that I have turned his head. We talked of your lordship. The lawyers of Bastia have sent him certain revelations made by a good-

for-nothing fellow whom they keep under lock and
key, which are of a nature to destroy your last suspicions; your enmity, which sometimes made me
uneasy, ought to cease henceforward. You cannot
conceive what pleasure it gave me. When you took
your departure with the fair *voceratrice*, gun in hand,
with sombre looks, you appeared more Corsican than
usual—too Corsican even. *Basta!* I trouble you
with this long letter, because I have nothing better
to do. The Préfet is going to leave, alas! We will
send you a message when we are on the point of
starting for your mountains, and I shall take the
liberty of writing to Mademoiselle Colomba, begging
her to make me a *bruccio*. Meanwhile, give her my
best love. I make great use of her stiletto to cut
the leaves of a new novel; but the terrible iron
scorns the service, and tears my book in a pitiable
way. Adieu, monsieur; my father desires his best
regards. Attend to what the Préfet says; he will
give you none but good advice, and he is going out
of his way, I believe, on your account. He is
to lay a first stone at Corte; I can fancy that it ought
to be a very imposing ceremony, and I greatly regret
that I cannot witness it. A gentleman in an embroidered coat, silk stockings, a white sash, with a
trowel in his hand—and a speech! The ceremony
will conclude with shouts of *Vive le Roi!* nine times
nine. You will be very vain of having made me fill
four pages of letter paper; but, as I told you before,
monsieur, I am aweary, and for that reason I allow
you to write to me at considerable length. Apropos,

it is extraordinary that you have not informed me of your happy arrival at Pietranera Castle.

'LYDIA.

'P.S. I beg you to listen to the Préfet's advice, and to do what he tells you. We agreed together that you ought to do so; and it will give me great pleasure.'

Orso read this letter three or four times over, accompanying each reading with innumerable mental commentaries. Then he wrote a long reply, which he gave to Saveria to take to a man of the village, who started for Ajaccio that same night. He had almost forgotten his discussion with his sister respecting his grievances, true or false, with the Barricini; Miss Lydia's letter caused him to behold everything in rose-coloured hues; his suspicions and his hatred had melted away. After waiting some time for his sister to come down, and not seeing her make her appearance, he went to bed, with his heart lighter than he had felt it for some time previous. Chilina having been dismissed with secret instructions, Colomba passed the greater part of the night in searching through old piles of paper. A little before daybreak a few small pebbles were thrown against her window; at which signal she went down into the garden, opened a private door, and let into the house a couple of exceedingly ill-looking men. Her first care was to take them into the kitchen and give them something to eat. Who these persons were the reader will shortly be informed.

XV.

In the morning, about six o'clock, one of the Préfet's servants knocked at the door of Orso's house. Received by Colomba, he told her that the Préfet was on the point of leaving, and that he awaited her brother. Colomba replied, without hesitation, that her brother had just fallen down stairs and had sprained his ankle; that, being unable to set a step, he begged Monsieur le Préfet to excuse him, and would be very grateful if he would condescend to take the trouble to step over to him. Very soon after this message Orso came down stairs and inquired of his sister whether the Préfet had not sent for him. 'He begs you to wait for him here,' she answered, with the greatest assurance. Half an hour elapsed without the slightest movement being visible in the direction of the Barricini's house; meanwhile, Orso asked Colomba if she had made any discovery; she replied that she would explain herself before the Préfet. She affected great calmness, but her complexion and her eyes betrayed a state of febrile agitation.

At last, the door of the Barricini's house was seen to open; the Préfet, in travelling costume, came out the first, followed by the Mayor and his two sons. What was the stupefaction of the inhabitants of Pietranera, (who had been on the look-out ever since sunrise to witness the departure of the first magistrate of the department,) when they saw him, accompanied by the three Barricini, cross the Piazza in a direct line and enter della Rebbia's house! 'They are making peace!' shouted the village politicians.

'I told you so,' remarked an old man; 'Orso Antonio has lived too long on the continent to settle matters like a man of courage.'

'Nevertheless,' replied a Rebbianist, 'you see it is the Barricini who have made the first move. They are begging pardon.'

'The Préfet has got them all under his thumb,' the old man answered. 'In these days there is no such a thing as courage; young people care nothing about their father's blood.'

The Préfet was not a little astonished to find Orso walking about without any symptom of pain. Colomba briefly avowed the falsehood, and begged his pardon for it. 'If you had been staying in any other house, Monsieur le Préfet, my brother would have gone yesterday to pay his respects.'

Orso made repeated excuses, protesting that he had nothing to do with this ridiculous trick, at which he felt deeply mortified. The Préfet and old Barricini appeared to believe in the sincerity of his expressions of regret, which were, moreover, confirmed by his confusion and the reproaches which he addressed to his sister; but the Mayor's sons did not appear satisfied. 'They are making game of us,' said Orlanduccio, loud enough to be heard.

'If my sister had played me such a trick as that,' said Vincentello, 'I would soon cure her of attempting it again.'

These words, and the tone in which they were uttered, displeased Orso, and a little damped his good intentions. He exchanged glances with the young Barricini which denoted anything but kindly feelings.

Meanwhile, every one was seated, with the exception of Colomba, who remained standing close by the door of the kitchen. The Préfet opened the business of the interview, and, after a few general observations on the prejudices of the country, reminded them that the greater part of the most inveterate feuds had no other cause than misunderstandings. Then, addressing the Mayor, he said that M. della Rebbia had never believed the Barricini family to have taken part, directly or indirectly, in the deplorable event which had deprived him of his father; that, in truth, he had retained some doubts relative to a detail in the lawsuit which had existed between the two families; that this doubt was excusable by M. Orso's long absence and the nature of the information which he had received; that, being now enlightened by recent revelations, he was perfectly satisfied, and wished to live on terms of friendship and good neighbourhood with M. Barricini and his sons.

Orso bowed with an air of constraint; M. Barricini stammered a few words which no one could catch; the sons looked up to the joists of the ceiling. The Préfet, continuing his harangue, was about to address to Orso the counterpart of what he had been saying to M. Barricini, when Colomba, taking some papers from beneath her handkerchief, gravely advanced between the contracting parties.

'It would give me very great pleasure,' she said, 'if hostilities between our two families were to cease; but for the reconciliation to be sincere, an explanation must be come to which can leave no manner of doubt. Monsieur le Préfet, I was right in suspecting Tomaso Bianchi's declaration, coming as it did from a person of evil reputation. I said that your sons had perhaps seen this man in prison in Bastia—'

'That is false,' interrupted Orlanduccio, 'I have not seen him.'

Colomba glanced at him a look of disdain, and continued with great apparent calmness: 'You have explained the interest which Tomaso had in threatening M. Barricini in the name of a formidable bandit, by the desire which he felt to keep his brother Theodore in the mill which my father allowed him to occupy at a low rental?'

'That is evident,' said the Préfet.

'On the part of a wretch such as Bianchi appears to be, such conduct is perfectly intelligible,' said Orso, deceived by his sister's air of moderation.

'The forged letter,' continued Colomba, her eyes beginning to sparkle with increased excitement, 'is dated the 11th of July. Tomaso was then staying with his brother at the mill.'

'Yes,' said the Mayor, rather uneasily.

'What interest had Tomaso Bianchi in the matter then?' exclaimed Colomba, with an air of triumph. 'His brother's lease was out; my father had given him notice to quit on the 1st of July. Here is my father's register, a minute of the notice given, and the letter of a land-agent at Ajaccio, proposing a fresh tenant for the mill.'

So saying, she delivered to the Préfet the papers which she held in her hand.

There was a moment of general astonishment. The Mayor visibly turned pale ; Orso, knitting his brows, stepped forward to look at the papers, which the Préfet was reading with great attention.

'They are only making game of us !' Orlanduccio again exclaimed, rising angrily. 'Come away, father ; we never ought to have entered this house !'

An instant sufficed for M. Barricini to recover his presence of mind. He requested to examine the papers ; the Préfet handed them to him without saying a word. Then, raising his green spectacles over his forehead, he looked them over with seeming indifference, whilst Colomba watched him with the eyes of a tigress who beholds a deer drawing near to the den of her whelps.

'But,' said M. Barricini, replacing his spectacles, and returning the papers to the Préfet, 'Tomaso, knowing the late Colonel's good-nature, thought—he must have thought—that the Colonel would reconsider his determination to turn him out. In fact, he did remain in possession of the mill ; and therefore'—

'It was I,' said Colomba, with a tone of disdain, 'who allowed him to retain possession of the mill. My father was dead, and in my position I had need to conciliate the clients of my family.'

'Nevertheless,' said the Préfet, 'Tomaso acknowledges that he wrote the letter. That is clear.'

'What is clear to me,' interrupted Orso, 'is that there has been most infamous conduct mixed up with the whole of this affair.'

'I must again contradict one of these gentlemen's assertions,' said Colomba. She opened the door of the kitchen, and immediately Brandolaccio, the Licentiate in Theology, and the dog Brusco, entered the room. The two bandits were without arms, at least apparently so; they had their cartridge-boxes at their girdles, but not the pistol which is its regular accompaniment. On entering the room they respectfully took off their caps.

The effect of their sudden appearance may be imagined. The Mayor nearly fell flat on his back; his sons bravely advanced to shelter him, thrusting their hands into their coat pockets to feel for their stiletti. The Préfet took a step or two in the direction of the door, whilst Orso, seizing Brandolaccio by the collar, shouted, 'What business have you here, you rascal?'

'We are caught in a trap!' exclaimed the Mayor, trying to open the door; but Saveria had double-locked it outside, according to the bandits' directions, as they afterwards learned.

'Good people!' said Brandolaccio, 'you have nothing to be afraid of; I am not half so black a devil as I look. Monsieur le Préfet, your humble servant. Lieutenant, gently, if you please; you are choking me. We are come here to give evidence.

So, say your say, Curé; you have the gift of the gab.'

'Monsieur le Préfet,' said the Licentiate, 'I have not the honour to be known to you. My name is Giocanto Castriconi, more frequently called the Curé. Ah! you recognise me! Mademoiselle, whom I also had not the advantage of knowing, begged me to give her some information respecting a certain Tomaso Bianchi, with whom I was confined, three weeks ago, in the prison of Bastia. This, then, is what I have to state—'

'Save yourself the trouble,' the Préfet said; 'I can listen to nothing from a man like you. Monsieur della Rebbia, I wish to believe that you have no hand in this odious conspiracy. But are you master in your own house? Order this door to be opened. Your sister, perhaps, will have to give an account of the strange connection which she maintains with bandits.'

'Monsieur le Préfet,' exclaimed Colomba, ' deign to hear what this man has to say. You are here to render justice to all, and your duty is to seek the truth. Speak, Giocanto Castriconi.'

'Don't hear him!' shouted the three Barricini in chorus.

'If everybody speaks at once,' said the bandit, smiling, 'that is not the way to come to an understanding. In prison, then, I had for my companion, not for my friend, this very Tomaso now in question. He was frequently visited by M. Orlanduccio.'

'That is false,' cried the two brothers at once.

'Two negatives make an affirmative,' Castriconi

coldly observed. 'Tomaso had money; he ate and drank the best of everything. I was always fond of good cheer (it is my most excusable failing), and, in spite of my repugnance to come in contact with the fellow, I consented to dine with him several times. In return, I offered to let him escape with me. A young woman, with whom I am on friendly terms, supplied me with the means. I do not want to compromise anybody. Tomaso refused, telling me that he was sure of his business, that the Advocate Barricini had recommended him to all the judges, and that he would come off as white as snow, and with money in his pocket. As for myself, I thought the best thing I could do was to take the air. *Dixi.*'

'Every word he has spoken is a heap of lies,' repeated Orlanduccio resolutely. 'If we were out in the country, each with our gun, he would not dare to talk in this way.'

'What stupid nonsense!' exclaimed Brandolaccio. 'Don't quarrel with the Curé, Orlanduccio.'

'Will you let me go, Monsieur della Rebbia?' said the Préfet, stamping with his foot impatiently.

'Saveria! Saveria!' shouted Orso, 'open the door, I command you.'

'One instant,' said Brandolaccio, : we have first to cut and run in our direction. Monsieur le Préfet, it is customary, when people meet at the house of a common friend, to give each other half-an-hour's grace at leaving.'

The Prefet darted a glance of disdain.

'My service to all the company,' said Brandolaccio.

Then stretching out his arm horizontally, 'Come, Brusco,' he said to his dog, 'jump for M. le Préfet!'

The dog jumped; the bandits hastily seized their arms in the kitchen, made their escape by the garden-gate, and, at the sound of a shrill whistle, the door of the saloon was opened as if by enchantment.

'M. Barricini,' said Orso, with concentrated fury, 'I look upon you as guilty of forgery. This very day I will send my complaint against you to the Procureur du Roi, for forgery and conspiracy with Bianchi. Perhaps I shall have a still more terrible accusation to make.'

'And I, Monsieur della Rebbia,' said the Mayor, 'will make my complaint against you for *malice prepense* and for conspiracy with bandits. Meanwhile, Monsieur le Préfet will recommend you to the care of the gendarmerie.'

'The Préfet will do his duty,' replied that personage with severity. 'He will see that order be not disturbed at Pietranera; he will take care that justice be done. I am speaking to all of you, messieurs!'

The Mayor and Vincentello had already left the room, and Orlanduccio was following them, walking backwards, when Orso said to him in a low voice, 'Your father is an old man whom I could crush with a blow: but I have something in store for you and for your brother.'

In reply, Orlanduccio drew his stiletto, and rushed on Orso like a madman; but, before he could make use of his weapon, Colomba seized him by the arm,

which she twisted violently, whilst Orso, striking him
in the face with his fist, drove him back several paces,
and knocked him rudely against the door-post. The
stiletto fell from Orlanduccio's hand, but Vincentello
had his, and was re-entering the room, when Colomba,
seizing a gun, proved to him that the match was not
equal ; at the same time the Préfet threw himself
between the combatants. 'I shall see you soon, Ors'
Anton' !' shouted Orlanduccio ; and, slamming the
door after him, he locked it outside, to give himself
the time to effect his retreat.

Orso and the Préfet remained a quarter of an hour
without speaking, each at the further end of the
room. Colomba, with the pride of triumph on her
brow, gazed at them alternately, leaning on the gun
which had decided the victory.

'What a country! What a country !' exclaimed
the Préfet at last, rising abruptly. 'Monsieur della
Rebbia, you are in the wrong. I require your word
of honour that you will abstain from all violence, and
will wait till justice has come to a decision respecting
this ill-starred piece of business.'

'Yes, Monsieur le Préfet, I was wrong to strike
the wretch ; but, in short, I have struck him, and I
cannot refuse him the satisfaction which he has demanded.'

'No, no! he does not want to fight a duel with
you ! But if he assassinates you—you have done all
that was needed to bring him to that.'

'We will take good care of ourselves,' said Colomba.

'Orlanduccio,' said Orso, 'does not seem to want for courage, and I expect better things of him than that, Monsieur le Préfet. He was rather in a hurry to draw his stiletto, but in his place perhaps I should have done the same. It is fortunate for me that my sister has not exactly a fine lady's wrist.'

'You shall not fight!' exclaimed the Préfet; 'I forbid you!'

'Allow me to say, monsieur, that in affairs of honour I recognise no other authority than my own conscience.'

'I tell you that you shall not fight.'

'You can arrest me, monsieur; that is to say, if I allow myself to be taken. But if that should happen you would only delay an affair which is now inevitable. You are a man of honour, Monsieur le Préfet, and you know that it cannot be otherwise.'

'If you were to arrest my brother,' added Colomba, 'half the village would take his part, and we should have a pretty fusillade.'

'I give you warning, monsieur,' said Orso, 'and I entreat you to believe that it is no bravado; I warn you that if M. Barricini abuses his authority as mayor to have me arrested, I will defend myself.'

'From this day,' said the Préfet, 'M. Barricini is suspended from his functions. He will justify himself I hope. Listen, monsieur; I take an interest in your welfare. What I ask is a very trifling request. Remain quietly at home till my return from Corte. I shall be only three days absent. I will bring back

K 2

with me the Procureur du Roi, and we will then completely disentangle this sad affair. Will you promise me to abstain from all hostilities till then ?'

'I cannot promise it, monsieur, if, as I think, Orlanduccio sends me a challenge.'

'How, Monsieur della Rebbia! you, an officer in the French army, would you fight a duel with a man whom you suspect of forgery ?'

'I struck him, monsieur.'

'But if you had stricken a galley slave and he called you out, would you fight a duel with him? Come, Monsieur Orso. Well, I will make even a less request: do not seek Orlanduccio. I allow you to fight him if he requires a rendezvous.'

'He will require one, I have no doubt; but I will promise you not to strike him again to provoke him to fight.'

'What a country!' repeated the Préfet, pacing backwards and forwards in the room. 'When shall I get back again to France ?'

'Monsieur le Préfet,' said Colomba, in her gentlest voice, 'it is rather late in the morning, will you do us the honour to breakfast here ?'

The Préfet could not help laughing. 'I have already stayed here too long: it may look like partiality. And that vexatious first stone! I cannot avoid going. Mademoiselle della Rebbia, for what sorrow you have probably laid the foundation to-day !'

'At least, Monsieur le Préfet, you will do my sister the justice to believe that her convictions are profound, and I am certain of it now; you yourself believe that they are not unfounded.'

'Adieu, monsieur,' said the Préfet, waving his hand. 'I warn you that I am going to order the brigadier of the gendarmes to keep his eye upon your movements.'

When the Préfet was gone, 'Orso,' said Colomba, 'you are not here on the continent. Orlanduccio knows nothing about your practices of duelling; and besides, he is a wretch who does not deserve to die a brave man's death.'

'Colomba, my love, you are a powerful woman. I am greatly obliged to you for saving me from a stab. Give me your little hand to kiss. But, look you, allow me to do as I please. There are certain things which you do not understand. Let me have some breakfast, and as soon as the Préfet has taken his departure send for little Chilina, who seems to do her errands admirably. I want her to carry a letter.'

Whilst Colomba was superintending the preparations for breakfast, Orso went up to his room and wrote the following note:—

'No doubt you are in a hurry to have a meeting: the same is also the case with myself. To-morrow morning at six o'clock we can both be in the valley of Aquaviva. I am very expert with the pistol, and therefore do not propose that weapon. I am told that you are a capital shot with the gun. Let us each bring a double-barrelled gun. I shall be accompanied by a man of the village. If your brother wishes to be with you, bring a second witness, and let me know. In that case only I shall have two witnesses.

'ORSO ANTONIO DELLA REBBIA.

The Préfet, after remaining an hour with the Adjoint du Maire, or Deputy Mayor, and stepping in for a few minutes at the Barricini's, started for Corte, escorted by a single gendarme. A quarter of an hour afterwards Chilina carried the letter which has just been communicated to the reader, and put·it into Orlanduccio's own hands.

The answer was a long time coming, and did not arrive until the evening. It was signed by M. Barricini, senior, and informed Orso that he had forwarded to the Procureur du Roi the threatening letter addressed to his son. 'Strong in my conscience,' he added in conclusion, 'I wait for justice to pass sentence on your calumnies.'

Meanwhile five or six shepherds, summoned by Colomba, arrived to garrison the tower of the della Rebbias. In spite of Orso's remonstrances they made *archere* in the windows looking on to the piazza, and during the whole afternoon and evening he received offers of service from different persons of the town. A letter even came from the theological bandit, promising, in his own name and in that of Brandolaccio, to interfere if the Mayor called in the gendarmerie to his assistance. He concluded with the following postscript: 'May I venture to ask what is Monsieur le Préfet's opinion of the excellent education which my friend has given to his dog Brusco? After

Chilina I don't know a more docile pupil, or one who shows a better capacity.'

XVI

The next day passed without hostilities. Both parties remained on the defensive. Orso did not leave the house, and the Barricini's door was constantly closed. The five gendarmes left to garrison Pietranera walked about the piazza or the outskirts of the village, assisted by the Garde Champêtre, the sole representative of the urban militia. The Deputy Mayor wore his sash all the day long; but except the *archère* in the window-shutters of the two hostile houses, nothing betrayed a state of warfare. A Corsican alone would have remarked that in the piazza around the evergreen oak women only were to be seen.

At supper-time Colomba joyously displayed to her brother the following letter, which she had just received from Miss Nevill :

'MY DEAR MADEMOISELLE COLOMBA,

I learn with great pleasure, through a letter from your brother, that your enmities are come to an end. Pray receive my congratulations. My father cannot bear Ajaccio ever since your brother left, and he has no one to talk to about the army and the chase. We leave to-day, and we propose sleeping on the road at your relation's, for whom we have a letter of introduction. The day after to-morrow, about eleven o'clock, we shall come to beg a luncheon off that mountain *bruccio* which you say is so superior to what we get in town.

'Adieu, dear Mademoiselle Colomba.

'Your friend,

'LYDIA NEVILL.'

'She cannot have received my second letter!' Orso exclaimed.

'You see by the date of hers, that Mademoiselle Lydia must have started when your letter reached Ajaccio. Did you tell her not to come?'

'I told her we were in a state of siege. It seems to me that it is not exactly the time to receive visitors.'

'Nonsense! The English are singular people. The last night that I passed in her room she told me that she should be sorry to leave Corsica without having seen a good *vendetta*. If you like, Orso, we can treat her to the spectacle of an assault upon our enemy's mansion.'

'I must tell you,' said Orso, 'that nature blundered when she made you a woman. You would have made an excellent soldier.'

'Perhaps so. At any rate I must go and prepare my *bruccio*.'

'It will not be wanted. We must send some one to warn them of the state of affairs, and to stop them before they have set off.'

'Yes, indeed! You want to send a messenger in such weather as this, for a torrent to sweep him away, your letter and all. How I pity the poor bandits, exposed to such a storm! Happily they have good *piloni.** I will tell you what you had better do, Orso. If the tempest is over, start very early to-morrow morning and reach our relation's house before our friends have left it. You can easily do that; Miss Lydia always gets up rather late. You will tell them what is passing here, and if they still persist in coming, we shall be most happy to receive them.'

Orso immediately assented to the proposal, and Colomba, after a few moments' silence, continued, 'You think, perhaps, that I was joking when I mentioned an assault on the Barricini's house; but do you know that we are in force—two to one at the very least? Ever since the Préfet has suspended the Mayor all the men here are on our side. We could hack them to pieces. It would be easy to open the business. If you liked I would go to the fountain, I would ridicule their women ; they would not come out, perhaps, for they are such cowards. Perhaps they would fire at me from their *archere ;* they would be sure to miss me. In that case the thing is done, they are the assailants. Heaven help the vanquished party! In an affray like that who could point out the exact person who had dealt the hardest blows? Believe what your sister says, Orso. The gentlemen of the long robe who are coming will spoil a great deal of paper, and will spend a great deal of useless breath. It will all end in nothing. The old fox would find the means of making them see the stars at noon-

* Cloaks made of very thick cloth, and furnished with a hood.

day. Ah! if the Préfet had not stepped before Vin-centello there would have been one of them the fewer.'

All this was said with the same coolness as she had just been talking about making of them the *bruccio*.

Orso, stupefied, gazed at his sister with admiration mingled with fear.

'My gentle Colomba,' he said, rising from table, 'make yourself easy. If I do not contrive to hang the Barricini I will manage to get at them some other way. A hot bullet or cold iron!* You see I have not forgotten my Corse.'

'The sooner the better,' said Colomba with a sigh. 'Which horse will you ride to-morrow, Ors' Anton'?'

'The black. Why do you ask me that?'

'Only to give him a feed of barley.'

When Orso had retired to his chamber, Colomba sent Saveria and the shepherds to bed, and remained alone in the kitchen, where the *bruccio* was making. From time to time she listened, and seemed to be waiting impatiently for her brother's going to bed. When she believed he was at last asleep, she took a knife, made sure that it was sharp, thrust her small feet into a pair of large shoes, and without making the slightest noise, went into the garden.

The garden, surrounded with walls, was contiguous to a large piece of ground, enclosed by a hedge, into which the horses were turned—for Corsican horses scarcely know what a stable is. In general they are let loose into a field, trusting to their own

---

* *Palla calda u farru freddu*, a very common expression.

intelligence to find food and shelter from the cold and the rain.

Colomba opened the garden-door with the same precautions; went into the enclosure, and with a low whistle called the horses, to whom she often gave bread and salt. When the black horse was within her reach, she seized him violently by the mane, and slit his ear with her knife. The horse made a terrible plunge, and rushed away uttering the shrill scream which acute pain sometimes extorts from animals of his species. Satisfied with this, Colomba was re-entering the garden, when Orso opened his window and cried, 'Who goes there?' At the same time she could hear him cock his gun. Happily for her, the garden door lay in complete obscurity, and was half concealed by a large fig-tree. Very soon, from the intermittent glare which shone in her brother's room, she concluded that he was endeavouring to light his lamp. She hastened then to close the garden door, and gliding along the side of the wall, so that her black dress became confounded with the dark foliage of the espaliers, she contrived to reach the kitchen a few moments before Orso made his appearance.

'What is the matter?' she inquired.

'I thought,' said Orso, 'I heard some one open the garden door.'

'Impossible. The dog would have barked. At any rate, let us go and see.'

Orso walked all round the garden, and having made sure that the outer door was properly closed, he felt a little ashamed of his false alarm, and prepared to return to his chamber.

'I am glad to see, brother,' said Colomba, 'that you are becoming prudent, as a man in your position ought to be.'

'You are finishing my education,' Orso replied. 'Good night.'

The next morning, Orso rose at daybreak ready to take his departure. His costume announced the pretensions to elegance of a man about to present himself to a woman whom he desires to please; at the same time with the prudence of a Corsican on *vendetta*. Over a blue cloth frock-coat which tightly fitted his waist, he wore, slung across his shoulder, a small tin box containing cartridges, suspended by a cord of green silk; his stiletto was placed in a side-pocket, and he held in his hand the handsome Manton laden with ball. While he hastily took a cup of coffee which Colomba offered, a shepherd went to saddle and bridle his horse. Orso and his sister followed him into the enclosure. The shepherd had caught the horse, but he let the bridle and saddle fall to the ground, seemingly horror-stricken, whilst the animal, remembering how he had been wounded the preceding night, and fearing for his other ear, reared, kicked, and neighed.

'Come! Be quick then!' shouted Orso.

'Ha! Ors' Anton'! ha! Ors' Anton'!' exclaimed the shepherd. 'Blood of the Madonna!' etc. It was a string of imprecations without number or end, the majority of which defy translation.

'What is the matter now?' inquired Colomba.

They all went up to the horse, and seeing him bleeding and with his ear slit, there was a general burst of surprise and indignation. The reader ought to know that to mutilate an enemy's horse is, for the Corsicans, at once a vengeance, a defiance, and a menace of death. Nothing but a gun-shot can expiate such a crime as this. Although Orso, who had spent a great deal of his life on the continent, felt less keenly than another the enormity of the outrage, nevertheless, if at that moment any Barricinist had made his appearance, it is probable that he would have caused him to expiate immediately an insult which he attributed to his enemies.

'The cowardly rascals!' he exclaimed, 'to wreak their vengeance upon a poor brute, when they dare not meet me face to face!'

'What do you wait for?' cried Colomba, impetuously. 'They come and provoke us, and mutilate our horses, and we make no reply! Are you men?'

'Vengeance!' answered the shepherd. 'Let us show the horse all round the village, and let us give the assault to their house.'

'There is a barn covered with thatch adjoining their tower,' said old Polo Griffo; 'in the twinkling of an eye I will set it in flames.' Another proposed to go and fetch the ladders from the church steeple; a third, to batter in the doors of the Barricini's house by means of a beam of timber, which was lying in the piazza for the construction of a building there. In the midst of all these furious voices, Colomba's was heard predominant, inviting her satellites, before they went to work, to treat them each to a beaker of anisette.

Unfortunately, or rather fortunately, the expected effect of her cruelty to the poor horse was in great part lost on Orso. He had no doubt that this savage mutilation was the work of one of his enemies, and he more particularly suspected Orlanduccio; but he did not feel that the young man, whom he had provoked and struck, had effaced the affront by slitting a horse's ear. On the contrary, this base and ridiculous revenge increased his contempt for his adversaries; and he now thought, with the Préfet, that such people as those did not deserve to measure weapons with him. As soon as he could make himself heard, he declared to his astounded partisans that they must renounce their warlike intentions; and that the authorities who were about to arrive would amply avenge his horse's ear. 'I am the master here,' he added, in a severe tone of voice, 'and I expect to be obeyed. The first who dares to talk again of killing and burning, stands a very good chance of having his brains blown out. Come, saddle me the grey.'

'How, Orso!' said Colomba, drawing him on one side. 'You allow yourself to be insulted! In our father's time, never would a Barricini have dared to mutilate an animal of ours.'

'I promise you they shall have cause to repent it; but it is for gendarmes and jailers, and not for us, to punish a set of wretches who only dare to fight with animals. I tell you, the authorities will grant me ample vengeance:—or if not—you will have no need to remind me whose son I am.'

'Patience!' said Colomba, with a sigh.

'Bear well in mind, sister,' continued Orso, 'that if, on my return, I find that any hostile proceedings against the Barricini have been taken, I will never forgive you for it.' Then he added more gently, 'It is very possible, even very probable, that I may return with the Colonel and his daughter: try to get their rooms in order, and to have a good luncheon, that our guest may suffer as little discomfort as possible. It is all very well, Colomba, to have plenty of courage, but a woman ought also to know how to manage a house. Come, kiss me, and be a good girl. The grey is saddled.'

'Orso,' said Colomba, 'you will not go alone?'

'I have no need of any one,' said Orso; 'and I promise you I will not let them slit my ear.'

'Oh! never will I let you start alone in time of war. Here! Polo Griffo! Gian Francè! Memmo! Take your guns; you will escort my brother.'

After a rather sharp discussion, Orso was obliged to yield and accept the attendance of an escort. He selected from amongst the most excited of his shepherds those who had most loudly counselled him to commence the war; then, after repeating his injunctions to his sister and to the shepherds who remained, he set off on his journey, making a circuit this time, to avoid the Barricini's house.

They were already at some distance from Pietranera, and were advancing at a rapid pace, when on crossing a little brook which lost itself in a marsh, old Polo Griffo perceived several hogs comfortably reclining in the mud, enjoying at the same time the warmth of the sun and the coolness of the water. Instantly, taking aim at the largest, he shot him in the head and killed him on the spot. The defunct's companions started up and took to flight with surprising activity, and although another shepherd fired a second shot, they contrived to reach a thicket safe and sound, in which they disappeared.

'You idiots!' exclaimed Orso; 'you mistake hogs for wild boar.'

'No, indeed, Ors' Anton',' replied Polo Griffo; 'but this herd belongs to the Advocate, and I want to teach him to mutilate our horses.'

'What, you rascals!' cried Orso, in a transport of rage; 'you copy the infamous conduct of our enemies! Leave me, you wretches. I have no need of you. You are only good to fight with hogs. If you dare to follow me, I will break your heads!'

The two shepherds looked at each other in utter astonishment. Orso put spurs to his horse, and disappeared at full gallop.

'Well!' said Polo Griffo, 'that's a good one! Set your heart upon people, to be treated in this way! The Colonel, his father, was angry with you, because you levelled your gun at the Advocate—you were a great fool not to fire!—and the son—you saw what I did for him—he talks of breaking my head, as if it were no better than a leaky wine-gourd. That's what they learn on the continent, Memmo!'

'Yes; and if they find out that it was you who

killed the hog, they'll go to law with you; and Ors' Anton' will neither speak to the judges, nor yet pay the advocate. Luckily, nobody saw you, and Saint Nega will help you out of the business.'

After a short deliberation, the two shepherds concluded that the wisest plan would be to bury the hog in a quagmire; which they duly executed, be it understood, after taking each of them a few slices to grill from the innocent victim of the feuds of the della Rebbias and the Barricini.

XVII.

Relieved of his undisciplined escort, Orso continued his journey, thinking more about the pleasure of seeing Miss Nevill again, than fearing to encounter his enemies. 'The lawsuit which I shall have with those wretches, the Barricini,' he said to himself, 'will oblige me to go to Bastia. Why should not I go there with Miss Nevill? Why, from Bastia, should we not go together to the baths of Orezza?' And all at once the recollections of his childhood pictured to his mind's eye that lovely site. He fancied himself transported to a spot of verdant turf, at the foot of ancient chestnut-trees. On a bank of lustrous grass, scattered with blue flowers resembling those eyes which smiled at him, he beheld Miss Lydia seated by his side. She had taken off her hat, and her fair hair, finer and softer than silk, shone like gold in the sunshine, which glanced through the foliage. Her eyes were of so pure a blue, that they seemed bluer than the firmament. With her cheek resting on her hand, she listened pensively to the words of love which he addressed to her with trembling lips. She had on the same muslin dress which she wore the last time he saw her at Ajaccio. From beneath the folds of this dress there peeped out a little foot in a black satin shoe. Orso said to himself how happy he should be to kiss that foot; but one of Miss Lydia's hands was ungloved, and held a daisy. Orso took the daisy, and Lydia's hand pressed his hand; and he kissed the daisy, and then the hand, and nobody scolded him for it. And all these sort of thoughts and fancies diverted his attention from the road along which he was travelling, and he meanwhile trotted on and on. He was about to kiss a second time in imagination Miss Nevill's white hand, when he was near kissing in reality his horse's head, which suddenly stopped short. It was little Chilina who barred the way by seizing his horse's bridle.

'Where are you going to, Ors' Anton'?' she said. 'Don't you know that your enemy is close by?'

'My enemy!' exclaimed Orso, in a rage at being interrupted at such an interesting moment. 'Where is he?'

'Orlanduccio is not far off. He is waiting for you. Go back. Go back!'

'Ah! he is waiting for me! Did you see him?'

'Yes, Ors' Anton'; I was lying in the fern when he passed. He was looking in all directions with his spyglass.'

'In which direction was he going?'

'He went down there, in the same direction as you are going.'

'Thank you.'

'Ors' Anton', had you not better wait for my uncle?
He will not be long; and with him you can travel in
safety.'

'Fear nothing, Chili; I have no need of your
uncle.'

'If you like, I will go before you.'

'No I thank you; no I thank you.'

And Orso, urging on his horse, proceeded rapidly
in the direction which the little girl had indicated.

His first feeling was a blind transport of rage; and
he said to himself that fortune offered him an excellent opportunity of chastising the coward who muti-
lated a horse, in revenge for a blow. Then, as he
was advancing all the while, the sort of promise
which he had made to the Préfet, and especially the
fear of missing Miss Nevill's visit, modified his sentiments, and almost made him wish that he might not
encounter Orlanduccio. But soon, the remembrance
of his father's death, the insult perpetrated on his
horse, and the Barricini's threats, renewed his angry
feelings, and urged him to seek his enemy in order to
provoke him to fight a duel. Thus agitated by con-
flicting resolutions, he continued to march forwards,
but now with precaution, examining the thickets and
the hedges, and sometimes even coming to a halt, to
listen to the vague noises which are heard in the open
country. Ten minutes after having parted from little
Chilina (it was then about nine o'clock in the morning), he found himself on the slope of a very steep
hill. The road, or rather the scarcely-traced path

L 2

which he followed, traversed a mâquis that had been
recently burnt. At this spot the ground was covered
with whitish ashes; and here and there shrubs and a
few large trees, blackened by the fire and entirely
stripped of their leaves, remained standing, although
they had ceased to live. At the aspect of a mâquis
which has been burnt, you may fancy yourself transported to a northern locality in the midst of winter;
and the contrast between the places which have been
ravaged by the flames, and the luxuriant vegetation
surrounding them, makes them appear still more sad
and desolate. But in this melancholy landscape,
Orso, for the moment, only beheld one thing, important, it is true, in his position: the ground, being
naked, could cover no ambuscade; and the man who
has to fear that every instant a gun-barrel levelled
at his breast may protrude from a thicket, regards as
a sort of oasis any smooth piece of land where there
is nothing to arrest the view. To the burnt mâquis
succeeded several cultivated fields, enclosed, according to the custom of the country, with breast-high
walls of uncemented stone. The path passed between
these enclosures, where enormous chestnut-trees, irregularly planted, presented at a distance the aspect
of a thick grove.

Obliged to dismount by the steepness of the path,
Orso, who had left the bridle on his horse's neck,
descended rapidly by sliding over the ashes; and he
was scarcely five-and-twenty paces from one of these
stone fences to the right of the road, when he perceived, exactly in front of him, at first a gun-barrel,

and then a human head rising just above the top of the wall. The gun was levelled, and he recognised Orlanduccio on the point of firing. Orso immediately put himself on his defence; and the two, taking aim at once, regarded each other for several seconds with that poignant emotion which the bravest man feels at the moment of inflicting or receiving a mortal wound.

'Despicable coward!' Orso exclaimed. Before the words were completely uttered, he saw the flash of Orlanduccio's gun, and almost at the same time a second shot was fired on his left, from the other side of the path, by a man whom he had not perceived and who aimed at him from behind another wall. Both the bullets hit him : one, Orlanduccio's, went through his left arm, which he had exposed while taking aim ; the other struck him in the chest, and tore his coat, but fortunately meeting with the blade of his stiletto, it flattened thereupon, and only inflicted a slight contusion. Orso's left arm dropped motionless at the side of his thigh, and his gun-barrel was lowered for an instant; but he immediately raised it again, and directing his weapon with his unaided right hand, he fired at Orlanduccio. His enemy's head, which was only exposed as far as the eyes, disappeared behind the wall. Orso, turning to the left, fired a second shot at a man enveloped in smoke whom he could scarcely distinguish. This figure also disappeared in turn. The four shots had succeeded each other with incredible rapidity ; practised soldiers never fired in file with shorter intervals of time. After Orso's last shot, all was silent. The smoke issuing from his weapon rose slowly towards the sky; nothing stirred behind the wall, nor was the slightest sound audible. Had it not been for the pain which he felt in his arm, he might have believed that the men at whom he had just fired were the phantoms of his imagination.

Expecting a second attack, Orso took a few steps to place himself behind, one of the dead trees which remained standing in the maquis. Screened by this, he put his gun between his knees and hastily reloaded it. Meanwhile, his left arm gave him acute pain, and felt as if loaded with a heavy weight. What had become of his adversaries? He could not understand it. If they had made their escape, if they had been wounded, he must assuredly have heard some sound, some rustling amongst the leaves. Were they dead then? or rather were they not awaiting, behind their wall, the opportunity of firing at him again? In this uncertainty, and feeling his strength beginning to fail, he placed his right knee on the ground, supported his wounded arm on the other, and made use of a branch still remaining on the trunk of the burnt tree to sustain his gun. With his finger on the trigger, his eyes fixed upon the wall, his ear attentive to the slightest sound, he remained motionless during several minutes, which appeared to him an age. At last, far, far behind him, a distant shout was heard; and soon a dog, running down the hill with the swiftness of an arrow, halted close to him wagging his tail. It was Brusco, the disciple and the companion of the bandits, announcing doubtless his master's arrival: no honest man was ever more impatiently expected. The dog, sniffing the air in the direction of the nearest fence, appeared to scent some cause of uneasiness. Suddenly he uttered a smothered growl, leaped over the wall, and almost instantly jumped back to its top, from which he stared at Orso fixedly, with astonishment in his looks as clearly as a dog's countenance is able to express it. He then held his muzzle to the wind, this time in the direction of the other fence, over which he again leaped. In a second, he reappeared on the top of the wall, manifesting the same astonishment and distrust; he then bounded into the mâquis, with his tail between his legs, constantly regarding Orso, and retreating from him with slow steps and a side-long march, till he found himself at a considerable distance. Then, resuming his course, he remounted the hill almost as swiftly as he had descended it, to meet a man who was descending rapidly in spite of the steepness of the slope.

'Help, Brando!' shouted Orso, as soon as he believed him within reach of his voice.

'Ho! Ors' Anton'! you are wounded!' asked Brandolaccio, running up completely out of breath. 'In your body or in your limbs?'

'In the arm.'

'In the arm! That's nothing. And the other fellow?'

'I think I have hit him.'

Brandolaccio, following his dog, ran to the nearest fence and leaned over, to look on the other side of the wall. Then, taking off his cap, he said—

'Health to Signor Orlanduccio.' And then, turning

towards Orso, he saluted him in turn with an air of gravity, 'That's what I call dishing up a man in proper style.'

'Is he still alive?' asked Orso, breathing with difficulty.

'Oh! he knows better than that; he is too much annoyed at the bullet which you have put into his eye. Blood of the Madonna, what a hole! Yes, a capital gun! What a calibre it has! It will squash you a fellow's brain! I say, Ors' Anton', when I first heard "Pif! Pif!" I said to myself, Sacrebleu! they are bonneting my poor lieutenant. Then I heard "Boum!. Boum!" Ah! says I, the English gun has got a word to say; it gives them their answer. But, Brusco, what do you want with me now?'

The dog led him to the other fence. 'By your leave!' exclaimed Brandolaccio, stupified. 'A double shot! That's all! Plague take you! 'Tis clear that gunpowder is dear, for you use it sparingly.'

'What is it—tell me?' Orso asked.

'Come! No nonsense, Lieutenant! You bring down your game, and want other people to pick it up for you. Somebody will have an odd sort of dessert to-day! And that's the Advocate Barricini. If you want butcher's meat, here it is! Now, who will come to your property?'

'What! Is Vincentello also dead?'

'Very dead. Good health to us!* It was very

* _Salute a noi!_ An exclamation which ordinarily accompanies the employment of the word _dead_, and which serves as a sort of corrective to it.

kind of you to put them so soon out of their misery.
Come and look at Vincentello; he is still on his
knees, with his head leaning against the wall. He
looks as if he were asleep. You may call it a dead
sleep! Poor devil!' ·

Orso turned aside his head with horror. 'Are
you sure he is dead?'

'You are like Sampiero Corso, who never gave but
a single blow. Do you see, there—in the chest, on
the left side? Look, just as Vincileone was hit at
Waterloo. I would bet that the bullet is not far
from the heart. A double shot!—Ah! I will throw
away my gun. Two men at two shots!—with ball!
The two brothers! If he had had a third barrel,
he would have killed the papa. You will do better
another time. What a shot, Ors' Anton'! And then,
to think that a fine fellow like me should never have
the chance of getting a double shot at the gendarmes!'

All the while he was talking, the bandit examined
Orso's arm, and ripped open the sleeve with his
stiletto.

'It is a mere nothing,' he said. 'The coat will
furnish Mademoiselle Colomba with a little work for
her needle. Hein! What's this I see?—this scratch
on the breast? Did anything get in that way? No,
you would not be so plucky. Come, try and move
your fingers. Do you feel my teeth when I bite your
little finger? Not much? It is all one, it will be a
mere nothing. Let me take your handkerchief and
your cravat; your frock-coat is done for. Why the

devil did you make yourself so smart? Were you going to a wedding? There, drink a drop of wine.— Why don't you wear a gourd? Does a Corsican ever travel without his gourd?' Then, in the midst of his surgical operation, he stopped to exclaim, 'A double shot! Both shot dead! Won't the Curé laugh? A double shot! Ah! here comes that little tortoise Chilina at last.'

Orso made no reply. He was as pale as death, and trembled from head to foot.

'Chili,' cried Brandolaccio, 'go and look on the other side of the wall. Hein?' The child, by the help of her hands and feet, climbed up the wall, and as soon as she perceived Orlanduccio's body, she made the sign of the cross.

'That's nothing,' continued the bandit. 'Go and look there, a little further off.'

The child made a second sign of the cross.

'Was it you, uncle?' she timidly inquired.

'I! I am an old good-for-nothing, Chili; that is monsieur's performance. Offer him your compliments.'

Mademoiselle will be finely glad,' said Chilina; 'and she will be very sorry to learn that you are wounded, Ors' Anton'.'

'Come, Ors' Anton',' said the bandit, after he had bandaged the arm; 'Chilina has caught your horse. Get up, and come with me to the mâquis of la Stazzona. He will be a clever fellow who finds you there. We will treat you as well as we possibly can. When we come to the cross of Saint Christina you must dismount. You must give up your horse to Chilina, who will go and acquaint mademoiselle with what has happened, and in the mean time you can confide your errands to her. You may tell the little one anything you please, Ors' Anton'; she would let herself be chopped in pieces rather than betray her friends. Be off, you little hussy,' he said, in affectionate tones. 'The devil take you, excommunication seize you, trumpery baggage!' Brandolaccio, superstitious, like many bandits, was afraid of fascinating children by addressing them in terms of praise or benediction; for it is well known that the mysterious powers who preside over the *Annochiatura* * have the evil habit of executing exactly the contrary of any wish we may express.

'Where do you wish me to go, Brando?' said Orso, in a scarcely audible voice.

'Parbleu! you may take your choice; either to prison or to the mâquis. But a della Rebbia does not know the way to prison. To the mâquis, Ors' Anton'.'

'Farewell, then, to all my hopes!' sorrowfully exclaimed the wounded man,

'Your hopes! Do you hope to do better with a double-barrelled gun? I say, how did they hit you? They must have had as many lives as a cat.'

'They fired first,' said Orso.

'That's true; I forgot. Pif! pif! boum! boum!

* An involuntary fascination which is effected either by the eyes or by word of mouth.

A double shot with one hand!* When any one beats that I will go and hang myself! Come, we have managed to get you on horseback—before leaving take a look at your performance. It is not polite to leave the company in this way without bidding them good-bye.'

Orso set spurs to his horse; for no consideration in the world would he look at the unhappy men whom he had recently slain.

'I say, Ors' Anton',' said the bandit, taking the horse by the bridle, 'do you wish me to speak frankly to you? Well, no offence to you—I am sorry for these poor young fellows. I beg your excuse—so handsome —so young—so strong! Orlanduccio, with whom I have shot so often. Three or four days ago he gave me a bundle of cigars. Vincentello, who was always so merry! 'Tis quite true you have done what you ought to do—and, besides, the shot is too famous to regret it. But I, for my part, had nothing to do with your vengeance. I know you were right; when you have an enemy, you must get rid of him. But the Barricini were an old family—another family who can't come up to the scratch!—and that by means of a double shot! It's capital.'

Delivering thus the funeral oration of the Barricini, Brandolaccio hastily conducted Orso, Chilina,

---

* If any incredulous sportsman is inclined to doubt M. della Rebbia's double shot, I advise him to go to Sartena, and inquire how one of the most distinguished and most amiable inhabitants of that town extricated himself alone, and with his left arm broken, from a position at least as dangerous.

and the dog Brusco, towards the mâquis of la Stazzona.

XVIII.

Meanwhile, shortly after Orso's departure, Colomba
had learned through her spies that the Barricini were
out and abroad ; and, from that moment, she suffered
the most extreme uneasiness. She ran about the house
in all directions, going backwards and forwards from
the kitchen to the rooms prepared for her guests, doing
nothing, yet always busy, and constantly stopping to
look if there were any unusual movement in the
village. About eleven o'clock a tolerably numerous
cavalcade entered Pietranera; it was the Colonel,
his daughter, their servants, and the guide. Colomba's
first words on receiving them were, 'Have you seen
my brother?' She next asked the guide which road
he had taken, and at what hour they had started?
and, from the answer she received, she could not
understand why they had not met.

'Perhaps your brother went by the heights,' said
the guide. 'We came by the path through the
valley.'

But Colomba shook her head and repeated her
questions. In spite of her natural firmness, which
was augmented by the pride of concealing her weakness from the eyes of strangers, it was impossible for
her to hide her apprehensions, which were shared by
the Colonel, and especially by Miss Lydia, as soon as
she had acquainted them with the attempt at reconciliation which had resulted in such an unfortunate
issue. Miss Nevill became agitated, wanted to send

messengers in all directions, and her father offered to remount his horse and set off with the guide in search of Orso. Her guests' alarm reminded Colomba of her duties as the mistress of the house. She forced a smile, pressed the Colonel to sit down to table, and found a score of plausible reasons for her brother's absence, which she demolished herself a moment afterwards. The Colonel, believing it was his duty as a man to reassure the ladies, gave an explanation of his own.

'I would wager anything,' he said, 'that della Rebbia fell in with game; he could not resist the temptation, and we shall see him come back with a prodigious bagful. By Jove!' he added, 'on the road we did hear four gun-shots. Two of them were louder than the others, and I said to my daughter, "I am sure that's della Rebbia; no gun but mine would give such a report."'

Colomba turned pale, and Lydia, who watched her narrowly, easily guessed what sort of suspicions the Colonel's conjecture had suggested. After a silence of several minutes, Colomba anxiously inquired whether the two louder detonations had preceded or followed the others. But neither the Colonel, his daughter, nor the guide, had paid any great attention to this capital point.

About one o'clock, none of Colomba's messengers having yet returned, she summoned all her courage and compelled her guests to sit down to table; but, with the exception of the Colonel, no one could touch a morsel. At the slightest noise in the piazza

159

Colomba ran to the window, and then sadly resumed
her seat, and still more sadly forced herself to continue
with her friends an unmeaning conversation to which
nobody paid the least attention, and which was interrupted by long intervals of silence.

All at once a horse was heard to gallop in. 'Ah!
this time it must be my brother!' cried Colomba,
rising. But when she saw Chilina riding astride on
Orso's horse, 'My brother is dead!' she exclaimed,
in heart-rending tones.

The Colonel dropped his glass, Miss Nevill uttered
a scream, and they all hurried to the house door.
Before Chilina could dismount from her steed, she was
lifted like a feather by Colomba, who hugged her so
tight as almost to stifle her. The child understood
her terrible looks, and her first word was that of the
chorus in Otello, 'He lives!' Colomba loosened her
grasp, and Chilina slipped to the ground as adroitly
as a young kitten.

'The others?' asked Colomba, in a hoarse voice.

Chilina made the sign of the cross with her fore
and her middle fingers. Instantly Colomba's deadly
paleness was succeeded by a vivid flush, which over-
spread her countenance, she darted a burning glance
at the Barricini's house, and said to her guests with
a smile, 'Let us go in and take our coffee.'

The bandits' Iris had a long tale to tell. Her
patois, translated by Colomba into more or less correct Italian, and then into English by Miss Nevill,
extorted more than one impatient exclamation from the
Colonel, more than one sigh from Lydia; but Colomba

listened with an impassible air, only she twisted her damask napkin in a way which threatened to tear it in pieces. She interrupted the child five or six times to make her repeat that Brandolaccio said the wound was not dangerous, and that he had seen many much worse in his time. In conclusion, Chilina reported that Orso had urgently requested some writing-paper, and that he charged his sister not to allow a lady, who perhaps would be staying in the house, to depart before she had received a letter from him. 'That,' added the child, 'is what tormented him the most; and I had already set off when he called me back to tell me to be sure to deliver the message.' At this report of her brother's injunctions, Colomba slightly smiled, and squeezed the Englishwoman's hand, who melted into tears, and did not feel that there was any necessity to translate this portion of the narrative to her father.

'Yes, you will stay with me, dear friend!' cried Colomba, embracing Miss Nevill, 'and you will give us your aid.'

At this, taking a quantity of old linen out of a closet, she began to tear it up to make bandages and lint. To see her sparkling eyes, her animated complexion, and her alternations of coolness and pre-occupation, it was difficult to say whether she was most afflicted by her brother's wound, or enchanted at the death of her enemies. Sometimes she poured out coffee for the Colonel, vaunting her skill in its preparation; sometimes distributing work to Miss Nevill and Chilina, she directed them how to prepare the bandages and roll them up; she inquired for the twentieth time whether Orso's wound made him suffer much. Continually she stopped in the midst of her work to say to the Colonel, 'Two such able, such terrible men! And he, all alone, wounded, with only one arm to make use of, brought them down both. What courage, Colonel! Is he not a hero? Ah! Miss Nevill, what a blessing it must be to live in a quiet country like yours! I was sure you did not yet know my brother. I said, the hawk will spread his wings. You were deceived by his gentle mien; but when he was with you, Miss Nevill—ah! if he could see how busily you are at work for him. Poor Orso!'

Miss Lydia did not get on very fast with her task, and could not find a word to say. Her father asked why they did not immediately go and make a complaint before a magistrate. He talked about coroner's inquests, and a variety of other things equally unknown in Corsica. Finally, he wanted to know whether that good M. Brandolaccio's country seat was very far distant from Pietranera, and whether he could not go himself and visit his friend.

And Colomba replied with her usual calmness that Orso was in the bush; that he had a bandit for his nurse; that he would be running great risks if he were to show himself before they had made certain how the Préfet and the judges were disposed in the matter; and, lastly, that she would contrive to get a clever surgeon to go and see him by stealth. 'Above all things, Colonel,' she said, 'be sure you remember that you heard the four shots, and that you told me that Orso fired after the others.' The Colonel understood nothing about the business, and his daughter only sighed and wiped her eyes.

The day was very far advanced, when a sad procession entered the village. They brought back to the Advocate Barricini the bodies of his children, each lying across a mule that was led by a peasant. A crowd of retainers and idle people followed the melancholy cortège. They were accompanied by the gendarmes, who always arrived too late, and by the Deputy Mayor, who raised his arm to the sky, incessantly repeating, 'What will Monsieur le Préfet say?' Several women, amongst whom was Orlanduccio's nurse, tore their hair, and uttered savage howls. But their noisy grief produced a much feebler impression on the spectator than the mute despair of a personage on whom every eye was fixed. It was the unhappy father, who went from one body to the other, raising their heads, which were soiled by the dirt, kissing their purple lips, and sustaining their limbs which were already stiff, as if to save them from being jolted on the road. Sometimes he opened his mouth to speak, but not a cry, not a word came forth. With his eyes constantly fixed on the corpses, he ran against stones and trees and every other obstacle that lay in his way.

The lamentations of the women and the curses of the men redoubled when they came in sight of Orso's house. Some Rebbianist shepherds having ventured to utter an exclamation of triumph, their adversaries could not contain their indignation. 'Vengeance! vengeance!' shouted several voices. Stones were thrown; and two gun-shots, aimed at the windows o the room in which Colomba and her guests were sitting, pierced the shutters, and scattered splinters of wood on the very table at which the two ladies were at work. Miss Lydia screamed aloud, the Colonel seized a gun, and Colomba, before they could stop her, rushed to the house door, and opened it impetuously. Then, standing on the raised threshold, with her hands outstretched to curse her enemies:

'Cowards!' she cried, 'to fire at women! to fire at strangers! Are you Corsicans? Are you men? Wretches, who only dare smite people in the back, come forward! I defy you. I am alone; my brother is far away. Kill me, kill my guests; the action is worthy of you. You dare not, cowards that you are! You know that we avenge ourselves. Go; go, and weep like women, and be thankful that we do not exact more blood than we have done!'

In Colomba's voice and attitude there was something imposing and terrible: the crowd retreated in affright, as if it had beheld one of those malevolent fairies, of whom the Corsicans tell such dreadful tales when they meet to spend their winter evenings. The Deputy Mayor, the gendarmes, and a certain number of women, took advantage of this movement to throw themselves between the two parties; for the Rebbianist shepherds were already making ready their arms, and at one moment it was to be feared the Piazza would become the scene of a general

M 2

engagement. But the two factions had lost their leaders; and the Corsicans, disciplined in their very fury, rarely come to actual blows in the absence of the principal authors of their intestine wars. Besides, Colomba, rendered prudent by success, restrained her little garrison. 'Leave those poor people to weep,' she said; 'let the old man fetch home his own flesh and blood. What would be the good of killing an old fox who has no more teeth to bite with? Giudice Barricini! remember the second of August! remember the bloody pocket-book, in which your false hand wrote a forged name! My father had entered your debt therein; your sons have paid it. I give you my quittance, old Barricini!'

Colomba, with folded arms and a smile of disdain upon her lips, saw the bodies carried into the house of her enemies, and the crowd slowly dispersed afterwards. She closed her door, and, returning to the Colonel, said:

'I have to beg your pardon, monsieur, in behalf of my countrymen. I would never have believed that Corsicans would fire at a house which sheltered strangers, and I am ashamed of my country.'

At night, when Miss Lydia had retired to her chamber, the Colonel followed her, and asked her whether they had not better, the very next day, leave a village in which they ran the chance of having a bullet lodged in their head at any instant, and get away as soon as possible from a country where nothing was to be seen but treachery and murder.

Miss Nevill remained some time without replying,

and it was evident that her father's proposition caused her considerable embarrassment. At last she said :

'How can we leave this unfortunate young person at a moment when she stands in such need of consolation? Does it not strike you, papa, that it would be very cruel on our part?'

'It is on your account that I speak, my child,' said the Colonel; 'and if I knew you were in safety at the hotel at Ajaccio, I assure you I should be very sorry to leave this cursed island without first shaking hands with that brave fellow, della Rebbia.'

'Well then, papa, let us wait a little longer; and before we leave, let us make sure that we cannot be of service to them.'

'Good-hearted girl!' said the Colonel, kissing his daughter's forehead. 'I am pleased to see you sacrifice your own comforts for the sake of relieving the misfortunes of others. You will never repent of having done a good action.'

Miss Lydia tossed in her bed, unable to sleep. Sometimes the vague noises she heard sounded like the preparations for an attack on the house; sometimes, reassured on her own account, she thought of the poor sufferer, probably at that moment stretched on the cold ground, with no other help than what he could expect from the charity of a bandit. She pictured him to herself covered with blood, writhing in horrible tortures; and what is singular was, that every time that Orso's image presented itself to her imagination, he always appeared exactly as she had beheld him at the moment of his departure, pressing to his lips the talisman which she had given him. Then she thought of his bravery. She said to herself that the terrible danger from which he had just escaped had been incurred on her account, in order that he might see her a little sooner. She was very near persuading herself that it was in her defence that Orso's arm had been broken. She reproached herself as being the cause of his wound, but she admired him all the more for it; and if the famous double shot had not, in her eyes, quite the same merit as it had in Brandolaccio's and Colomba's, she nevertheless believed that very few heroes of romance would have displayed equal intrepidity and presence of mind in case of like peril.

The chamber which she occupied was that of Colomba. Over a sort of oaken prayer-desk, by the side of a blessed palm-branch, was suspended to the wall a miniature portrait of Orso in his Sous-Lieutenant's uniform. Miss Nevill took down the portrait, examined it attentively, and at last laid it by her bedside, instead of replacing it. She did not fall asleep till the point of day; and when she awoke, the sun was already high above the horizon. In front of her bed she perceived Colomba, who awaited motionless the moment when she opened her eyes.

'Well, mademoiselle, you are miserably off in our wretched house!' said Colomba. 'I fear you have scarcely been able to sleep.'

'Have you had any news, dear friend?' said Miss Nevill, sitting up in the bed.

She caught sight of Orso's portrait, and hastily tossed a handkerchief to conceal it.

'Yes, I have news, answered Colomba, smiling. And taking the portrait, she asked, 'Do you think it a good likeness? He is better looking than that.'

'Good Heavens!' said Miss Nevill, in great confusion,' I took down—in my thoughtless way—that portrait. I have the bad habit of pulling everything about. and putting nothing in its place. How is your brother?'

'Tolerably well. Giocanto came here this morning before four o'clock. He brought me a letter—for you, Miss Lydia; Orso has not done me the favour to write to me. Certainly, there is on the direction, "To Colomba;" but lower down, he has put, "To Miss N——." Sisters are not jealous of each other. Giocanto tells me that writing gave him considerable pain.. Giocanto, who writes a magnificent hand, offered to write at his dictation. He refused the offer. He wrote with a pencil, as he lay on his back. Brandolaccio held the paper. My brother was constantly trying to sit up; and then, at the slightest movement, he suffered most acute pain in his arm. It grieved one to see him, Giocanto said. Here is the letter.'

Miss Nevill read the letter, which was written in English, doubtless as an additional precaution. Its contents were as follows :—

' MADEMOISELLE,

'I have been the victim of an unhappy fatality : I know not what my enemies will say, nor what calumnies they will invent. To me it is a

matter of indifference, provided you, mademoiselle,
give no credence to them.   Ever since I first saw
you, I have been flattering myself with senseless
dreams.   It required this catastrophe to show me my
folly ; I am reasonable now.   I am aware what sort
of future awaits me, and shall meet it with resignation.
This ring which you gave me, and which I believed
to be a talisman of happiness, I dare. keep no longer.
I fear, Miss Nevill, that you will feel regret at having
bestowed your gifts so badly ; or rather, I fear its
reminding me of the time when I had lost my senses.
Colomba will return it to you.   Adieu, mademoiselle ;
you are about to leave Corsica, and I shall see you no
more ; but tell my sister that I still enjoy your
esteem.   I assure you, with truth, that I still deserve it.   O. D. R.'

Miss Lydia had turned on one side to read the
letter ; and Colomba, who watched her attentively,
put into her hands the Egyptian ring, with inquiring
looks as to what it all might mean.   But Miss Lydia
did not venture to raise her head ; she gazed sadly at
the ring, which she alternately put on her finger and
took off again.

'Dear Miss Nevill,' said Colomba, 'may I not
know what my brother says ?   Has he mentioned the
state of his health ?'

'But,' said Lydia, blushing, 'he says nothing about
it.   His letter is in English.   He requests me to tell
my father.   He hopes the Préfet will be able to settle
the business—'

Colomba, with a cunning smile, seated herself on

the bedside, took both Miss Nevill's hands in hers, and looking at her with her piercing eyes, said, 'Won't you be a good-natured girl? Won't you let my brother have an answer? You would do him such a deal of good! At one time I had the idea of waking you when his letter arrived, but I did not dare.'

'You were very wrong,' said Miss Nevill. 'If a word from me could—'

'Now I have no means of sending him letters. The Préfet is come, and Pietranera is full of his hangers-on. By-and-by we will see what can be done. Ah! if you only knew my brother, Miss Nevill, you would love him as I love him, he is so good, so brave! Just think what he did; one against two, and he wounded!'

The Préfet had returned. Informed by an express from the Deputy Mayor, he came with a body of gendarmes and voltigeurs, accompanied also by the Procureur du Roi, with clerks, and secretaries, and all the rest, to investigate this fresh and terrible catastrophe, which complicated, or, if you will, which terminated the enmities of the families of Pietranera. Shortly after his arrival he saw Colonel Nevill and his daughter, and did not conceal from them his fears that the affair might take an unfavourable turn. 'You are aware,' he said, 'that the combat took place without witnesses, and the unfortunate young men's reputation for skill and courage was so well established, that every one refuses to believe that Monsieur della Rebbia could have killed them both without the assistance of the bandits with whom he is said to have taken refuge.'

'That is an impossibility,' exclaimed the Colonel. 'Orso della Rebbia is an honourable young man : I will answer for him.'

'Such is my own belief,' said the Préfet ; 'but the Procureur du Roi (those gentlemen are always suspicious) does not appear to be very favourably disposed. He holds in his hands a document which goes against your friend. It is a threatening letter addressed to Orlanduccio, in which he appoints a rendezvous, and the rendezvous, in his ideas, look very like an ambuscade.'

'But Orlanduccio,' said the Colonel, 'refused to fight like a man of honour.'

'It is not the custom here. People lie in wait for each other and shoot each other in the back : such is the fashion of the country. There is one favourable point in the evidence : a child affirms that she heard four shots, of which the two last, louder than the others, were fired by a weapon of large bore, like M. della Rebbia's gun. Unfortunately this child is the niece of one of the bandits who are suspected of being accomplices, and she has been tutored, it is thought, to make that statement.'

'Monsieur,' said Miss Lydia, blushing up to the eyes, 'we were on the road when the shots were fired, and we remarked the same circumstance.'

'Really ? That is very important. And you, Colonel, you doubtless made the same observation ?'

'Yes,' replied Miss Nevill eagerly ; 'it was my

father, who is accustomed to guns, who said, " That's
M. della Rebbia shooting with my Manton.'

'And the shots which you recognised, were they
really the last?'

'The two last, were they not, papa?'

The Colonel's recollections were not exactly clear,
but on all occasions he made a point of never contra-
dicting his daughter.

'We must immediately acquaint the Procureur du
Roi with that. Moreover, we expect a surgeon this
evening, who will examine the bodies, and will ascertain whether the wounds were made by the weapon
in question.'

'It was I who gave it to Orso,' said the Colonel,
'and I wish it had been at the bottom of the sea.
That is to say, the brave fellow! I am very glad he
happened to have it, for without my Manton I hardly
know how he would have got out of the scrape.'

XIX.

The surgeon arrived rather late: he had met with
an adventure on the road. Encountered by Giocanto
Castriconi, he had been requested with the greatest
politeness, to go and pay a visit to a wounded man.
They took him to Orso, and he gave the first dressing
to the wound. Afterwards the bandit accompanied
him for a considerable distance on the way back, and
greatly edified him by talk about the most eminent
professors at Pisa, who he stated were his intimate
friends.

'Doctor,' said the theologian, on taking leave,

' you have so highly prepossessed me in your favour
that it is superfluous for me to remind you that a
medical man ought to be as discreet as a confessor.'
At the same time he played with the lock of his gun.
' You have quite forgotten the spot where we had the
honour to meet. Adieu; delighted to have made
your acquaintance.'

Colomba urgently entreated the Colonel to be present at the post-mortem examination of the bodies.
' You know my brother's gun better than any one
else, and your presence will be very useful. Besides there are so many ill-natured people here
that we might run great risks if we had no one to
take our part.'

Left alone with Miss Lydia, she complained of
having a severe headache, and proposed a short walk
just outside the village. 'The open air will do me
good,' she said; 'it is so long since I have breathed
it.' On the way she began talking about her brother,
and Miss Lydia, who took great interest in the subject, did not notice that they had left Pietranera far
behind them. The sun was setting when she observed it at last, and requested Colomba to return.
Colomba knew a bypath, she said, which would
shorten the distance considerably; and leaving the
path they had hitherto followed, she took another apparently much less frequented. Soon she began to
climb a hill so steep that she was continually obliged
to hold on to the branches of trees with one hand,
whilst with the other she dragged her companion
after her. After a long quarter of an hour passed in
making this difficult ascent, they found themselves

on a small platform covered with myrtles and arbu-
tuses, in the midsr of which large blocks of granite
protruded through the soil in all directions. Lydia
was extremely fatigued ; nothing was to be seen of
the village, and it was almost night.

'Do you know, my dear Colomba,' she said, 'but I
fear that we have lost our way'?

'Don't be alarmed,' Colomba replied. 'Let us
walk on. Follow me.'

'But I assure you that you are mistaken; the
village cannot be in this direction; I would bet anything that we are turning our backs on it. Look
there, do you see those lights in the distance ? certainly that's where Pietranera is.'

'My dear friend,' said Colomba, with some excitement, 'you are right; but a couple of hundred paces
off, in the mâquis—'

'Well ?'

'Is my brother. I could see him and embrace
him if you liked.'

Miss Nevill started.

'I left Pietranera,' pursued Colomba, 'without
being remarked, because I was with you, otherwise
they would have followed me. To be so near him
and not to see him! Why should not you come
with me and see my poor brother ? it would be such
a consolation to him.'

'But, Colomba, it would not be proper on my part.'

'I understand. You city ladies are always tormenting yourselves about what is proper—we country
women only think of what is right.'

'But it is so late. And your brother, what will he think of me?'

'He will think that he is not abandoned by his friends, and that will give him the courage to support his sufferings.'

'And my father—he will be so anxious.'

'He knows you are with me. Well, make up your mind. You were looking at his portrait this morning,' she added, with a cunning smile.

'No, really, Colomba, I dare not. Those bandits who are there—'

'Very well. Those bandits do not know you, and what does it signify? You were wishing to see some!'

'Good heavens!'

'Come, mademoiselle, take your choice. To leave you alone here is quite impossible; no one can tell what might happen. Either let us go and see Orso, or let us return to the village together. I shall see my brother—God knows when—perhaps never.'

'What's that you say, Colomba? Well, then, come along; but only for one minute. We will return home immediately.'

Colomba pressed her hand, and without replying, walked forward so rapidly that Lydia could scarcely follow her. Happily Colomba soon came to a halt, saying to her companion, 'We must not advance any further without giving the notice; we might perhaps expose ourselves to be shot.' She whistled between her fingers. Soon a dog was heard to bark, and the bandit's advanced guard shortly made his appearance. It was our old acquaintance, the dog Brusco, who immediately recognised Colomba, and undertook to act as her guide. After many windings in the narrow paths of the thicket, they were met by a couple of men armed up to the teeth.

'Is that you, Brandolaccio?' asked Colomba, ' Where is my brother?'

'Down there,' replied the bandit. 'But walk softly; he is fast asleep for the first time since his accident.'

The two ladies approached cautiously, and close to a fire, whose glare had been prudently masked by a low wall of dry stones built around it, they beheld Orso lying on a bed of fern and covered with a *pilone*. He was very pale, and his breathing was audibly oppressed. Colomba sat down by his side and gazed at him in silence, with her hands joined as if she were praying mentally. Miss Lydia, covering her face with her handkerchief, pressed close to her; but from time to time she raised her head to look at the wounded man over Colomba's shoulder. A quarter of an hour elapsed without any one uttering a syllable. At a signal from the theologian, Brandolaccio retreated with him into the thicket, to the great satisfaction of Miss Lydia, who, for the first time, thought that the bandits' long beards and accoutrements had too much local colour.

At last Orso made a movement; Colomba immediately leaned over him and kissed him repeatedly, overwhelming him with questions about his wound,

his sufferings, and his requirements. After replying
that he was as well as could be, Orso in turn inquired
whether Miss Nevill were still at Pietranera, and if
she had written to him. Colomba, stooping over her
brother, completely concealed her companion, whom
the darkness also would have prevented him from
recognising. She held one of Miss Nevill's hands,
whilst with the other she gently raised the patient's
head.

'No, brother; she has given me no letter for you;
but you are always thinking about Miss Nevill; do
you really love her?'

'Do I love her, Colomba!—But she—perhaps she
despises me now!'

At that moment, Miss Nevill made an effort to
withdraw her hand; but it was not easy to make
Colomba let go her hold; and though small and well
formed, her hand was gifted with a degree of strength
of which we have had sufficient proof.

'Despise you!' exclaimed Colomba, 'after such an
exploit. On the contrary, she speaks highly of you.
Ah! Orso, I should have never have done talking to
you about her.'

The hand was constantly trying to escape, but
Colomba succeeded in drawing it closer and closer to
Orso.

'But, in short,' asked the patient, 'why has she sent
me no answer? One single line, and I should have
been content.'

By constantly pulling Miss Nevill's hand, Colomba
at last contrived to place it in her brother's. Then

suddenly retreating with a burst of laughter, 'Orso,'
she cried, 'take care how you speak ill of Miss Nevill,
for she understands Corsican perfectly.'

Lydia instantly withdrew her hand, and stammered
a few unintelligible words. Orso believed he was in
a dream.

'You here, Miss Nevill! Oh! how did you
venture? Ah! how happy you make me!' Raising
himself with difficulty, he endeavoured to draw close
to her.

' I accompanied your sister,' said Lydia, 'that they
might not suspect where she was going. And besides,
I also wished to be assured that— Alas! how uncomfortable you must be here!'

Colomba was sitting behind Orso. She cautiously
lifted him, so as to support his head on her knees.
She put her arms around his neck, and motioned
Lydia to approach. 'Nearer, nearer! she said; 'a
wounded man ought not to have to raise his voice.'
And as Lydia hesitated, she took her hand, and forced
her to sit so close that her dress touched Orso, and
that her hand, of which she still kept hold, rested
upon Orso's shoulder.

'He is comfortable so,' said Colomba, gaily. 'You
are not so very badly off, are you, Orso, bivouacking
in the mâquis such a lovely night as this?'

'Oh, yes! a most lovely night!' said Orso; 'I
shall never forget it!'

'How you must suffer!' said Miss Nevill.

'My suffering is over,' said Orso; 'I should like
to die where I am.' And his right hand approached

Miss Nevill's, which was constantly held imprisoned by Colomba.

'You must absolutely be transported to some place Monsieur della Rebbia, where you can receive proper attention. I shall not be able to sleep, now that I know in what a wretched state you are lying—out in the open air—'

'If I had not feared to meet you, Miss Nevill, I would have endeavoured to return to Pietranera, and give myself up as a prisoner.'

'Eh! why should you fear to meet her, Orso?' inquired Colomba.

'I had disobeyed you, Miss Nevill, and I should not have dared to look you in the face at that moment.'

'Do you know, Miss Lydia, that you can make my brother do just as you please?' said Colomba, laughing. 'I shall not allow him to see you.'

'I hope,' said Miss Nevill, 'that this unfortunate affair will be cleared up, and that you will soon have nothing to fear. I shall be very glad, when we depart, to know that they have done you justice, and that your loyalty has been acknowledged as well as your courage.'

'You are going to depart, Miss Nevill! Do not say that word again.'

'It cannot be helped. My father cannot shoot for ever. He wishes to leave.'

Orso let fall his hand, which touched Miss Lydia's, and there was a moment's silence.

'Nonsense!' resumed Colomba. 'We shall not

allow you to quit in such a hurry. We have still a
great deal to show you at Pietranera. Besides, you
have promised to take my portrait, and you have not
yet begun it. And then I have promised to compose
you a *serenata* in seventy-five couplets, And then—
but what is Brusco growling at?—Brandalaccio is
running after him; I must go and see what is the
matter.'

She immediately rose, and placing, without the
slightest ceremony, Orso's head on Miss Nevill's lap,
she ran after the bandits.

A little astonished at finding herself thus supporting a handsome young man, tête-à-tête with him in
the midst of a copse-wood, Miss Nevill scarcely knew
what to do; for by withdrawing abruptly, she feared
that she should hurt the patient. But Orso gave up
of his own accord the soft pillow to which his sister
had just transferred him, and raising himself on his
right arm, said, 'So you are going to leave soon, Miss
Lydia? I never thought that you would make a
long stay in this unhappy country; and yet, ever
since your arrival here, it makes me a hundred times
more sorry to think that I must say adieu. I am a
poor lieutenant — without prospects — and now pro-
scribed. What a moment, Miss Lydia, to tell you I
love you!—but it is doubtless the only opportunity I
shall ever have, and I fancy that I am less wretched
now that I have relieved my heart.'

Miss Lydia turned her head on one side, as if
the darkness did not suffice to conceal her blushes.
'Monsieur della Rebbia,' she said with a trembling

voice, 'should I have come to this place if——'
And as she spoke, she placed the Egyptian talisman
in Orso's hand. Then making a violent effort to
resume her habitual tone of pleasantry, 'It is very
unkind of you, Monsieur Orso, to talk so. In the
midst of the mâquis, surrounded by your bandits, you
know I should never dare to be cut of temper with
you.'

Orso made a movement to kiss the hand which
restored the talisman; and, as Lydia withdrew it
rather hastily, he lost his balance and fell on his
wounded arm. He could not suppress a painful
groan.

'You have hurt yourself, my dear friend?' she
exclaimed, raising him up. 'It is my fault! Pardon
me.' They had been talking together for some time
past, in a low voice, and very close to each other,
when Colomba, who rushed in hurriedly, found them
in exactly the same position in which she had left
them.

'The voltigeurs!' she cried. 'Orso, try and get
up, and walk; I will help you.'

'Leave me,' said Orso. 'Tell the bandits to make
their escape; let them arrest me; it is of little consequence. But take care of Miss Lydia; in Heaven's
name, don't let them see her here!'

'I will not leave you,' said Brandolaccio, who followed Colomba. 'The serjeant of the voltigeurs is
one of the Advocate's godsons. Instead of arresting
you he will kill you, and will afterwards say that he
did not do it on purpose.'

Orso made an effort to rise; he even took a few steps; but soon stopping short, he said, 'I cannot walk. Make your escape, all the rest of you. Adieu, Miss Nevill; give me your hand,—and adieu!'

'We will not leave you!' exclaimed both the ladies.

'If you cannot walk,' said Brandolaccio, 'I must carry you. Come, Lieutenant, pluck up your courage; we shall have time to decamp by the valley, down there. M. le Curé will furnish them with a little employment.'

'No, leave me,' said Orso, lying down on the ground. 'Colomba, get Miss Nevill away!'

'You are strong, Mademoiselle Colomba,' said Brandolaccio; 'lift him up by the shoulders; I have got good hold of the feet. Capital! Straight forward! March!'

They were carrying him away at a rapid pace, in spite of his protestations; Miss Lydia followed them, horribly frightened, when a shot was heard, to which five or six others immediately replied. Lydia uttered a scream, Brandolaccio an imprecation; but he doubled his pace; and Colomba, following his example, ran through the thicket without minding the branches which whipped her face and tore her dress.

'Stoop, my dear, stoop,' she said to her companion, 'a bullet might hit you.' In this way they marched, or rather they ran, some five hundred paces, when Brandolaccio declared that he could go no further, and dropped on the ground, in spite of Colomba's exhortations and reproaches.

'Where is Miss Nevill?' Orso inquired.

But Miss Nevill, alarmed by the gun-shots, arrested at every moment by the tangled copse, soon lost all trace of the fugitives, and was left alone in a state of extreme agitation and anxiety.

'She is lagging behind,' said Brandolaccio, 'but she is not lost; women are always found again. Only listen, Ors' Anton', what a row the Curé is making with your gun. Unluckily it is as dark as pitch, and they may shoot all night without doing each other much harm.'

'Hush!' cried Colomba; 'I hear a horse; we are saved.'

'In fact, a horse which was grazing in the mâquis, frightened by the noise of the guns, was making its way in their direction.

'We are saved!' repeated Brandolaccio. To run up to the horse, to seize him by the mane, and slip the noose of a rope into his mouth by way of a bridle, was for the bandit, with Colomba's assistance, the work of a moment. 'We had better now let the Curé know,' he said. He whistled twice; a distant whistle responded to the signal, and the Manton's deep-toned voice ceased to be heard. Brandolaccio jumped on the horse's back. Colomba placed her brother before him; the bandit held him tight with one arm while he directed his steed with the other. In spite of his double load the horse, excited by a couple of good kicks in the stomach, set off at a rapid pace, and galloped down a steep hill on which any other than a Corsican horse would have killed himself a hundred times.

Colomba then retraced her steps, calling Miss Nevill with all her strength ; but no voice replied to hers. After wandering some time at hazard, endeavouring to find the path by which she had come, she fell in with a couple of voltigeurs, who challenged her with, ' Who goes there ?'

' Well, gentlemen !' said Colomba, in a bantering tone, ' you have made a great deal of noise. How many slain ?'

' You were with the bandits,' said one of the soldiers ; ' you must come with us.'

' With great pleasure,' she replied : ' but I have a friend hereabouts, and we must find her first.'

' Your friend is already caught, and you and she will go and sleep in prison.'

' In prison ? We will see about that ; but meanwhile conduct me to her.'

The voltigeurs led her to the bandits' encampment, where they collected the trophies of their expedition, namely the *pilone* which had covered Orso, an old boiler, and a jug full of water. At the same spot was also Miss Nevill, who, found by the soldiers half dead with fear, replied only by tears to all the questions which they put to her respecting the number of the bandits and the direction they had taken.

Colomba threw herself into her arms and whispered in her ear, ' They are saved !' Then addressing the serjeant of the voltigeurs, she said, ' Monsieur, you clearly see that mademoiselle knows nothing of what you are asking her about. Allow us to return to the village, where we are impatiently expected.'

'We shall take you there, and that quicker than you like, my darling,' said the serjeant; 'and you will have to explain what you were doing in the wood at this time of night with the brigands, who have just made their escape. These rascals must be wizards and sorcerers, for they fascinate young women irresistibly. Wherever there are bandits you are sure to find pretty girls.'

'You are very gallant, Monsieur le Serjeant,' said Colomba, 'but you had better be careful what you say. This young lady is related to the Préfet, and I advise you not to carry your jokes too far.'

'Related to the Préfet!' murmured a voltigeur to his commanding officer; 'in fact she does wear a hat.'

'I don't care for the hat,' said the serjeant; 'they were both of them with the Curé, who is the biggest scoundrel in the neighbourhood, and my duty is to take them prisoners, consequently we have no further business here. If it had not been for that cursed Corporal Taupin—the drunken Frenchman showed himself before I had surrounded the copse— if it had not been for him we should have caught the whole of them at one sweep of the net.'

'There are seven of you, I think?' asked Colomba. 'Do you know, gentlemen, that if by chance the three brothers, Gambini, Sarocchi, and Theodore Poli, should happen to join Brandolaccio and the Curé at St. Christina's Cross, they might give you a little trouble. If you are likely to have any conversation with the *Commandante della Campagna*,*

* The title assumed by Theodore Poli.

I should not care to make one of the party. By night
bullets have no respect of persons.'

The possibility of an encounter with the redoubt-
able bandits whom Colomba had just named appeared
to make a considerable impression on the voltigeurs.
All the while swearing at Corporal Taupin, that dog
of a Frenchman, the serjeant gave the order to retreat, and his little troop took the road to Pietranera,
carrying with them the *pilone* and the boiler. As
for the jug, they passed sentence on it with a hearty
kick. A voltigeur wanted to take Miss Lydia's arm,
but Colomba instantly repulsed him, with ' Let
nobody dare to touch her. Do you think we shall
try to run away ? Come, Lydia, my dear, lean on
me, and don't cry like a child. You have had an
adventure which will not end badly. In half an hour
we shall be sitting down to supper. For my own
part I shall be very glad to get it.'

' What will they think of me ?' said Miss Nevill in
a whisper.

' They will think you lost your way in the wood,
that's all.'

' What will the Préfet say ? what will my father
especially say ?'

' The Préfet ? You will tell him to mind his préfecture. Your father ? From the way in which you
were talking with Orso I should have thought you
had something to say to your father.'

Miss Nevill pressed her arm without replying.

' Does not my brother,' murmured Colomba in her
ear, ' deserve to be loved ? Don't you love him a little ?'

'Ah, Colomba!' answered Miss Nevill, with a smile in spite of her confusion, 'you have betrayed me—me who had such confidence in you!'

Colomba put her arm round her waist, and kissing her on the forehead, said, very low, 'My dear little sister, will you forgive me?'

'I cannot help it, my terrible sister,' said Lydia, returning her kiss.

The Préfet and the Procureur du Roi lodged at the house of the Deputy Mayor of Pietranera, and the Colonel, extremely anxious about his daughter, was coming for the twentieth time to ask for news, when a voltigeur, who had been sent forward by the serjeant as an avant courier, gave them an account of a terrible battle with the brigands, in which there were, it is true, neither killed nor wounded, but in which they had taken a boiler, a pilone, and a couple of girls, who, he said, were the friends or the spies of the bandits. Thus announced, the two prisoners made their appearance in the midst of their armed escort. You may imagine Colomba's radiant countenance, her companion's shame, the Préfet's surprise, and the Colonel's joy and astonishment. The Procureur du Roi took a malicious pleasure in subjecting poor Lydia to a sort of interrogatory, which he continued till he had put her completely out of countenance.

'I think,' said the Préfet, 'that we may set the parties at liberty. These young ladies went out for a walk—nothing more natural when the weather is fine; they chanced to meet with a very amiable young man who is suffering from a wound—again nothing more natural.' Then taking Colomba aside, he added, 'Mademoiselle, you may send word to your brother that his affairs are turning out better than I expected. The examination of the bodies and the Colonel's deposition have made it clear that he only repelled an attack, and that he was alone at the time. The matter will be arranged satisfactorily, but he must quit the mâquis as soon as possible, and give himself up as prisoner.'

It was nearly eleven o'clock when the Colonel, his daughter, and Colomba sat down to a supper that had got quite cold. Colomba ate heartily, making game of the Préfet, the Procureur du Roi, and the voltigeurs. The Colonel ate without uttering a word, but constantly looking at his daughter, who never lifted her eyes from her plate. At last, in a gentle but grave tone of voice, he asked, in English, 'Lydia, are you engaged to della Rebbia?'

'Yes, papa, this very day,' she replied, blushing, but in a firm voice. She then raised her eyes, and not perceiving in her parent's physiognomy any signs of anger, she threw herself into his arms and kissed him, as well-bred young ladies do on similar occasions.

'That's all very well,' said the Colonel; 'he is a brave fellow, but, child, we will not stop in this infernal country, or I refuse my consent.'

'I don't know English,' said Colomba, who gazed at them with extreme curiosity, 'but I will wager that I have guessed what you are saying.'

'We are saying,' answered the Colonel, 'that

we mean you to come with us to take a trip to Ireland.'

'Yes, with pleasure; and I am to be *surella Colomba*, sister Colomba. Is it agreed, Colonel? Are we to touch hands upon it?'

'We ought to kiss in such a case as this,' said the Colonel.

XX.

Several months after the wonderful shot which plunged the *commune* of Pietranera into consternation, as the journals say, a young man, with his left arm in a sling, rode out of Bastia in the afternoon, in the direction of the villa of Cardo, celebrated for its fountain, which, during summer, supplies the delicate persons in town with most delicious water. A young woman of tall stature and remarkable beauty accompanied him on a little black horse, whose strength and elegance would have been the admiration of a connoisseur, but who unfortunately had an ear slashed by some singular accident. In the village the young woman sprang lightly to the ground, and after helping her companion to dismount, unfastened some tolerably heavy bags that were hanging at her saddle-bow. The horses were given in charge to a peasant, and the lady, laden with the bags, which she concealed under her mezzaro, and the young man carrying a double-barrelled gun, proceeded towards the mountain by a steep and narrow path, which did not seem to lead to any human dwelling. On arriving at one of the higher slopes of Monte Quercio they halted and seated themselves on the grass. They seemed to be expecting some one, for they gazed incessantly at the mountain, and the lady frequently consulted a handsome gold watch, perhaps as much for the sake of admiring a trinket, which appeared to be new to her, as of knowing whether the hour fixed for a rendezvous had arrived. They were not kept long waiting. A dog emerged from the thicket, and at the name of Brusco, pronounced by the young woman, he ran up to caress them. Shortly afterwards two men appeared, with bushy beards, their gun on their arm, their cartridge-box at their girdle, and the pistol by its side. Their clothes, torn and covered with patches, contrasted strongly with their arms, which were the production of a maker enjoying a continental reputation. In spite of the apparent inequality of their position these four personages accosted each other with the familiarity of old acquaintances.

'Well, Ors' Anton',' said the elder of the bandits, 'your affair is settled, the case dismissed. My compliments. I am sorry the Advocate has left the island, so that we cannot see what a rage he is in. And your arm—?'

'In a fortnight,' replied the young man, 'the doctors tell me I may do without my sling. Brando, my good fellow, to-morrow I leave for Italy, and I wished to bid you adieu, as well as M. le Curé. That is the reason why I begged you to come.'

'You are in a great hurry,' said Brandolaccio. 'You were only acquitted yesterday, and you are going away to-morrow.'

'Business obliges us,' said the young lady gaily. 'Messieurs, I have brought you some supper, and don't forget my old friend Brusco.'

'You spoil Brusco, Mademoiselle Colomba, but he is a grateful dog. You shall see. Come, Brusco,' he said, holding out his gun horizontally, 'jump for the Barricini!' The dog stood stock still, licking his muzzle and looking at his master. 'Jump for the della Rebbia!' and he jumped a couple of feet higher than was necessary.

'Listen, my friends,' said Orso; 'yours is a very bad trade, and if you do not happen to finish your career in the Piazza which we see down there,* the best luck you can possibly meet with is to fall in a mâquis by a gendarme's bullet.'

'Well,' said Castriconi, 'it is a death like any other, and which is better than a fever which kills you in a bed, in the midst of the more or less sincere weepings and wailings of your heirs and legatees. When once one is used to an open-air life as we are, there is nothing like dying in one's shoes, as they say in the village.'

'I should like to see you leave this country,' continued Orso, 'and lead a quiet life. For instance. why should you not go and settle in Sardinia, as many of your countrymen have done? I could assist you with the means.'

'In Sardinia!' exclaimed Brandolaccio. '*Istos Sardos!* Those wretched Sardinians! The devil

* The Piazza, where executions take place in Bastia.

fly away with them and their lingo too. They are
too bad company for us.'

'There are no resources in Sardinia,' added the
theologian. 'For my own part I despise the Sardinians. In order to hunt the bandits they have a
mounted militia, which is a double disgrace to the
bandits and to the country.* A fig for Sardinia ! What
surprises me most, Monsieur della Rebbia, is, that
you, who are a man of taste and learning, did not adopt
our life in the woods after having tried it as you did.'

'But,' said Orso, smiling, 'when I had the advantage to be your messmate, I was not exactly in a
state to appreciate the charms of your position; and
my ribs still ache when I call to mind the ride I took
one fine evening, when I was thrown like a sack of
sand across a horse without a saddle, on which my
friend Brandolaccio was mounted.'

'And the pleasure of escaping pursuit,' resumed
Castriconi, 'do you reckon that for nothing? How
can you be insensible to the charms of absolute liberty
in a fine climate like ours? With this *porte-respect*
(he pointed to his gun) a man is a king, as far as it
will carry ball. You give your orders, you redress
grievances. It is a very moral and a very agreeable
diversion, monsieur, which we do not deny ourselves.

---

* I owe this critical remark on Sardinia to one of my
friends, an ex-bandit, to whom I leave the entire responsibility
of it. It means, that bandits who allow themselves to be
caught by horsemen are idiots ; and that a force who run
after bandits on horseback have not much chance of meeting
with them.

What life can be better than that of a knight-errant when one is better armed than Don Quixote and has a little more common sense? Look here: the other day I learnt that little Lilla Luigi's uncle—the old thief that he is—would not give her a dowry; I wrote to him without using any threats—that's not my way. Well, he was convinced of his mistake in an instant: he portioned her off. I thus made two people happy. Believe me, Monsieur Orso, there is nothing like a bandit's life. Stuff! you would have been one of us, perhaps, if it had not been for a certain English girl, of whom I only caught a glimpse, but of whom every one at Bastia is talking with raptures.'

'My future sister-in-law is not fond of the mâquis,' said Colomba, laughing; 'she is too much afraid of it to like it.'

'In short,' said Orso, 'have you made up your minds to remain where you are? Be it so. Tell me if I can do anything for you.'

'Nothing,' said Brandolaccio, 'except to bear us in mind. You have overwhelmed us with kindness. Chilina has a dowry provided, and to settle her in life nothing more is needed than for the Curé to write a letter or two, without threats. We know that your farmer will give us bread and gunpowder in our necessities; and so adieu. I hope to see you again in Corsica one of these days.'

'In time of need,' said Orso, 'a few pieces of gold prove extremely useful. Now that we are old acquaintances, you will not refuse this little cartridge, which may help you to procure others.'

'No money between us, Lieutenant,' said Brando-laccio resolutely.

'Money is all-powerful in the world,' said Castriconi; 'but in the mâquis people only pay attention to a brave heart and a gun that never misses fire.'

'I should not like to leave you,' resumed Orso, 'without some little token of remembrance. Come, what would you like best, Brando?'

The bandit scratched his head, and, casting a side-long look at Orso's gun, said, 'Lieutenant—if I dare—but no; you hold to it too much to—'

'What is it that you wish?'

'Nothing—the thing itself is nothing—you must know how to make use of it. I am always thinking of that splendid double shot with a single hand. Oh! that does not happen twice.'

''Tis the gun you wish for? I brought it you; but make use of it as little as you possibly can.'

'Oh! I don't promise you to make use of it as you did; but, make yourself easy, when any one else is master of it, you may say that Brando Savelli has gone over to the left.'

'And you, Castriconi, what shall I give you?'

'Since you absolutely will leave me a material souvenir, I will frankly ask you to send me the smallest published edition of Horace. It will amuse me, and prevent my forgetting my Latin. There is a young woman who sells cigars on the quay at Bastia; give it to her, and she will forward it.'

'You shall have an Elzevir, my learned friend; there is precisely one amongst the books I meant to take away with me. Well, my friends! we must part at last. Give me your hands. If one of these days you think of Sardinia, write to me; N—, the Advocate, will give you my address on the Continent.'

'Lieutenant,' said Brando, 'to morrow, when you are outside the port, look towards the mountain, at this spot; we shall be here, and we will signal to you with our handkerchiefs.'

They separated; Orso and his sister returned to Carlo, and the bandits retreated up the mountain.

XXI.

On a fine April morning Colonel Sir Thomas Nevill, his daughter, married a few days previously, Orso and Colomba, drove out of Pisa in an open carriage, to inspect an Etruscan hypogeum that had lately been discovered, and which every stranger made a point of visiting. On descending into the interior of the ruin, Orso and his wife pulled out their pencils, and set to work to sketch the ornaments; but the Colonel and Colomba, neither of them caring about archæology, left the young people to themselves, and took a walk in the environs.

'My dear Colomba,' said the Colonel, 'we shall never get back to Pisa in time for luncheon. Do you not begin to be hungry? Orso and his wife are up to their necks in antiquities; and when they once begin to draw together they never have done.'

'Yes,' said Colomba; 'notwithstanding which, they never have a scrap to show.'

'My advice,' continued the Colonel, 'is, that we go

to that little farm-house yonder. We shall at least find some bread, and perhaps *aleatico;* possibly even strawberries and cream, which will help us to wait patiently for our sketchers' return.'

'You are right, Colonel. You and I, who are the sensible members of the family, should be greatly to blame to make ourselves martyrs to a couple of lovers who live on poetry. Give me your arm. Don't I get on with my education? I take a gentleman's arm; I wear hats and fashionable dresses; I bedeck myself with jewelry; I have learnt a hundred fine things; I am not the least bit of a savagess. Just look how gracefully I have put on my shawl. That light-haired fellow, that officer in your regiment who is looking out for a wife—I can never remember his name; a tall curly-headed person, whom I could dash to the ground at a blow—'

'Chatworth?' said the Colonel.

'Yes, that's the man! But I shall never be able to pronounce it. Well! he is desperately in love with me.'

'Ah! Colomba, you are turning coquette. We shall have another wedding before long.'

'I marry! Who then will there be to bring up my nephew, when they present me with one? Who will there be to teach him Corsican? Yes, he shall learn to talk Corsican, and I will make him a little pointed cap on purpose to put you in a rage.'

'Wait till you have a nephew; when you have got him, you may teach him how to handle the stiletto if you like.'

'Adieu to stiletti,' said Colomba, gaily; 'I have a fan now, to give you a rap on the knuckles when you speak ill of my country.'

Chatting in this way they reached the farm, where they found wine, strawberries, and cream. Colomba helped the farmer's wife to gather strawberries, whilst the Colonel drank some *aleatico*. At the corner of a walk in the garden, Colomba remarked an old man sitting in the sunshine in a straw chair, apparently ill; for his cheeks were hollow, his eyes were sunken, he was excessively thin; and his immobility, his paleness, and his fixed stare, made him look more like a corpse than a living creature. For several minutes Colomba gazed at him with such marked curiosity as to attract the attention of the farmer's wife. 'That poor old man,' she said, 'is one of your countrymen; for I am sure, by your talk, mademoiselle, that you come from Corsica. He met with misfortunes in his own country; his children died in a terrible fashion. They say—I beg your pardon, mademoiselle—that your people are not too tender in their hatreds. The poor gentleman, therefore, being left alone in the world, came to Pisa, to live with a distant relation of his, to whom this farm belongs. The worthy man is a little cracked—'twas his misfortunes and his sorrow that did it—which is inconvenient for madame, who keeps a great deal of company; so she sent him here. He is very harmless, and not at all troublesome; he does not speak three words in the course of the day. But the truth is he has lost his wits. The doctor comes to see him once a week; he says that he cannot last long.'

'Ah! they have given him up?' said Colomba. 'In such a state as his it will be a happy release.'

'You should talk to him a little, mademoiselle, in Corse; it might cheer him, perhaps, to hear his native tongue.'

'At any rate we'll try,' said Colomba, with an ironical smile; and she approached the old man till her shadow screened him from the sun. The poor idiot raised his head and fixedly stared at Colomba, who stared at him in like manner, but constantly smiling. In a moment or two the old man passed his hand over his forehead, and closed his eyes, as if to escape from Colomba's gaze. Then he opened them again, but immoderately wide; his lips trembled; he tried to stretch out his hands; but, fascinated by Colomba, he remained fixed to his seat. unable either to speak or to move. At last, big tears flowed from his eyes, and heavy sobs burst forth from his chest.

'This is the first time I have ever seen him taken so,' said the farmer's wife. 'Mademoiselle is one of your countrywomen; she is come to see you.'

'Mercy!' he cried in a hoarse voice; 'mercy! are you not satisfied yet? That leaf—which I burned— how did you contrive to read it? But why both of them? Orlanduccio, you could read nothing against him. You should have left me one—only one— Orlanduccio—you did not read his name—'

'I would have both of them,' said Colomba, in a

low voice, and in the Corse dialect. 'The branches are lopped; and if the stump were not rotten I would have grubbed it up. Go; make no complaint; you have not long to suffer. I had to suffer for two long years!'

The old man uttered a cry, and his head fell upon his breast. Colomba turned her back on him, and slowly walked towards the house, chanting some incomprehensible words from a *ballata*, 'I must have the hand which pulled the trigger—the eye which took aim, the heart which plotted.'

Whilst the farmer's wife was rendering the old man assistance, Colomba, with a heightened complexion and sparkling eyes, sat down to table opposite to the Colonel.

'What is the matter with you?' he asked. 'You look exactly as you did at Pietranera, the day when the bullets were flying about your dining-room.'

'Some recollections of Corsica have come into my head. But it is all over now. I am to be the godmother, am I not? Oh! what fine names I will give him; Ghilfuccio Tomaso Orso Leone!'

At that moment the farmer's wife came in. 'Well!' asked Colomba with the greatest coolness, 'is he dead, or only in a swoon?'

''Tis nothing, mademoiselle; but 'tis singular what an effect the sight of you had upon him.'

'And the doctor says that he cannot last long?'

'Not a couple of months, perhaps.'

'It will be no great loss,' observed Colomba.

'Who are you talking about?' asked the Colonel.

'About an idiot, one of my countrymen,' said Colomba with an air of indifference, 'who is boarding and lodging here. I will send from time to time to inquire how he is. But, Colonel Nevill, do leave the strawberries for my brother and Lydia.'

When Colomba left the farmhouse, and stepped into the carriage, the farmer's wife followed her movements with her eyes, and at last observed to her daughter, 'You see that very handsome young lady. Well! I am sure she has the evil eye.'

ALFRED DUVERNOY'S STORY.

THE DIAMOND CLASP.

SUNDAY intervened, and of course no tale was told on that day. Nor is it necessary to say how it was passed. It was passed properly; you know, reader, how that is—for it is the way I·hope you pass your own Sunday.

So we will pass to the next day. The task was now Duvernoy's.

'You know,' said he, 'that the confessional is an institution which does not exist in our church, and therefore our clergy have not in the course of their ministry the same opportunities for gathering the materials of an interesting tale as have our brethren of Rome. (Murmurs.)   Brethren, I repeat, for I hope that no one here will deny that ours is but one branch of the church of Christ, and that all the members of it are brethren in spirit, though in some certain unhappy differences, and in others, serious errors have hitherto kept them too much asunder. But although the confessional is not one of our institutions, every clergyman must necessarily have many communicants who come to him, and unburden their consciences.   The great majority of the narratives we hear under such circumstances are of too heart-rending or solemn a nature to permit me for a moment to think of reproducing them here; but one confession which was lately made to me by a lady of high rank and fashion forms, with some slight alterations and adaptation to this occasion, the groundwork of the tale I propose to read, entitled 'The Diamond Clasp." '

'Ten postage stamps,' said D'Aubrey.

' Why so ? '

' You are going to give us some "shop,"' replied D'Aubrey, inexorably.

' O, well,' said Duvernoy, 'there's a shilling; pray keep the change as a reward for your zeal.   The tale is as follows :—

THE DIAMOND CLASP.

I HAD been a wanderer all my life, though at the time I speak ·of many years of that were yet before me. I was an only child, and at eighteen was left an orphan, free to go where my fancy led me; and this time it was towards *home*—not my own, I never had one, never realized the blessedness of that word, never tasted of its calm unvarying happiness.

For family reasons my parents had lived abroad, and for their own pleasure moved from place to place, till we had lost sight of all old friends, and were almost forgotten in the old home world.

Such a life is practical in its tendencies. New scenes and faces for ever passing before our weary eyes—a life of ceaseless change—a few calm restful hours, tells upon the inner part of our character, preparing us for every startling emergency, as the stagnation of an every-day country life induces an opposite degree of quiet indolence, to which a tinge of romance or love of superstition is the condiment that enlivens the dish, the flash of sunlight that sparkles over the most sluggish and gloomy waters.

So far, then, my education had not been one that predisposed me to a dreamy love of the marvellous. Naturally of a thoughtful disposition, my life had never given me an opportunity for indulging in mystical reveries or weak fanciful castle building. I was going home—there was something sweet in the words, though everything was strange to me there; yet it had been my mother's home, and for her sake, her dead memory, its doors were opened now for me.

It was a merry party of cousins, children home for the Christmas holidays, of all ages and sizes, from the tall self-conscious collegian and the dignified young lady of my own standing, to the lisping pet of the family, numbering but four or five summers. The old dining-room looked bright with all those young careless faces in it. It wanted nothing to make it a more perfect picture. I was outside the circle as it were. I could look back with my mother's eyes (for she used never to weary of telling me of her young days), I could watch them now with my own, and I could even look on, far on to the future with the power which a life of reasoning from past and passing events gave me, to the time when the shadows would fall on this group too, when other children would brighten up this dark old room, and those here now should each have outgrown his youth, and be plodding sadly under each separate burden. It was a mood which suited me, though a woman's philosophy is often at fault; yet throughout my stirring life I had been often accustomed to sketch the passing scene, filling up with tints of my own choosing—sometimes vivid and intense, sometimes sober and grey, as the case might be.

I was not wanted to talk. 'Cousin Annie was tired,' mamma urged in her kindly tone from the head of the table, a tone so full of tender motherly feeling that it brought to mind the long 'For ever' of this world that came between that tone and me and the foreign cemetery where my mother lay at rest.

And while the chat (for it was of too mixed a nature to be termed 'conversation') went on around me, I watched the fire leap up among the glowing logs, I marked the home comforts, the warm dark oak panelling, the rich subdued lamplight, the gleam of old silver flagons on the high carved sideboard, the branching antlers above, and the well-filled bookshelves stored with many a rare black letter and many a treasured 'Elzevir,' which made my heart beat with the anticipated delight of studying them. The row too of family portraits—the quaint upright figures of one generation, the easy gracefulness of another, and the assumed state of a later period— were there before me. I knew them all by heart, my mother had talked of them many an hour when we sat together on winter nights in some half-empty French hotel, or when we stood together on some lonely vine-clad hill, looking down on the autumn glory of an Italian view, or while gazing up at some grand chain of snowy peaks we rested near a shrine in the shadow of a dark pine wood. Her heart was always travelling back to the old times and places, and she never wearied of telling me of the things she had most reverenced as a child. I knew exactly the large picture over the fireplace — the boyish young face beneath the heavy powdered curls suggesting to our present minds a contrast painfully startling of youth and age. The long-flapped waistcoat and ruffled sleeve, the sad eyes following every movement, as though they strove to warn us to use the present well. The fair young sister standing by with a basket heaped with roses in one slender hand, a spray of jessamine held archly up in the other, the emblem, perhaps, of a romance never told, a tale never finished. The stern dark woman next, whose rich lace and lustrous satin could not soften the hard handsome lines of her proud face. And next the slight figure in the dark-blue velvet robe, with the broad lace frill shading the small white neck and shoulders, her long powdered tresses drawn back, with a tiny branch of star-flowers fastened on one side, and a thick wave of hair floating to the other, the large hazel eyes, full, and dark, and wistful, and the pale oval face from which the painter's vermilion had long ago faded. I knew her story well. 'The Fairy,' as they called her, she was so bright and lovely, her destiny so strange and weird a one. There was some horrid mystery, some dark, dark doubts that her end was come by fairly; there was deep cruel jealousy at work. Two sisters loving *one*,—the younger, the fairy of the picture, was found dead, drowned in a few feet of water, amongst the mud and weeds in the lake below the house. There had been a token sent from a distant land, but no lover returned to claim it. No smiles parted the lips of the elder sister again.

It was so long ago, the rights of the tale were almost forgotten; but there was a dread still of passing the lake at night, and no servants would sleep in what had been the Fairy's room.

As I gazed upon the picture the wondering thought came over me, if, when it was taken, the fair and living original had any foreknowledge of the fate it was hers to meet. They say those who are to die young have an expression in their eyes unmistakable to those who have once marked the sign. I thought the painter must have caught it here, something there was so sad, so shrinking, so appealing in their mournful, shadowy depths.

But the other (the companion picture), the haunting misery in the other's pale, passionate, eager face! I could not keep my eyes from wandering to it. I shuddered inwardly as I remembered the dreary years that were given *her* to live, the desolate old age, the hours (they said) of raving agony that filled her solitude with moans, and cries, and fearful phantom forms!

English as I was in many of my tastes and prejudices, I yet inherited in a strong degree my mother's dislike of the prevailing custom of wearing large quantities of useless jewellery; but one I always wore—a diamond clasp on a black velvet ribbon—round my arm. I never parted with it for one moment, but at night, when it lay nestled in its bed of white satin locked in my dressing-case. It had been given me by my mother almost in her last hour, with a solemn charge never to lose possession of it, as it had been an heirloom in our family for generations, and had descended through the

female branch from eldest daughter to eldest daughter
till it at length became mine. Sacred as it was,
it had yet another value in my sight—it was the
'Token' sent to my fairy ancestress—fatal indeed
to her—but without which, it was said, its rightful
possessor would be overtaken by peril and misfortune.

Dessert and wine had been set upon the table, and
my uncle having filled my glass that I might, as he
said, 'join in drinking the toasts of the evening,' observed, 'What splendid diamonds those are Annie!
the old bracelet, is it not? May I look at it?'

It was difficult to unfasten, and to avoid delay I
raised my arm upon the table that he might examine
the stones more closely. As I did so I caught an
expression of scorn on my cousin John's handsome
features. His opinion had been formed respecting
me in that moment. He was a hard judge, though
I could not blame him.

I had been 'educated abroad;' 'well, what then?'
of course I was a weak superficial French coquette,
cold and bright as the diamonds, taking advantage of
the occasion to show my round white arm and delicate tapering fingers.

And if he thought so there was nothing I could do
that would convince him otherwise. And I saw
Marion's lip curl, and even aunt's sweet good face
shadowed over.

'The Fairy's Clasp, children,' said my uncle,
'you have all heard of it often enough.'

And while the others pressed round to examine it,

with eager exclamations, he turned to inquire of me, if I was 'endowed with strong nerves?'

My answer being a satisfactory one, he proceeded to tell me, with a smile lurking about his mouth and a twinkle in the corners of his keen eyes, of a tradition, that on some particular nights during the year, when the moon had reached a certain point, that the owner of the 'Diamond Clasp,' must beware of sleeping in the Fairy's chamber.

Aunt smilingly declared, 'that it was too bad to frighten me so,' but he continued:

'I don't know if this is a charmed night, but I heard mamma say, you were to have the "Oak-room," as, with all these young ones at home, we are nearly full, so you must be on your guard!'

I answered, laughing, with an assurance that I was 'perfectly at ease on the subject,' and a timid voice at my side which said, 'Cousin, do you like ghosts?' turned the laugh against little Nelly.

When tea was over, and Marion had sung two or three songs, and Eta and Nelly had played their grand duet, aunt thought my eyes looked heavy and tired, and she kindly proposed that I should retire before the servants made their appearance for prayers.

I was not tired, but still I was glad of rest. I needed quiet, to restore me, after much that I had gone through and suffered of late, and I thankfully followed her to my room, where she left me with many warmly expressed words of welcome, and hopes that I should be happy and comfortable whilst remaining under her roof.

The Fairy's room! There was nothing terrible about it, seen by the cheerful firelight and the tall candles lit upon the dressing-table. It was small and cosy-looking, with an open peaked roof and rows of black beams, black oak doors and window frame, a light modern paper on the walls. A black twisted-legged table, with a low old-fashioned bedstead to match, in the centre of the head-piece of which two long-tongued antediluvian monsters, carved in oak, stood ready to do battle at a given signal, and two fleur de lys, the family cognizance, kept guard at the foot. The whole was enshrouded in curtains of warm-hued damask, against which the soft white quilt and pillows stood out like drifted snow, and promised luxuriant rest for aching head and weary limbs.

I set to work, vigorously at first, to reduce chaos to order, unpacked various things that I required, and wrapping myself up in my dressing-gown, I drew my chair close to the flickering blaze, and loosening the heavy braids of my hair, prepared to give up an hour to quiet thought over the changes which had come across my life.

The world seemed to grow very still. The household sounds of closing doors and moving feet had died away. The last good nights! had been said, some time before, upon the stairs, and only the wind moaned hoarsely in the chimney, and shivered amongst the nearest tree tops, only the heavy rain pattered on the roof, with a saddened hushing murmur, which made me draw still nearer to the hearth with a sigh of thankfulness that I was safe, and warm, and at home.

It was strange to find myself at last amongst scenes which had been so often painted for me in words; amongst those whose names were all familiar, whose birth and other holydays, whose tastes and interests, whose hopes and fears, whose handwriting I had known for years, but who, individually, were as far from me as the chance acquaintance of an hour! Strange, how forming one of the family circle, the one, perhaps, outwardly most cared for and attended to, I was yet the least known, the least loved, the least thought for of all. 'With them, but not of them.' What a different and melancholy meaning one little word changed can convey!

Strange! how it happens, that the *one* treasured hope of many changing years may at length be suffered to be realized, but under circumstances so altered, that the fulfilment of it may become a great trial rather than a season of rejoicing! Strange! that sickness and death, the long passage of years bridged over thus, should bring me a lonely orphan into my mother's home, when the picture I had formed of our realization of that Jacob and Esau-like meeting should have glowed with such different colours!

Did any man or woman's life yet ever pass, as they hoped, or prayed, or believed it would pass?

This old room! I thought what strange scenes its walls must have witnessed, of change and disappointment, and grief and death! The little cares and pains—the daily ebb and flow of life's tide. To its century-stored experience what a little thing was one human life! what a mere shadow its most desperate struggle, its most harrowing suspense!

But these old rooms do not give up their dead! not even to teach lessons to the living! Their 'dead past buries its dead,' and they 'make no sign,' and generation after generation go down in turn to the same dark tenantless burying-ground! The candles had long ago been extinguished. The fire, though still warm, gave little light, and the falling together of the ashes recalled me from my wandering mood. The wind had died away, not a whisper stirred the ivy branches against the window, and even the rushing rain was over. It was very still, and the room looked dark;— so still, and dark, and solemn, that, childlike, I wished I had not stayed up 'mooning' so late, but had gone to bed at once, and been comfortably asleep then, instead of sitting crouching there fearful of breaking the painful calm by any movement of mine.

It seemed as though Nature lay still, watching, waiting, expecting some grand convulsion—the fulfilment of some long-predicted destiny—and I must not rise or turn, I must not breathe a deeper breath, lest the spell should break.

I do not know why I thought so—we are all weak and fanciful at times, but such an idea had never crossed me before, and I had spent many a still and lonely night in many a still and lonely place.

I was not usually fanciful or nervous, on the contrary I was accustomed to, and generally preferred, solitude, and reason and the sense of a higher and overruling Power had hitherto been at all times, and in all places of peril, a sufficient guarantee of safety.

I knew, in the ordinary course of events there could be no danger here. I was not aware of any cause for apprehension, but such an overpowering—such a shuddering sense of dread, came over me, that I could endure the silent feeling of it no longer. With an effort beyond anything I can describe, I rose from my chair, and went towards the dressing-table, and then I first became conscious of an excessive coldness in the air of the room, which caused me to turn abruptly, in order to ascertain whether the door had been by mistake left open ; but it was close shut, and the same dreary stillness appalled me again. With an involuntary shiver I bent forward to unfasten the clasp of my bracelet, and in so doing. I caught a glimpse of myself in the glass before me, with white cheeks and large frightened eyes.

But something there was, *beyond*, that at once arrested my trembling fingers and my glance—something faint and shadowy, standing behind me—a face, laid close beside mine ! Too indistinct and misty to be the reflection of a living person—and yet, so ghastly, so mournful, so despairing in its dim expression, that it could not have been the creature of a dream—the mere distorted vision of an over-excited imagination. The glass was perfectly smooth and ieven. There was nothing in the room which, reflected on its surface, could by any possibility—by any stretch of inventive power—by any freak or peculiarity of colour or position,—assume such a shape or appearance, even to the most weak and credulous— to the most weary and sleep-laden eyes ! I assured myself of this instantly ; I did not give in without a hard fight for the wise representations, and still wiser disbelief, of those eerie nursery-fireside tales we have all heard in our day, which those who taught me had neither knowledge or experience of. My nerves were rarely troublesome ; I had been too long and too constantly accustomed to meet danger and difficulty at every turn—to act independently ; and, young as I was, to be the chief stay and support of others, older than myself,—to allow myself, under any circumstances, to suffer from groundless alarm, and mere temporary depression of spirits.

But—it stayed there ! How long I cannot tell— but long enough for me to note the dark velvet robe and gilded braid ; long enough for my terror-stricken eyes to mark the dripping tresses, of long brown hair, twisted with green and shining water-weeds ; long enough for me to see, that one slender arm, which was lifted wildly upwards, was torn and wounded near the wrist, and that drops of dark-red blood were slowly flowing from it.

How much longer I could have held up I do not know, when something pressed my arm—a cold, wet, clammy weight ; so cold, that though fifty years have come between that hour and me, yet the thought of it still sends a shiver to my heart ; so cold, that the remembrance of that icy touch has chilled my frame beneath an Indian sun, and returned to me, like the touch of death, while scorched and weak with fever.

I sank suddenly to the floor, and the sun was shining on the frosted lawn, and the rooks cawing at their morning parliament, when I came back from that long and dreary faint.

I was broken in health and spirit for long, long afterwards. I do not care to speak of that time—to recall the memory of that dim mournful face—but oh, it was *not* a dream! for the velvet ribbon had been nearly torn from my bruised and blackened arm.

It was not a dream! for there lay a knotted tangle of wet and shining pool-weeds on the floor.

It was not a dream! for fifty long years, with their load of engrossing care, have passed over my head since then; and many sore trials, I never thought to have bowed under, have filled my heart, without ever taking one shade from the dreadful freshness and reality of that night in 'The Fairy's room.'

'Is that *all*, grandmamma?'

'Yes, all, my darling—except you may write down that Cousin John and I made friends after that; and that I became his wife, and we went out to India for many years, and came back to live here again at last; and that, some day or other, you will have to keep and guard "The Diamond Clasp."'

CHARLES VERNEY'S SECOND STORY.

REMINISCENCES OF WALPOLE AND STRAWBERRY HILL.

VERNEY was now pressed to fulfil his promise of
a tale relating to Walpole and Strawberry Hill.
D'Aubrey had been the general spokesman in all the
previous movements; but now all the guests spoke
at once (except Scott, who was absent), and demanded
Verney's tale.

Verney was so very shy and diffident a man, that
the idea of giving two stories, when the others had
only given one each, made him feel rather bashful
and ashamed. He feared that, unknown to himself,
he had led his guests into asking him for a second
tale; and that it was not fair or right of him to ask
them to his house and then dose them with his own
stories. He could have told them a tale himself
of Strawberry Hill, and better perhaps than the one
he eventually read; but he was determined that if he
must intrude on them a second time, it should not be
with anything of his own composition; and at the
same time he felt bound to apologise for giving them
something which was not his own.

'You are really very kind,' said he; 'though I
should feel I deserved the compliment more, if my
tales were like those you have been so generous as
to contribute, my own composition, or even my own
rendering from a foreign language; but you see, I
must make amends for my deficiency in originality,
by the riches of my library. I own to have spent a

great deal of the time since we were at Cambridge together, in book-collecting, and I am fond above all things of attending book-auctions.* I have picked up a great many literary curiosities in this way ; and I have been especially particular never to let anything about Twickenham slip through my fingers.   There is nothing, however, in my collection I prize more than a manuscript account of a visit to Horace Walpole at Strawberry Hill.   I cannot quite ascertain either the author or the date.   The latter, however, is comparatively immaterial, for there was substantially no change in Walpole's mode of life, from the time he settled at Strawberry Hill, to the day of his death.   He went on increasing his Abbey-castle, and its stores of curiosities ; and supplying the place of his old friends, as death picked them off, by new ones.   In fact, it would be more correct to say, that this is an account of several visits condensed into one. They must have been made, I conjecture, from two or three other little indicia, at very different times— the longest, while Walpole was still in the prime of life ; the rest, when he was already on the wane— but before, as I think, he had got into that gloomy old age which came over him, and which made him exchange the character of the Baron of his Castle, for the Monk of his Abbey.   I have often wondered

* In the days of Verney, book-auctions used constantly to be attended by gentlemen, now the booksellers form the entire " company."

whether my old age is to be as gloomy as that : when
you are all great men,—D'Aubrey, my Lord Chief
Justice; Angerstein, my Lord Chancellor; Rebow,
Home Secretary; Scott, Prime Minister; Duvernoy,
Archbishop of Canterbury; and our friend who is
looking out of the window, Ambassador at Paris;—
why then, you know, you'll all be too much occupied
to be visiting, or still less writing to the old recluse
at Twickenham; and I shall have to say of myself,
as Walpole said of himself to the Countess of Ossory
in 1797 :—" I scarce go out of my own house; and
then only to two or three private places, where I see
nobody that really knows anything : and what I learn
comes from newspapers, that collect intelligence from
coffee-houses—consequently, what I neither believe
nor report. At home I see only a few charitable
elders—except about fourscore nephews and nieces
of various ages, who are each brought to me once
a-year, to stare at me as the Methusalem of the
family; and they can only speak of their own con-
temporaries, which interest no more than if they
talked of their dolls, or bats, or balls." '

'Oh,' said D'Aubrey, 'even when we attain the ex-
altation which you have been good enough to pro-
phesy for us, and which of course we all shall attain,
there will be no fear of your hanging loose apart from
the world, like Walpole. He was a man without a
vocation. When he had built up his lath-and-
plaster gim-crack toy-house, and stuffed it full of

curiosities, and shown it to all the great lords and ladies of his day, there was nothing more left for him to do. Nobody cared about him, except a few old retainers ; old Cole, the stupidest of stupid antiquaries; Hannah More, and the two Miss Berrys; and this was rather a small circle to live in. Walpole was always ashamed to be a literary man; and perhaps would never have made a really eminent one, but—'

'He was quite right,' burst in Rebow, who flushed and grew excited; 'who would exhibit himself and his antics—be they on the boards or on the page—if he could afford to live like a gentleman without the bookseller's or the manager's pay?'

'I think, my dear Rebow,' said Verney, 'that you don't sufficiently allow for the great change that has taken place in an author's position. I grant that Gray and Walpole were right in their aversion to the degraded imputation of being an author; but then, what had degraded it? The soliciting subscriptions—the perpetual carrying round of the begging-box ; and, what was worse than all, the collection of subscriptions for works which—perhaps fortunately—never had, and never were intended to have any existence. Whenever an author came to a noble house for a subscription to his forthcoming book, the first question to be asked and answered was, "Is he a rogue?—does he mean to obtain money under false pretences?—has he paid his rent for the last week?" As means to the ascertainment of the truth respecting these matters, it was usual to look at the elbows of the author's coat, the hue of his linen, and the complexion of his nose. If he was found a ragged, drunken scoundrel, he was told to carry elsewhere his distinguished brains, pregnant with immortal verse; but if he was found passably respectable, a few odd guineas were sent out to him, by the hand of my Lord's door-keeper, who flung them to him with the same air as if he were relieving a beggar—and in fact he was doing so. The *genus* author being of this nature, no wonder that men of birth, like Walpole—or even of education, like Gray—shunned to be classed among them; but now an author is, in my judgment, {the most magnificent and lofty specimen of the productive classes. I suppose we must still, in this slow, old-prejudiced country of ours, give for a little while longer some sort of indefinable prestige to the unproductive classes; and after despising the honest hard-working merchant, who has scraped the fortune together, look up to the prodigal son who squanders the income of it, at least, in vulgar show and splash. Well, let that be so for a time; things will right themselves anon; but still, even as it is at present, what *productive* class can you put above an author? Others produce silks and cottons, by the toil of their hands, or the use of their capital; he, by the labour of his brains produces thoughts, and the beautiful expression of thoughts. The lawyer lives by producing thoughts—so also the parson—but then their thoughts are more directed to the concrete; the one thinks only on behalf of his client, and his thoughts are narrowed to the little field of his client's actions and property; the other thinks chiefly about his parish, and his thoughts are too often restricted to its metes and bounds. Now the author, on the contrary, thinks for human nature in general : he is the orator of the human race ; and he produces what is as ennobling to those who partake in it, as it is incorruptible.'

'What a pity it is,' broke in D'Aubrey, when Verney had at last finished, 'that we must knock down that pretty nine-pin of yours, but an author happens not to belong to the *productive* classes at all ! The country is not a bit richer for his efforts, unless his work happens to sell abroad largely, and so bring money into the country, which, except in the case of such very popular writers as Rebow, is scarcely ever the case ; and even then, in strictness, an author is not *productive*, for he does not increase the wealth of the world, he only draws some of it from one kingdom to another.'

'I am shocked to hear you,' said Verney, 'repeat the cant of the Political Economists, as they call themselves, the excellent inventors of the Science of the Breeches Pocket.'

'Well, well,' again interrupted Rebow, 'don't let us be hard upon the Chrematologists. We must all line our breeches pockets, if it isn't already done for us, as it is for you, Verney; and for my part I'd rather do it by picking cotton or unravelling silk-coons than by ripping up my own brains and exposing them for sale. Fah! it always puts me in mind of what the Abyssinians do with their cattle. After they've been driving them all day in the waggons, when they put up the tent at night, and begin to think they want dinner, they go to the poor beasts and cut—steaks out of their haunches. The wound is sewn up and presently heals. What is this which I do, but when I want to feed the twelve mouths that yawn upon me at home, I go and slice out my brains to get them bread?'

'But you don't lay the brains on the platter for them,' said Angerstein, beginning, like a true Chancery man, to dissect the simile, and reason about a trope. The rest of the company shuddered, when poor Rebow talked so seriously and sadly, and yet so absurdly, and it began to dawn upon them, that though he had not served out his brains for his children's dinner, he had disordered them in the hard struggle of earning that dinner.

'I always thought,' said Duvernoy, anxious to change the subject, 'that that habit of collecting subscriptions had a great tendency to demoralize and degrade both authors and patrons. In the old days of patronage to authorship, it was decidedly a noble

Q 2

thing for a great man to place a poet on his establishment. The poet felt no more degraded by such an
engagement than did my lord's chaplain, when he
undertook to do duty in the Castle chapel, and keep
the conscience of my lord and my lady. True that
they were both employés, and did not always dine
at the high table, but then why should they? Were
they not persons earning their bread, and could they
hope to be quite on a level with those who were born
to own and to spend? The feeling of those days
said, 'No.' I often think the life of an author in
those days must have been superlatively happy.
Sure of his turret chamber, endless leisure, magnificent gardens to walk in, the company of the rich,
the beautiful, the famous; and, so far as there
was refinement in those days, refined; what more
could he have wished for?'

'Independence, liberty, the birthright of man,'
shouted Rebow. 'Bad as the subscription-gatherers
were, authors you describe were worse. The "poet"
wrote what the "fool" acted. Was there any difference between them, except that one was a fine bold
fellow who did his work in public, and didn't mind
being seen in his true hues, while the other was a
sneaking hireling, who couldn't patch up his verses
unless he secluded himself from what principally
elevates and refines mankind—society, the converse
and clash of thoughtful minds?'

'For my part,' said D'Aubrey, 'I think the "paid author of the establishment" and the "subscribed-to author" are both good riddances, though I must confess that our greatest writers and thinkers have been included in the former class, and some of them in the other class too. Certainly, I agree with Duvernoy, that the first was the better of the two, for it is always better to be sure of your pay, and have no bother about getting it—however small it may be, and however dirty the work you do for it—than to be always sending round the begging-box, and to have to rack your brains, not merely in doing your work, but also in getting the pay for it.

'But it's all very well for Verney to lead us into discussions about authors and subscriptions; but I should like to know when we are going to have our story about Walpole?'

'Directly,' replied Verney; 'I have only been waiting till Scott, who is in my study, has read it through. It was written, you see, at the end of the last century; and the taste of that time was, as we all know, so coarse as to permit jokes and allusions that we should not think of now. I have read the tale several times myself, and am pretty sure there is nothing of the kind in it. Indeed, I didn't think of it, till Scott asked me to be very particular about the point; so I thought the best way of being particular was to make him read the tale himself, which he has been doing for the last-hour.'

' Aw,' drawled Graham, ' that's always the way with—aw—those fellows; what d'ye call 'em ?—sanctimonious sort of—aw—puritans—aw—and that like. They get all the reading of—aw—that sort of thing—to themselves, and—aw—never let anybody else have a scrap of it.'

' Well, what could you expect,' said D'Aubrey, ' when a man gets the habit of sacking the undergraduates' rooms of the French novels, and taking them away, under pretence that it isn't safe to burn them all at once——.'

' I'll go to him,' said Rebow, who was sitting next the door, and was off before Verney could stop him.

I wish this record to be, so far as consistent with truth, a record of harmonious intercourse between old college friends; and I don't consider myself bound to tell the 'whole truth.' So what took place in Verney's study between Rebow and Scott I had rather, with your kind permission, reader, leave unwritten. Rebow, as you know, had been writing there all the morning, and had left his papers open just as he had written them. He found that they had been all looked at by somebody, though they were put back very much in the same way as they were before, in the hope of avoiding detection; and he found Scott with the last sheet of Rebow's writing open before him, and finishing a long series of notes which he made from the papers that he—or somebody, let us give him the benefit of a doubt if there is one—had perused. I say again, nothing shall be introduced here to raise the slightest surmise that the most entire harmony and respect did not exist between Scott and Rebow, or any others of Verney's visitors; and so I will not for a moment even hint what took place, and how it happened that Scott returned to Verney's drawing-room very pale and trembling, and having just that sort of indescribable look—so familiar to D'Aubrey—which comes over a prisoner when an eye-witness of his crime has given his evidence, and the judge turns to the prisoner's counsel and says, ' After that, Mr Surrebutter, do you think it advisable that the case should continue ?'

' Well—aw—really,' said Graham, ' there must —aw—have been something very bad—aw, and wonderfully—aw—what dy'e call it—coarse you know in the tale to make you—aw look so—aw—deuced ill. 'Pon my word—honour bright—well I never! Gwood gwacious !' and Graham became moved in a most unwonted manner at Scott's deadly pallor. Every one else felt that Rebow, and not the tale, must have been the cause of it; but Graham thought the tale had been so dreadfully shocking as to make the college don quite ill.

Rebow returned, after he had gathered up and put

away his writings; and he had a quantity of paper in his hand he was tearing into the most minute fragments. D'Aubrey's curiosity was excited, and he took a cruise about the room. The wind or something else led him beside Rebow's chair; and he could there see that the paper Rebow was tearing contained Scott's handwriting. Rebow looked relieved when he came in, as one does after having convicted a thief.

Verney began without further preface.

REMINISCENCES OF WALPOLE AND STRAWBERRY HILL.

I<small>F</small> the question, 'What is genius,' can only be answered, as I fear it must, by pointing to examples, I should certainly select Strawberry Hill as the work of one of those examples. Genius, we are apt in this age to think, must show itself in some form of writing, but a time will soon I suspect come when people in our country will not suppose that to be a great genius a man must have written unexceptionable verses or immortal prose. Is there no genius shown in painting? When I was ambassador* at The Hague nothing gave me more delight than visiting the collections of paintings by native artists, with which the rich Dutch citizens love to adorn their pleasure-houses. Many examples of the Flemish, and not a few also of the Venetian schools, are in that country; and is it possible to stand before some chef-d'œuvre of Rubens, Rembrandt, Vandyke, Titian, or Giorgione, and not acknowledge the genius of the artist? May there not be genius in inventions? Was it not by a stroke of genius that printing and the mariners' compass were invented? Is

---

* It seems from this and other allusions in the paper that it was written by a nobleman at the close of the last century, who forbade its being opened till after the death of all his children.

there no genius shown in the field? Are Cæsar, Hannibal, Eugene, and Marlborough, inferior to Mr. Pope or Mr. Gray? But I will not say more, for my grandson or granddaughter, you whose eyes will first of human eyes after mine own see these pages, will, I am sure, have no need of such admonitions, but you will, in the greater enlightenment of your age, readily admit that genius may be practical as well as literary.

Now what Mr. Walpole has done at Strawberry Hill is to write down in brick and timber, and lath and plaster, the general idea which remains in an educated and tasteful mind after a tour among Gothic Abbeys and Gothic Cathedrals. An architect or a painter may have more definite and particular ideas connected with each example that he sees. He can point out to you in detail the most perfect example of the Early English, the Pointed Style, the Norman, and so on; but a gentleman is not expected to care about these intricacies of carving: it is sufficient for him to saunter along their lofty aisles, and range about their deserted halls and galleries, and give way to the poetry and romance of the situation, and carry off with him the general air and aspect of the scene, so that when he reads Froissart or Philippe de Comines, or some tale of modern times, peopled with the personages of chivalry and ceremonious piety, he requires no artist to draw pictures for him of the scene which the chronicler or the novelist represents, but he can build in the domains of his own imagination fairy halls and castles, gloomy abbeys and secret cloisters, amid which the heroes whom he reads of can live and flit about by the light of the dim twilight of the memory, with more true romance than if the actual buildings in which the events took place were present to him, or were described and delineated in all their minute and accurate detail.

This general idea of the forms and mode of building in the middle ages is part of the furniture of every refined mind. It is partly for this that our young nobility go on the continent; it is partly, my dear descendants, for this that I sent your fathers on their travels as soon as they left college; and I hope they, in common with the rest of us, are able ever to repeople in their minds the times and manners of our Christian forefathers.

Now Mr. Walpole has done more than this; not merely has he imbued his own mind with the form and mien of the edifices of those ancient times, but this general idea he has reduced into actual existence. I often amuse myself, after I have been reading a dialogue of Plato, or a chapter of Aristotle, though I confess the latter writes such a crabb'd style that I prefer to make acquaintance with his ideas when somebody has given them a better set of clothes— even though it be a Latin one—I often, I say, amuse myself after I have been reading a page of these worthies, who discuss whether abstract ideas have a real existence or not, by thinking of Strawberry Hill, which I make bold to say is the abstract idea of Gothic architecture reduced into form and substance.

Let me only get hold of one of your Nominalists—the infatuated people who tell you that abstract ideas do not exist, and I could take him to Strawberry Hill, and confute him, unless he should perhaps turn upon me with the crazy arguments of Bishop Berkeley, who proves, if they tell me right, that nothing in the world has any real existence.

Mr. Walpole was born in the year 1717, and derived his first literary turn from that queen of schools—my old mental nurse—Eton. He there made the acquaintance of our excellent poet, Mr. Gray, whose fastidious elegance of mind was not without considerable influence on Mr. Walpole. One cannot but respect the poet's excessive fastidiousness, though it has deprived us of much magnificent and beautiful verse, and has made him the sole instance of a really great writer who has not been prolific. About the year 1734 Mr. Walpole proceeded to Cambridge to complete his education, and was again accompanied by Mr. Gray. The old blind tutor there—Saunderson, I think, was his name—soon found out that Mr. Walpole had no comprehension for mathematics, and told him frankly it was only robbing him of his money to take it under pretence of teaching him Euclid and algebra. So Walpole frittered away his time in elegant dissipation. He never was a Greek scholar, and this he always assigned as the reason for not printing any Greek books at his private press at Strawberry Hill.

When the time came for him to leave Cambridge, his father began to shower sinecures upon him. First he was Inspector-General of Exports and Imports; then he was Usher of the Exchequer—a post with 3000*l.* a-year: other places were soon after given to him to the additional value of 1700*l.*, a-year; so that Mr. Walpole soon found that his vocation in life was to live at ease, and spend his income like a gentleman. I often pity those younger sons of ours, who find themselves placed by birth in a position which renders it disgraceful for them to take to any professional calling, unless it be the army or the bar, and who have neither taste for the one nor industry enough for the other. What are they to do with their hours? Alas! too often they find nothing to kill time with but 'dissipation. They have none of those country occupations which their elder brothers have—no great estates to occupy them; no duties in the House of Parliament, no business about the Court (though that is but a questionable commodity in these days; and I would have none of you, my dearly-loved descendants, hold places about the Court unless they be the places of Ministers—if such can be called Court places—Secretaries of State or the like; or better than any, foreign Embassies). But our elder sons have indeed a noble and glorious work before them; and as I hope that all of you—and I do so enjoin you to do as you respect my memory—who shall be born after the first, will make for yourselves by the law, or the church, or the army, or whatever other calling shall be fit and proper for a gentleman in your day,—those estates which you inherit not, but which will make you equal to the first-

born; and then I do commend to you the wise and
excellent discourse of Grey Bridges, Lord Chandos,
who was made a Knight of the Bath at the creation
of Charles Duke of York, in 1604, and for his hospitality and magnificence was called King of Cots-
wold. He is one of the noble authors whom Mr.
Walpole has omitted; as probably no copy of Lord
Chandos' 'Horae Subsecivae,' an excessively rare
book, ever came in his way. There stands one in my
library; but that you may all listen to his wisdom
with the more respect and reverence, I will transcribe
here the passage where Lord Chandos tells how a
man of quality should behave and direct himself;
when living at his country estate :—

'To make living in the country,' says he, 'a veyle
or shadow for base and sordid sparing, becomes not
the thought of such a man as I propose, whom I name
not, as driven to live there for necessity, and neer-
nesse, but for honourable and vertuous endeavours.
Amongst which the first should bee to expresse free-
dome and hospitality in his house, and bountifull
liberality towards his poorer neighbours : these be
the true ornaments of a country housekeeper; an
honourable custume, so peculiar to our Nation that
that way we have outgone all others, and howsoever
of late it hath been declining and decaying, yet it is
worthy of renovation, being so great a stay to the
country, such a releefe to the poore, so honorable
for themselves, and exemplary for posterity, the very
knot which contracts society and conversation, a re-
ceptacle for one's friends and children, which be the

chiefest solaces of a man's life, and the surest way to make a man be loved of those that know, and esteemed by all that heare of him. . . . And having heere, and thus settled him, his life must not be wholly reserved to his owne quiet, and particular pleasures: but in that place whereunto he is called, and destined to live, to apply himselfe and service, for the common and publike good; which in such a life as this, will principally consist in these particulars.'

But it is too long for these old gouty fingers to write out—you must read for yourselves, my descendants, how the noble author inculcates—' the duty of suppressing and preventing all bold and contemptuous behaviour of one neighbour towards another, all seeds of seditions and quarrels, and how the man of quality is not only to prevent ill but to do good ; and that first by his example in equally bearing part of the burthen in country services with the rest of the gentlemen, and this not only in the private execution of his duty and place, but also in the solemn and public meetings for distribution of justice, and next in composing of differences and discontents between one neighbour or friend and another, which,' says Lord Chandos—and I say so too—' is the principal act of charity.'

To return to Mr. Walpole—when he was well supplied with places, he went upon his travels with Mr. Gray for his companion. He had just broke loose from the restraints of the University, with as much money as he could spend, and was willing to indulge

himself in all kinds of gentlemanly dissipation. He
was always for balls, plays, and the like, and made a
good figure at them himself, and still more drew
notice as the son of the minister. Mr. Gray was a
little man of very ungainly appearance ; he was
always for antiquities and museums; and so in the
end they quarrelled. The quarrel was made up
afterwards, and Mr. Walpole always took the blame
to himself—though the poet was, I am sure, not the
most pleasant of companions. He was haughty, impatient, and very intolerant of other people's ways ;
and let me recommend you when you go the Grand
Tour, to get your fathers to send with you some
regular stupid college fellow, who can trim Latin and
Greek verses well; you can make a good upper
butler or steward of such a fellow—indeed it's all he's
fit for ; but don't take a man of real genius, or even
a man fit for the ordinary professions of life ; you'll
find he won't have the patience to dance attendance
on you at your plays and balls, and other more violent dissipations, which it's only gentlemanlike and
proper you should go through in the foreign cities.

When I visited Mr. Walpole the first time, according to his invitation, at Strawberry Hill, he had not
finished his house—indeed he kept adding something
to it for many years—still less had he completed his
collection ; but I prefer to think of my first visit
rather than any later ones, because Mr. Gray was
then staying there, and his Pindaric Odes were passing through Mr. Walpole's private press. How much
of his house was then finished I can't exactly recol-

lect; but I have been so 'recently there, and seen it in its complete state, that I think it hardly worth while to retrace its imperfections, and so I shall describe it to you in the state in which it was best worth being seen.

It was originally a cottage built in 1698, in a close called Strawberry-hill Shot, by the coachman of the Earl of Bradford, who lived in Richmond House, Twickenham. The people said that the coachman had made his gains by chopping the straw of the Earl's horses, and so they called the cottage Chopped-Straw-Hall. Mr. Colley Cibber lived there for a time, and wrote one of his plays, 'The Refusal, or the Lady's Philosophy.' Talbot Bishop of Durham had it after him, and lived there eight years. Mr. Walpole tells me that the bishop kept a large table, though it is scarce conceivable, as he had no kitchen but the little place which is now converted into a china-room. Then Henry Bridges Duke of Chandos lived in it. From him Mrs. Chenevix the celebrated toy-woman took it, as a summer residence. Mr. Walpole, in a letter of his I have seen thus describes it:—

'It is a little plaything-house that I got out of Mr. Chenevix's shop, and is the prettiest bauble you ever saw. It is set in enamelled meadows, with filagree hedges:

'A small Euphrates through the piece is rolled,
And little finches wave their wings in gold.

Two delightful roads, that you would call dusty,

supply me continually with coaches and chaises: barges as solemn as barons of the exchequer move under my window; Richmond Hill and Ham Walks bound my prospect; but, thank God! the Thames is between me and the Duchess of Queensberry. Dowagers as plenty as flounders inhabit all around, and Pope's ghost is just now skimming under my window by a most poetical moonlight. I have about land enough to keep such a farm as Noah's, when he set up in the ark with a pair of each kind; but my cottage is rather cleaner than I believe his was after they had been cooped up together forty days.' Again he says, 'The house is so small that I can send it you in a letter to look at; the prospect is as delightful as possible, commanding the river, the town, and Richmond Park; and being situated on a hill, descends to the Thames through two or three little meadows, where I have some Turkish sheep and two cows, all studied in their colours for becoming the view.'

The two roads to which Mr. Walpole refers pass very near his house, and would have been to my taste a great objection to it. He however liked to have life and action brought as near him as possible; he was not one of those philosophers who wished to shut the world out. Strawberry Hill was not, any more than the neighbouring villa of Mr. Pope, an ebullition of any real sympathy with rural scenes, nor was it, like Mr. Pope's, a trading establishment for literary purposes, but it was a device to obtain a reputation for taste and singularity—an effort of genius to represent an idea floating in his mind, as I have before remarked; and still more perhaps a means to break through the pattering monotony of life. Dull is the life that consists of an unstrung series of days, with no long-enduring pursuit before it, but plods on taking thought each morning only for the daily bread; duller is the life that lives by jobs and knows long months of unwilling idleness; but dullest is the life that knows no work at all, and cannot carve play-work out for itself.

It is in this respect that Mr. Walpole excels his fellows: he makes work for himself.

His proximity to the road has likewise this advantage that, if so disposed, he can see his visitors approach. He saw my carriage at a distance, and was ready at the door to receive me.

It seems strange to me that I should be under the necessity of describing Mr. Walpole's appearance. There is positively no one who has not seen him and does not know him at least by sight; but I must remember that I am writing for those who will not be born in all probability till after he and I are gathered to our forefathers, and so you will thank me for telling you what sort of person he was.

In person he is slender but compactly formed. Though not tall he looks so from his slimness. His complexion is of an unwholesome paleness, and nothing can exceed the whiteness of his hands. His eyes are his most striking feature; they are dark and lively, and when he is animated in conversation, or says a good thing, they will flash full of intelligence. His voice, when he used it naturally, is pleasing, but

R 2

he is apt to put on a forced laugh which I confess is anything but pleasing. His gout makes his gait rather awkward, but in receiving company or entering a room where persons are assembled he managed to conceal this awkwardness in a manner which gives an appearance of affected delicacy. He will then hold his chapeau-bras between his hands or under his arm, bend his knees slightly and walk partly on tiptoe, as if afraid of a wet floor. His dress is that of the most elegant gentleman of the time. I will describe it for you, though you will have one of my suits as an heir-loom. In summer a lavender suit, the waistcoat embroidered with a little silver or of white silk worked in the tambour, partridge silk stockings, gold-buckles, ruffles and frill of lace. In summer he wears no powder, but his wig is crushed straight and shows his very smooth pale forehead, and has a queue behind. In winter he wears powder.*

Since he turned the brow of life he has been very abstemious, and he possesses a constitution which can bear great alternations of temperature. Though he sits up very late either writing or conversing he breakfasts as early as nine o'clock, in that charming breakfast-room of his which fronts the Thames. He is always preceded by the favourite little dog which the Marquise du Deffand left to him, and which certainly does not rival the slender and delicate appearance of its master. With assistance, which its

* It is satisfactory to find that this description very nearly corresponds with that left us by Miss Hawkins (Anecdotes, p. 106), and by Pinkerton in his ' Walpoliana.'

fatness renders necessary, the dog is deposited on the sofa by his side. Tea is served to him out of the most rare and costly Japanese porcelain; butter from his own dairy, and bread the choicest that Twickenham can supply form the staple of his repast.

Ere he finishes breakfast he mixes a basin of bread and milk, and opening the window, feeds the squirrels, who come bounding along as soon as they hear the signal.

Till dinner-time he is almost constantly employed in attending visitors and explaining to them all the curiosities of his galleries, and wandering about in the grounds. He is generally very particular in the orders which he gives to admit people to see his house, and scarce ever allows any one to see it who is not a personal acquaintance of his or accompanied by one. When, however, strangers do come, he retires to a little hermitage on the other side of the road, surrounded by a dense wood, but with some sly vistas in it, from which he can see his visitors, unseen himself, and there he sits sometimes a whole morning,—a veritable hermit at penance. He has been so much in the habit of having visitors in whose presence it was necessary to keep his chapeau under his arm, that now he has contracted the habit of going all over his galleries without putting it on, and when any one remonstrates with him on thus exposing himself and on keeping his throat so open as he does, he replies, 'My back is the same with my face, and my neck like my nose.'

About four o'clock he dines; a very moderate re-

past of chicken, game, or some other light food suf-
fices. No other beverage but iced water is admitted
on his table except for the benefit of visitors, and
then, if he partakes at all, it is with extreme moderation. The ice-pail stands under the table, and his
decanter of water is never out of it except when he
replenishes his glass. There being no wine to loiter
over, he rings the bell almost directly after dinner
to order coffee up stairs. Mr. Pinkerton, who has
seen him more often than I have, having indeed made
court to him to a greater extent than I think is
altogether becoming the character of a gentleman—
but then authors, you know, are but a sort of head
lacqueys—Mr. Pinkerton tells me that Mr. Walpole
generally resumes his place on the sofa about five
o'clock, and will sit till two o'clock in the morning
in miscellaneous chit-chat full of singular anecdotes,
strokes of wit, and acute observations, occasionally
sending for books, or curiosities, or passing to the
library, as any reference happens to arise in conversation. After coffee, as Mr. Pinkerton further informs
me, Mr. Walpole tastes nothing, and I certainly never
saw him do so; but the snuff-box of *tabac-d'etrennes*
from Fribourg's is not forgotten, and is replenished
from a canister lodged in an ancient marble urn of
great thickness, which stands in the window-seat, and
serves to secure its moisture and rich flavour.

I know nothing more delightful than an evening
with Mr. Walpole. One cannot fall upon any subject of conversation that is at all connected with
history or biography but he rings the bell and sends

for some antique, which serves as a sort of vignette to whatever tale we are telling. It is something which you may actually feel and look upon belonging to the very times and persons of whom you were speaking, however long past those times, however distant those persons. There is no better way of bringing the reality of ancient ages home to us, and making us feel that we are not talking about vain creatures of a distempered imagination, but about men and women who had the same frames, hopes, wishes, passions, trials, sorrows as ourselves. The trophy of the victor, the fractured skull of the vanquished, the marriage gift of the murdered wife, the relics of saints, the still-born thoughts of authors that never burst into the life of print, all these are heaped up in those memorial chambers, and make Strawberry Hill the puppet-show of the time.

Nothing delights Mr. Walpole more than to have a crowd of distinguished persons visiting his house. It is natural that when he has laid out so much time and money in accumulating these treasures he should not wish them to lie unseen, and he has expressed this feeling in a letter to a friend of mine, in the following terms: 'Strawberry Hill is grown a perfect Paphos; it is the land of beauties. On Wednesday the Duchesses of Hamilton and Richmond and Lady Ailesbury dined there; the two latter stayed all night. There never was so pretty a sight as to see them all three sitting in the shell.' The shell is a seat in the form of a huge bivalve, invented by Mr. Walpole.

Mr. Walpole, then, received me at his low monastic doorway, chapeau-bras in hand, as I have said. Ere we pass from the doorway to the entrance hall of the house, a small oratory bespeaks to us the quasi-sacred character of the edifice we are about to enter. A saint is enshrined in it. Beyond is a cloister, where stands the likeness of Leonora d'Este, 'Dia Helionora,' a bas-relief head in marble, and certainly not inspiring the impartial spectator with that admiration which beset Leonora's lover, Tasso. The vase in which 'the pensive Selina' was drowned stands by the side of the lady's portrait, and is inscribed with the first stanza of Mr. Gray's beautiful ode :—

> ' 'Twas on this lofty vase's side,
> Where China's gayest art has dyed
> The azure flowers that blow,
> Demurest of the tabby kind,
> The pensive Selina reclin'd,
> Gazed on the lake below.'

On the right [is a small garden called the Abbot's garden, parted off by an open screen, taken from the tomb of Roger Niger, Bishop of London, in old St. Paul's.

Before us stands the narrow front of the house, which was designed by Richard Bentley, only son of the celebrated Dr. Bentley. The hall is small and gloomy, paved with hexagon tiles, and lighted by two narrow windows of painted glass, representing St. John and St. Francis, or as Mr. Walpole is fond of calling them, 'lean windows fattened with rich saints in painted glass.' In the well of the staircase hangs a Gothic lamp filled with painted glass, 'which casts the most venerable gloom on the stairs that ever was seen since the days of Abelard.'

To the left, through a small passage, over the entrance of which is an ancient carving in wood of the arms of Queen Elizabeth, is the Refectory, or Great Parlour. The furniture is of the truest Gothic, designed by Bentley. A table of Sicilian jasper stands covered with the richest china and porcelain, and under it two Etruscan vases and a jar of Roman fugenie. Over the table hangs a hunting horn of enamel upon copper; but above all, the pictures which are ranged on the walls of the Refectory are its greatest attraction. I hope, when you furnish your mansions, my dear descendants, you will remember and follow the excellent rule of selecting portraits for your dining-room; and, if you can, family portraits. Let mine be over your mantelpiece, if it is not too much to be asked by me, whose achievements you will doubtless excel. In the hours of conviviality, when the 'feast of reason and the flow of soul' are most enjoyed, it is well to draw round you as many loved and revered faces as you can to beam down kindliness and sympathy upon you. However full your table may be of guests, *their* company will never incommode you. When the wit sparkles, and the fire of genius illuminates your saloon, you may lay *them* aside—*they* will not trouble you; but when conversation lags, when you dine perhaps in solitude, then *they* are there to keep you company, to claim their kindred with you; and when an hour of adversity has come, when you are a fallen minister, and the world sits at the portal of your rival, *they* will not desert you, but will recall to you many a lesson of troubles, and sorrows, and adversities, which have been manfully borne and nobly surmounted; then you will feel emboldened to do as they have done—to recover power and to reconquer fortune.

Mr. Walpole well understands this rule of inviting your ancestors to your banquets. His Refectory would be worthy of study, if for nothing else, for the portraits of Sir Robert Walpole, his first wife, the daughter of John Shorter, Esq., his second wife, Maria Skerret, and his sons and daughters. Several of his more remote kin are collected there too; some painted by Sir Godfrey Kneller, some by Jarvis, others by Richardson, others by Eckardt. In the waiting-room, attached to the Refectory, is placed a head, in artificial stone, of John Dryden, the poet, great-uncle of Catherine Shorter, Sir Robert's first wife.

The China room, replete with the most costly and rich porcelain, Turkish earthenware, Venetian glass, and the like, may occupy the minute attention of the curious. Mr. Walpole, knowing my taste, rather hurried me through this to the Yellow Bedchamber, or Beauty Room, rich in Sir Peter Lely's Beauties. Charles II. is of course there; and, by way of contrast, King William III. when Prince of Orange.

We ascend the fine broad ancient-looking staircase, and after climbing one pair of stairs, are ushered into the breakfast-room, furnished with blue paper

and blue and white linen. The bow-window has
black and yellow glass set in plain blue glass.
The room is full of curious portraits. The Digby
family are especially strong. He rescued several of
them from a garret in an old house in Wales. Sir
Kenelm's wife, Venetia Stanley, is represented no
less than three times during her life, and once as she
was found dead in bed. The picture is set in gold,
enamelled black, on which behind is a sphere—a
quaint mode of intimating that the world is mourning for her. Here too is preserved the watch that
the Parliament gave to General Fairfax. On one
side the general is represented on horseback, after
Vandyck's King Charles; on the other the House of
Commons; behind, the battle. More peaceful is the
picture of Rose, the royal gardener, presenting the
first pine apple raised in England to Charles II., who
is standing in a garden. To Mr. Walpole himself
few things are more interesting in his collection than
the washed drawing of Madame la Marquise du
Deffand, and the Duchesse de Choiseul giving her a
doll, which the former, who was blind, holds out her
hand to receive, alluding to her calling the duchesse
grandmamma. Mr. Walpole particularly commends
the exactness with which every part of the room is
represented, and the likeness of Madame du Deffand.
What a curious trait of our manners is recorded in
Lady Diana Beauclerc's masquerade at Vauxhall in
bistre ! She manages to throw wonderful expression
into the faces and attitudes. Some of the figures
are masked, some not.

The Green Closet is full of most interesting paintings and drawings, which I must not weary you with particulars.   One thing, however, struck me here first in Strawberry Hill, and I had the means in other rooms of confirming my impression—Mr. Walpole has one of the most distinguishing characteristics of a refined and educated mind, the love of the locality in which he lives.   I have often been struck, in wandering through our country homes, to find that there is not the slightest reference in all the works of art, the furniture, or the curiosities collected there, to the neighbourhood where the house stands.   The whole domain might be moved off bodily, as the vulgar phrase is, from Northamptonshire or Wiltshire to Cornwall or to Sussex, or any other county the owner might prefer to abide in, and the house and all its pictures, fittings, and collections, would be as appropriate in its new as in its old locality.   Now this, some persons might say, is an advantage—what is fit for all places is better than what is fit for only one ; but I hold it to be a grievous error.   Houses and castles are not made to be moved, they are built upon a spot where they will stand till they perish ; and they should do more than stand there, they should drive their roots deep into the soil, so that, when you roam through their galleries and saloons, you should feel that you are in an edifice which has grown out of and belongs to the soil—such an one as you must come hundreds and hundreds of miles to see, whose fellow you can nowhere find, and not some mere tent which has been pitched by a nomad family

that wants to rest awhile, and will take it up again
when they are rested, and pitch it on some other
accidental oasis in the dreary desert through which it
is the employment of their transitory life to wander.

There is not a spot of earth which has not some
peculiar beauty belonging to it—something which is
its own—its actual and inalienable property.   It may
be in the form and aspect of the scenery ; in the
rich product of the soil or of the mines ; in the associations of the place—the most eternal and precious
of property.   Robbers cannot steal them, rivals cannot imitate them, rapacious owners cannot buy them
and carry them away.   They stand immutable, for
man to use or to neglect.   Ever offered to each suc-
eeding generation, never growing stale or worse for
the carelessness or insensibility of those who have
thrown away the opportunity of using them, but becoming more precious as time advances—more hon-
oured as they grow more ancient.

There is, I say, an individuality in every spot and
patch of earth, which may be seized upon and represented by those who possess sensibility enough to
feel it ; but how much greater and more obvious
than all other kinds of individuality is the individuality belonging to the homes of genius.—'I scarce
know,' says Tully,* ' what it is that affects us when we

* Movemur nescio quo pacto ipsis locis in quibus eorum,
quos diligimus aut admiramur, adsunt vestigia.   Me quidem
ipsæ illæ Athenæ nostræ non tam operibus magnificis exqui-
sitisque antiquorum artibus delectant, quam recordatione
summorum virorum, ubi quisque habitare, ubi sedere, ubi

stand in the very places where are the footsteps of those whom we love or admire ; for myself, our famed Athens delights me not so much with the magnificent works and exquisite arts of its ancient people, as with the recollection of its mighty men—where each was wont to dwell, where each to sit, where each to hold his disputations :—even at their tombs I worship.' You will remember, I doubt not, that when Tully with his brother Quintus, Piso, and a few other young Romans of noble quality, who were studying philosophy at Athens, walked out together one day from Antiochus' lecture, to the then deserted groves of Plato's academy, and wandered about the dreary and solitary walks, which once had resounded with the discussions of those who thought, not for the benefit of Greece alone, or Macedon alone, or Athens alone, but for the improvement of the human race, and for the advancement of knowledge through every age and in every clime. Piso, struck with the religion of the place, says:*—'Do we owe it to nature, or

---

disputare solitus sit ; studioseque eorum etiam sepulchra contemplor.—*Cicero, de Legibus,* l. ii. c. 2.

* Tum Piso, Naturane nobis hoc, inquit, datum dicam, an errore quodam ut, cum ea loca videamus in quibus memoria dignos viros acceperimus multum esse versatos, magis moveamur, quam si quando eorum ipsorum aut facta audiamus aut scriptum aliquod legamus ? velut ego nunc moveor ; venit enim mihi Platonis in mentem, quem accepimus primum hic disputare solitum, cujus etiam ille hortuli propinqui non memoriam solum adferunt, sed ipsum videntur in conspectu meo ponere. Hic Speusippus, hic Xenocrates, hic ejus auditor Polemo, cujus illa sessio fuit, quam videmus.—*Cicero, de Finibus,* v. ci.

some weakness of our own, that when we behold places much frequented, as we believe, by men worthy of remembrance, we are more affected than if we either heard their acts recounted, or read aught that they had left in writing? In this way I am myself now affected, for I recollect to have heard that Plato himself was wont at first to hold his disputations in this place; his little gardens close by not only call him to my remembrance, but seem to place him before my eyes. Here Speusippus, here Xenocrates, here his pupil Polemo, whose seat was this which we see.'

To the like effect speaks Milton, proudly, in his discourse of Prelatical Episcopacy, which with all his other prose works (his poetry needs no commendation of mine), I commend to your best care and study, for their style; seize its manliness and spirit, but avoid its occasional turgidity, as you will, I know, avoid his detestable opinions. 'With less fervency,' says he, 'was studied what St. Paul or St. John had written, than was listened to one that could say— here he taught, here he stood, this was his stature and thus he went habited; and O, happy this house that harboured him, and that cold stone whereon he rested! this village wherein he wrought such a miracle, and that pavement bedewed with the warm effusion of his lost blood, that sprouted up into eternal roses to crown his martyrdom.' And that I may not weary you with examples I will give you but one more— the beautiful prophecy of Pliny the younger to the Emperor Trajan:—

'There will come a time when posterity will visit, and will commend to be visited to those who come after them, the field that has drank thy sweat, the trees that gave thee shelter, the overhanging crag that offered thee sleep, the house that thou, a mighty guest, didst occupy. Like as to thyself were shown the sacred footsteps of mighty leaders.'

I have been led into this reflection by the admirable manner in which Mr. Walpole has made Strawberry Hill a true Twickenham house. You will doubtless be familiar with the scene; its beauty will, after the long lapse of years when you will see it, be as splendid as it is now; but perhaps Strawberry Hill may be no longer standing, or at least its collection be no longer preserved. You will not then be able to appreciate, unless I record it for you, the taste and judgment of Mr. Walpole, in introducing into almost every room some sketch or picture of the surrounding scenery, or some portrait of the illustrious men who have lived there; so that while you wander through the maze of his infinite collections, and give way to the thoughts of ancient times and far distant countries, you come in every room upon some picture or some fragment which says to you, 'Yes—think of the absent and the long past; study, if you choose, the relics of lost empires, the trinkets of the beautiful, long withered to dust; the armour of the brave, who now lie beneath the same battle-field with those who trembled to meet them—yes, study these things, and think of them as long as you please; but you shall not leave this room and forget that you are in Twick enham. Here is Twickenham as it is seen from Richmond Hill; here, as it appears from Mrs. Clive's house: this is the view from Pope's; this from the terrace outside; this from Lady Diana Beauclerc's: here is the portrait of Pope's father as he lay dead; there is Pope's mother, and yonder Pope himself; and his villa in every one of its phases. You shall not forget you are in Twickenham, and you shall not forget what Twickenham is.'

I took the liberty of offering to Mr. Walpole my tribute of admiration at the delightful and graceful manner in which in every apartment the claims of Twickenham were thus kept ever present to the mind. He replied, 'I am glad, my lord, you are pleased with the idea; it is not every one who comes here who sees and understands it; but then, you know, I am most fortunate in the village whose claims to respect I thus advocate. Its scenery speaks for itself; but as you perhaps may not know all the great names with whom we are associated, I will take leave to offer to your lordship, when we come to my printing press, a copy of my Parish Register of Twickenham.' I need not say how delighted I was to think that Mr. Walpole had put together the associations about his village, for though I knew it had been for several ages the chosen home of celebrated characters, yet I had never been able to find even so much as a list of them. What he gave me was as follows:—

The Parish Register of Twit'nam.

Written about 1758.

Where silver Thames round Twit'nam meads
His winding current sweetly leads ;
Twit'nam, the Muses' favourite seat,
Twit'nam, the Graces' lov'd retreat.
There polish'd Essex* wont to sport,
The pride and victim of a court !
There Bacon† tun'd the grateful lyre
To soothe Eliza's haughty ire ;
—Oh ! happy had no meaner strain
Than friendship's dash'd his mighty vein !
Twit'nam, where Hyde,‡ majestic sage,
Retir'd from folly's frantic stage,
While his vast soul was hung on tenters
To mend the world, and vex dissenters ;
Twit'nam, where frolic Wharton § revell'd,
Where Montague,‖ with locks dishevell'd
(Conflict of dirt and warmth divine),
Invok'd and scandalized the Nine ;
Where Pope in moral music spoke
To th' anguished soul of Bolingbroke,
And whisper'd how true genius errs,
Preferring joys that pow'r confers ;
Bliss, never to great minds arising
From ruling worlds but from despising ;
Where Fielding¶ met his bunter muse,
And, as they quaff'd the fiery juice,
Droll nature stamp'd each lucky hit
With unimaginable wit ;
Where Suffolk** sought the peaceful scene,
Resigning Richmond to the queen,

---

* Robert Devereux, Earl of Essex.   † Sir Francis Bacon.
‡ Lord Clarendon.   § The Duke of Wharton.
‖ Lady Mary Wortley Montague.   ¶ Henry Fielding.
** Henrietta Hobart, Countess of Suffolk.

And all the glory, all the teasing,
Of pleasing one not worth the pleasing.
Where Fanny,* ever blooming fair,
Ejaculates the graceful pray'r,
And 'scap'd from sense with nonsense smit
For Whitfield's cant leaves Stanhope's† wit.
Amid this choir of sounding names
Of statesmen, bards, and beauteous dames,
Shall the last trifler of the throng
Enrol his own such names among?
    Oh! no enough—if I consign
To lasting types their notes divine—
Enough if Strawberry's humble hill
The title-page of fame shall fill.

Postscript added 1784.

Here genius in a later hour
Selected its sequester'd bow'r,   ·
And threw around the verdant room
The blushing lilac's chill perfume.
So loose is flung each bold festoon—
Each bough so breathes the touch of noon—
    The happy pencil ‡ so deceives,
That Flora, doubly jealous, cries
' The work's not mine—yet, trust these eyes,
    'Tis my own Zephyr waves the leaves.'

I have detained you indeed a long time with this
reverie in the Green Closet, let us pass rapidly through
the Blue Bed-chamber and the Red Bed-chamber, both
replete with paintings and works of art, and each containing views of Twickenham and portraits of persons

---

* Lady Fanny Shirley.
† Philip Stanhope, Earl of Chesterfield.
‡ Of Lady Diana Beauclerc.

connected with it, and come out again upon the Staircase.   In a niche stands the armour of Francis I.;
it is of steel gilt and covered with bas-reliefs.   The
lance is of ebony inlaid with silver, the sword steel
inlaid with gold.   Mr. Walpole is not, I think, wrong
in ascribing the workmanship to Benvenuto Cellini.
Many other curiosities of the same description line
the approach to the Armoury, which is an open vesti-
bule of three Gothic arches, lighted by a window
entirely of painted glass, and ornamented over the
doors and niches with quarterings of the family of
Walpole painted by Grout.   It is full of curious and
historical armour, and dispels the illusion which the
ground-floor of the house is calculated to create, that
the visitor is in an abbey.   It is certainly a feudal
castle, whose ancient and hereditary treasures are
now laid open to his view.

But something better awaits us than an abbey or
a castle.   I think it was Tully who said when he had
built a library to his Tusculan villa, 'A mind seems
added to my house.'   Mr. Walpole has nobly provided that the mind of his house should be well lodged.
I have got a print, which shall be carefully preserved
for you, of the painting made by one Muntz, a
poor artist in the employ of Mr. Walpole, but yet not
without merit, which represents Mr. Walpole in a
luxurious arm-chair, soft and shining with embroidered
silk; the shelves which contain his precious books
are just shown, and so is an ancient carved chest containing his most precious manuscripts.   The window
is open, and there lies expanded before him the green

enamel of the rich plain, through which a white sail upon the river gently glides along. A few books which he has been perusing lie scattered on the floor, and Mr. Walpole has a sort of startled, pleased look about him, as if he had just hit upon the solution of some Court anecdote which had often puzzled him, and had always been wrongly understood by the world at large; for it must be confessed, and it is a thousand pities, that though he reads literature of all kinds, he is most deeply interested in the light Court gossip of the day, or perhaps, if I may so say, of yesterday, the trivialities and fooleries of which he has heard so much in his father's time at the Minister's house, and which he now inquires about with all the zeal and energy of an antiquary. It is this, I think, which so much charmed him with old Lady Suffolk at Marble Hill. She was too deaf to hear a word he said, but she would talk without end of the scandal and back-stairs history of the Court in her day; and Mr. Walpole liked nothing better than to spend an evening with her, collecting from her lips the materials for the memoirs of the Court of the late King, which he is said to design, and indeed to have proceeded some way in writing.

To do justice to Mr. Walpole it must, however, be said, that he respects more serious literature and collects it. His library consists of some 15,000 volumes, ranged in cases carved after the model of the choir of old St. Paul's. The chimney-piece is imitated from a tomb in Westminster Abbey, with some hints from Canterbury, so that an ecclesiastical air is thrown over the whole room, and makes me often think that I am in one of those old monastic libraries in which all the learning of the ancients was stored up and shut away during the dark ages. His literary curiosities are innumerable; but the most interesting to me is the identical copy of Homer used by Mr. Pope in his translation. It is a small edition, printed at Amsterdam in 1707, and we see that the poet had —if he chose to use it—the assistance of a Latin translation. There is writ in it in Mr. Pope's hand-writing, 'E Latini A Pope 1714,' and 'Finished ye translation in Feb. 1719-20 A Pope.' One of the pages contains a pencil-sketch of Twickenham Church, as seen from the poet's grotto, and drawn by the poet's own hand. Amid all the riches and fascination of that library, this is what Twickenham has to advocate its claims by; and Mr. Walpole tells me that it is more looked at and thought of than anything else the room contains.

If you wish to be made melancholy—that is, more melancholy than such a collection as that of Strawberry Hill must necessarily make you; if you wish to be made especially melancholy, and to distrust all your own hopes and reliances, walk up to the little clock of silver gilt, richly chased, engraved and ornamented with fleur-de-lys, while on the top sits a lion holding the arms of England. It was a present from Henry VIII. to Anne Boleyn on the morning of their marriage. On the weights are the initial letters of Henry and Anne, with true lovers' knots; at top, *Dieu et mon droit*—at bottom, *The most happy*.

The Star Chamber is rich in painted glass, and full of precious medals. It always detains me long, for there is nothing I love better than to pore over old coins; but I shall not give you the trouble of reading a long description of it. My own cabinet is better worth your study than any description by me of Mr. Walpole's, though I need not say that his collection far excels mine. The contents of the Holbein Chamber are selected according to a plan which I think the true one in all large collections of pictures. They relate almost exclusively to the time of Holbein—Sir Thomas More, Catharine of Arragon, Queen Elizabeth when a girl, Henry Howard, Earl of Surrey, the poet, are all represented there; and Wolsey's red hat, found in the great wardrobe by Bishop Burnet, when Clerk of the Closet, is an actual tangible relic of those days. It is truer, I say, in the arrangement of works of art and historical relics, to arrange them according to order of time, than to leave them, as is often done, to be sorted according to the size of their frames. In my own gallery I have attempted it, and I hope you will preserve the arrangement; so that one chamber is devoted to Albert Durer and his school, another to the Venetians, another to the Flemish, and another to the Dutch. You thus see brought together the examples of each school, and can catch at a glance the general characteristics belonging to the schools, and the individual peculiarities of the painters.

I have left still untold the most magnificent of the apartments—the Gallery, 56 feet long, 17 high, and

13 wide, with a ceiling imitated from Henry VII.'s chapel.   Five recesses are filled with the choicest treasures of antiquity—the magnificent Roman eagle found within the precinct of the baths of Caracalla at Rome, taking the lead.   The pictures which hang from the highly decorated walls have every variety of interest. In one is represented the marriage of Henry VII. to Elizabeth of York; in another is a group, by Janet, of Catherine de Medicis and her children, Charles IX., Henry III., the Duke of Alençon, and Margaret, Queen of Navarre. On the window side stands the portrait of Henry Carey, Lord Falkland, Deputy of Ireland, in white, by Vansomer, which suggested to Mr. Walpole the incident of the picture walking out of its frame in the 'Castle of Otranto.'

The Round Drawing-room next succeeds, full with magnificent paintings and China antiquities and objects of virtù.   From that we go to the Tribune, where there is a cabinet containing not less than a hundred miniatures by Petitot, and other great masters.   The whole room sparkles with gold and jewels.   Their splendour is only exceeded by the interest of some of them—the missal, for example, painted by Raffaelle and his pupils, for Claude de France, the queen of Francis the First.   It is covered with turquoises and rubies, and on each cover is an enormous cornelian, with an intaglio of the Crucifixion on one side, and a relievo on the other. Henry the Eighth's dagger, of Turkish work; the little bronze bust of Caligula, with silver eyes; the

Florentine boar, and the Jupiter Serapis, are all that I can stay to mention. The Great North Bed-chamber is filled again in the same way. Here Twickenham too vindicates its rights of the soil by the most interesting thing in the room. It is the original sketch by Hogarth of the Beggars' Opera, which, as you know, was writ in Pope's villa at Twickenham :—Walker as Macheath, Miss Fenton (afterwards Duchess of Bolton) as Polly, Hippisley as Peach'em, Hall as Lockit ; on one side, in a box, Sir Thomas Robinson, very tall and lean, Sir Robert Fagg, a famous horse-racer, fat, with short grey hair. Mr. Walpole bought it at the sale of John Rich, the well-known harlequin and master of the theatres in Lincoln's-Inn Fields and Covent Garden, for whom the picture was painted.

There remain to be mentioned the Beauclerc Closet, a hexagon, built expressly to receive seven incomparable drawings of Lady Diana Beauclerc, for Mr. Walpole's tragedy of the 'Mysterious Mother;' the Round Bedchamber, which contains a portrait of the Countess of Suffolk, by Jervas, with her house at Marble Hill, Twickenham ; the Great Cloister and the Chapel, with painted glass from the church of Bexhill, in Sussex, and a shrine from the church of Santa Maria Maggiore, in Rome.

I have thus, my dear descendants, given you a sketch—meagre enough—of the wonderful house of Mr. Walpole. At my principal visit I met Mr. Gray and Mr. Mason there. I subsequently have met there Mr. Cole. George Selwyn, the wit, and Mr.

Chute, a herald, have also, as I best recollect, been there at the same time with myself. I took rough notes of what passed at my visits, and in particular of Mr. Walpole's conversation, which was always lively and entertaining, though perhaps harping too much on light Court anecdote. These conversations you will not, of course, expect one of my quality to record with accuracy and minutenes; but I have directed my gentleman to take the notes I made to the poet who lives in my east turret, you may perhaps like to know the room—it is the one with the small window of six panes, and the sloping roof just over the butler's sleeping-room), and he will no doubt make something readable out of it, for the fellow has wit and sense. If I like what he does I will preserve it for you, with my original notes, in the same chest in which I intend to put this. Meanwhile I think you will like to read this ballad by William Pulteney, Earl of Bath, in praise of the house which I have been describing. The second, fourth, and fifth stanzas are by Mr. Walpole.

STRAWBERRY HILL—A BALLAD.

i.

Some cry up Gunnersbury ;
　　For Sion some declare ;
And some say that with Chiswick House
　　No villa can compare ;
But ask the beaux of Middlesex,
　　Who know the country well,
If Strawb'ry Hill, if Strawb'ry Hill,
　　Don't bear away the bell.

II.

Some love to roll down Greenwich hill
   For this thing and for that ;
And some prefer sweet Marble hill,
   Tho' sure 'tis somewhat flat;
Yet Marble hill and Greenwich hill,
   If Kitty Clive can tell,
From Strawb'ry Hill, from Strawb'ry Hill,
   Will never bear the bell.

III.

Tho' Surrey boasts its Oatlands,
   And Clermont kept so grim,
And some prefer sweet Southcotes,
   'Tis but a dainty whim ;
For ask the gallant Bristow,
   Who does in taste excel,
If Strawb'ry Hill, if Strawb'ry Hill,
   Don't bear away the bell.

IV.

Since Denham sung of Cooper's,
   There's scarce a hill around,
But what in song or ditty
   Is turn'd to fairy ground.
Ah, peace be with their memories !
   I wish them wondrous well,
But Strawb'ry Hill, but Strawb'ry Hill,
   Must bear away the bell.

V.

Great William dwells at Windsor,
   As Edward did of old,
And many a Saul and many a Scott
   Have found him full as bold.
On lofty hills like Windsor,
   Such heroes love to dwell,
Yet little folks like Strawb'ry Hill,
   Like Strawb'ry Hill as well.

They all observed that Rebow had listened with more attention to this narrative than to any of the other tales. He seemed to be constantly absent while they were read, just catching the thread of the story; but whenever any idea new to him was started, his mind immediately began to decompose it, and mix it with the material of ideas with which his brain was well stocked; and Rebow would immediately be thinking how he could introduce them into the book or the articles he was writing. This excessive fertility of mind made him a very slow and inaccurate reader when he was by himself. He could scarce catch an idea without its immediately suggesting others of the kind in his brain; and thus he was prevented from minutely observing how the original idea was expressed, and what context it was set in. He had, of course, a wretched memory for what he read, and never made much figure in college examinations in consequence. But to this narrative he listened with a rapt attention, though it was not such as a novelist, one would have thought, would have been nearly so much interested as in any of the others. When it was over, he turned to Verney and said,

'I think you said you don't know who wrote that narrative?'

'No—I wish I did; for though it may lack invention in an artistic point of view, it is most interesting to me.'

'And so it is to me; for I know the author. I ought to be one of those descendants to whom it is addressed, though my grandfather—if I dare call him such, who do not bear his name—would not acknowledge a poor scribbler, a wretch, like the poet whom he kept in his turret attic:—and—and, for other reasons.'

'My dear Rebow, is it then by the Earl of —— ?'

'Yes; there are allusions in it which make me certain about it.'

Well, you have conferred a great obligation on me by discovering its author ; but don't say anything more about garret-scribblers. We are all scribblers, now-a-days, and no one would have been more certain to have been a scribbler, if he had lived now, than the Earl himself.'

'He might have written for amusement,' replied Rebow, 'as you do, but not for bread.' A sigh which escaped him warned Verney to drop the subject as a hopeless one.

MRS. VERNEY'S STORY.

SEPPY WILL;

OR, THE BABE IN THE WOOD.

THE gentlemen had now all discharged their narrative duties; but one day remained; and they had become so accustomed to a tale as the evening amusement, that it would have seemed blank and dismal without one—so soon does what was at first a luxury become a necessity.

It was proposed, I think by Verney, that they should draw lots to determine upon whom the task of telling the last tale should devolve. D'Aubrey, however, moved as an amendment, that Mrs. Verney should be asked to favour them with a tale. This was carried by acclamation; and before there was time even to interpose an objection, Mrs. Verney found that she was doomed by her guests; and being determined not to disappoint them, if she could help it, she read in the evening the following tale :—

SEPPY WILL;

OR, THE BABE IN THE WOOD.

I.

Few towns enjoy so wide-spread a celebrity as Calais, both in respect to historic interest, and as a well-known halting-place on one of the grand European thoroughfares. Calais is not a household, but a cosmopolitan word. At the same time, few towns are so imperfectly understood, in proportion to their fame, as to the practical points of local peculiarity and social character. Calais retains the unmistakeable mark of ancestral polish and civilisation. She has an admirable library in charge of a learned and urbane archiviste; she has a small but extremely curious museum; she appreciates, and successfully cultivates, the arts; she is given to hospitality and accords confidence to strangers who can show the least pretensions to merit it; her markets are excellently-well supplied with fish, flesh, fowl, and fruit; and yet, were the best house in Calais offered me as a gratuitous residence, I would thank the liberal donor with a bow of refusal. Do you ask me, Why?

Calais, on the map, lies on the very edge of the shore. The town does so lie, in point of fact; but it stands very low, being raised only a few feet above high-water mark; it is surrounded by duplicate and triplicate lines of fortification; and the consequence is that, within the town itself, you see scarcely more of the sea than you would in a city fifty leagues inland. But few houses catch a view of the Straits of Dover from their windows; and, of those few, one or two are the haunts of infamy and vice, which no respectable person can approach or enter. In short, in Calais (if you resemble myself) you feel a pining after air and elbow-room. The streets are narrow, the houses high; while from certain ditches, which constitute a portion of the plan of defence, there exhales an odour which compels the perennial and hermetical shutting of many a window that would otherwise look out on the open plain and admit a fresh stream of country air. Thus, by a provoking paradox, the heart of the town is better ventilated than the offskirts. Certainly, there is the handsome and picturesque square for you to pace to and fro in; but it is a sort of a large unroofed apartment, wherein the town holds her levées and drawing-rooms. There is the shady public walk or garden on the ramparts; but it is a species of prisoner's garden, dull, flowerless, unfrequented, rectangular, bounded by a precipice of wall down which you may easily break your neck, and by dingy houses in which you might suppose debtors to lodge. From the best points of view, there is a foreground of formidable fortifications over which the eye must leap, before it can reach the free horizon. This solitary promenade gives you the idea of its having been laid out on the pattern, or by the aid of a parallel ruler; and at each end only there is a less limited and prison-like prospect, of the sea, and of the distant hills, of which latter more anon. Thirdly and lastly, there is the unusually long-extended jetty, which makes a charming walk and airing-place when the tide is up and the wind not too high; but even if the sea would oblige us by always remaining at high-water mark and even-tempered in respect to calmness, the eye would tire of constantly looking at heaving waves and a floor of planks. You want, for a change, rural sights and sounds; you long to behold a bit of green and to hear the voice of an animal or bird, even the hum of an insect or the croak of a frog.

'Take a walk in the country, then,' you say. Ay, there's the rub! Calais has no country round it; nothing but canals, intersecting sandy, or shingly, or swampy plains. Stretch out along the coast on the Dunkerque road, and you follow ever the same monotonous flat, till you are tired of walking, riding, or driving. In the other direction, southwards, it is not much better; for, when at last you do reach the upland slope which would conduct you to the Boulon-nais, it is treeless, hedgeless, a cultivated down, and nothing more. Add to this that, for security's sake in troubled times, there are only two issues from the town; one, immortalized by Hogarth, leading to the port; the other, on the opposite side, conducting to what should be the fields. But when you have crossed its several drawbridges, you find yourself

entering another town, St. Pierre-les-Calais (with a
church, a town-hall, and a maire of its own), which
has grown up beside and contiguous to the former,
and would coalesce with it, just as two drops, in
contact, melt into one, but for the separation effected
by rampart, ditch, and glacis. To find real sylvan
scenery, you must traverse the excrescential,
independent suburb, and reach the wood-crowned
hills which are visible from one end of the parallel-
ogram parade. At the foot of these, is the town of
Guines; beyond Guines, and at the distance of a
short ten miles English from Calais, is the village of
Campagne, lying just on the skirt of the forest,
which is the property of the State. Campagne is
also on the border of the famous Field of the Cloth
of Gold, and was for more than two hundred years
under the English sway. Campagne abounds in
shady lanes, in orchards, in farmhouses overshadowed
by lofty elms, in horseponds, cabarets, and cottages
rejoicing in little bits of leek and cabbage gardens.
But the whole of the above display of topographical
knowledge has been undertaken here, not for the
sake of disinterring any marrowless bone of antiquity,
but in order to explain to you clearly why it is that
so many wealthy Calaisians and St. Pierre people
have country houses or country lodgings in the
village of Campagne.

II.

In the Rue des Prêtres, at Calais, stands an
enormous house, built of that pale grey stone from

the quarries of Ferques whose natural complexion conceals the sober tintings of age. At first sight, you cannot tell whether this house is old or new ; it is of no order of architecture ; all you can say of it is, that it is large and flat-faced. There is a wide and lofty porte-cochère painted grey and always kept closed ; if on foot, you enter beneath its archway by a wicket-door cut in the larger one. There are large windows distributed over the façade at regular intervals, quite unrelieved by mouldings or other ornament; these windows are always completely screened inside by muslin blinds of most scrupulous whiteness, so that the edifice has the aspect of a gigantic quakeress veiled and muffled in linen to the tips of her fingers. Not a flower, not a bird-cage, not a picture, not a morsel of mirror is visible from without. Whatever amount of curiosity or speculation is exercised on outward things by those within, no external symptom of the same is perceptible by the casual passer-by. The mansion was built in the last century by a Russian nobleman, who resided in it for a long period of years, with what aim or object was never exactly known, and never will be, unless the Calais archives should contain some store of secret correspondence unknown to those who have hitherto held them in custody. He was too wealthy to be an exile ; too highly considered by illustrious travellers to be an ordinary spy ; had too discursive and cultivated a taste to choose such a residence, except under the influence of some strong motive. Suffice it, that on leaving Calais, he gave this house. as a

sort of parting legacy, to a long-tried confidential
retainer, who sold it to the grandfather of its present
owner and occupier, Mr. R—— N—— C——.

At Calais and its sister town St. Pierre, there are
several roads that lead to fortune. One of these, an
introduction from England, is the tulle trade, or the
manufacture of cotton lace. To this profession,
which gives employment to thousands, Mr. C——
devotes his energies, although what he has inherited,
added to what he has acquired himself, would enable
him well to live apart from business. His father was
pure English, his mother pure French. He is an
affectionate father, an indulgent husband, a genial
companion, and a good listener; he carves well—a
rare accomplishment for any one with French blood
in their veins—he gives exquisite wines, is of extremely quiet and unpretending habits, has a vast
fund of information which he keeps for use rather
than for show, has a broad and high bald forehead,
and is exactly three and forty years of age. Mrs.
C——, his excellent wife, is of precisely similar
parentage; namely, English by the father's and
French by the mother's side. Hence she is known
to certain of her admirers as La Belle Alliance. She
is tall, warm-tempered, with speaking eyes and tell-
tale mouth and cheeks, and is inclined to the Italian
or Michael Angelo mould of woman. She combines
charmingly the characters of mistress of the house
or hostess, wife, and mother. She makes you at
home instantly in the agreeable society by which she
is always surrounded. You meet there people whose

claims to admission you might perhaps have doubted, but you soon find that their merits entitle them to be received; you remark the constant absence of others whom you might expect to see there, but you feel convinced, you don't quite know why, that they are best away. Mrs. C—— has faith in, love and respect for, her husband; she has a lofty scorn of everything low or mean. Her children, seven, she idolizes. In short, though an admirable hostess she is more the wife than the mistress of the house, and still more the mother than the wife. There is, however, something instinctive, I was going to say animal, about her maternity. She seems ever to love the youngest best, fondling *them* doatingly, and allowing the elders to go to school or college without expressing any severe pang at the temporary parting; just as a lioness would send forth her firstlings to make their way in the world, while those to whom she still gives suck are the objects of daily affection and nightly care.

Thus, five of Mrs. C——'s children are away from home; well cared-for and never forgotten, but still away. The two younger, a boy of five, Charles, and a girl of three and a half, Septima, are rarely out of her sight an hour at a time during the day. These babes are continually being tossed and dangled by their mother into groups and attitudes and living pictures that would serve an artist for models to study from. Is she aware how handsome she looks at such moments? Does it enter into her calculations that the presence of a young child implies at least a youngish mother? For, by the way, Mrs. C—— owns to thirty-five, while her most jealous rivals do not give her more than forty. Are these children spoiled at all? you ask. The question is superfluous; they *are* spoiled, temporarily. But, as they grow older, the spoiling is gradually with-drawn, and a sort of reconstitutive process in their character takes place. Thus, Charley has much more common sense, in proportion, than his sister, whose whims are indulged to the very verge of wilfulness. It would almost seem as if the mother purposely encouraged and cultivated the spirit of contradiction in this infant's breast. Disobedient speeches, consisting mainly of 'Seppy will,' and 'Seppy won't,' at times when the words respectively indicate refusal and not assent, have often been listened to with fatal smiles of approbation. Every one has his fault; and so, I suppose, has, or rather had, my charming friend Mrs. C——, for she is lately changed for the better.

III.

I hardly know whether I have quite admitted you inside the mansion yet. A large marble hall would gave airyness to the house, but screens of stained glass, folding doors, and painted blinds, prevent it. All excess of light is excluded, as well as draughts and gusts of wind. A mat of tiger-skin lying in the hall is the favourite resting-place of a fragile Italian greyhound, Flibbertygibbet, whose limbs look scarcely strong enough to support him in his sprightly frolics up and down stairs. As soon as the drawing room door (or wherever the mistress is) is opened, the first thing you see is a small, plump King Charles' spaniel, whose wheezy bark and somewhat watery eye are the very symbols of indolence. A third domestic pet must not be forgotten, whose habitat is the nursery. Minet is a tall, strong-built, half Angora tom-cat, three years old, lean and lank, with light slaty-blue coat and clear yellow eyes, who takes a particular fancy to little Septima. Septima always feeds him, close to Septima's bed he sleeps; by Septima's side he walks in the garden; with Septima he travels from Calais to Campagne. If by chance he is left at home, he will go and sit for hours by the side of one of the little girl's frocks hanging on a peg, as a substitute for the reality, till the wearer returns in bodily presence. Cats are said to be attached to places, and not to persons. Minet is attached to two places, the Calais house and the Campagne house, making himself equally at home in either, and to one person, Miss Septima C——. The garden just mentioned is like the rest of the establishment, large and confined. It is surrounded by immensely lofty walls, ornamented at top, in summer, with vases of agaves and scarlet geraniums. No living creature can peep into it, except the swallows which circle overhead. Generally, not the slightest breath of a breeze is to be felt; but if a gale is blowing, and the wind once gets in, it goes whirling round and round, like mad, enraged at the impossibility of ever getting out.

One sultry morning last July, a small knot of friends were assembled in the breakfast-room at the Rue des Prêtres. Besides the family (including the two children and their nursemaid Eliza), there were Madame and Mademoiselle Van E— (Mrs. C——'s aunt and cousin), and Mr. Davies, a widower, the head of an important establishment and an old and trusty friend of the C——s. In short, the whole party were at home and perfectly at ease each with the other.

'How oppressively close it is in the town!' said Mrs. C——. 'For the last two days I have been haunted by one single idea.'

'I guess what it is,' said Louise Van E—.

'And so do I,' interposed her mother.

'And so do we, don't we, Davies?' added C——, smiling. 'But business is rather pressing just now. It is impossible we should migrate to Campagne at the present moment.'

'I know it,' replied Mrs. C——, 'and I would not ask it. But I think you can both be spared till to morrow morning, and we might spend at least a few hours amidst the flowers and the green leaves. Suppose we all start immediately, to enjoy a picnic in the forest. We, dear Richard, you and I, have the more solid part of the feast already provided, the cold meat, the bread and a fresh-cut salad; and we will start as soon as the carriage is ready. Wine, and everything of that kind, is on the spot at Campagne. I will hold Mr. Davies and my aunt responsible for some extra fruit and any other little

addition they can find. They will follow in their
own carriole, at their own convenience. We will all
be free to ramble wherever we please during the
afternoon, remembering dinner at six precisely on
the grass, under the old oak, where we gathered that
excellent dish of blackberries last autumn.

'We know!'—'Agreed!'—and, 'Agreed!' was the
unanimous vote.

'Seppy, and Minet, and Charley, will go too!'
pleaded the child, with tears in her eyes.

'Yes,' said mamma; 'certainly. But on one
condition, Eliza. I will not allow the children on
any account to gather those nasty sour and seedy
wild strawberries that grow in the wood. You shall
have as much ripe garden fruit as is good for you, my
dears; mind that, and attend to what I say.'

'But they are not to dine in the forest with us?'
asked Davies, in a tone of slight remonstrance.

'No, I think not,' answered the lady, undecidedly.
'That is, at least, if you do not wish—'

'But the weather, Davies,' interrupted Mr.
C——. 'What does your extra-sensitive barometer
say to that?'

'The barometer, for some hours past, has been in
a most capricious and precarious state. It might
suddenly either mount to "Set Fair," or drop to
"Tempest." I bet two to one on "Tempest," unless
my own personal feelings greatly deceive me.'

'We know you are a capital electrometer,' said Mrs.
C——, laughing. 'Supposing even "Tempest" to
carry the day, it does not greatly matter. The house

is so near, that we shall always have time to take shelter, and finish our dessert, and have our coffee, indoors.'

'It will be a good opportunity,' said C—— to his friend, 'for us to have a rat-hunt. A family of those agreeable vermin have settled somewhere in the granary over the stable; and I should like to be rid of them, young and old, before getting in the hay and corn this summer. We'll try what Alphonse's famous ferret will do.'

'Unfortunately, the day before yesterday, Alphonse was clumsy enough to let his ferret get away in a hungry fit: he had forgotten to feed it. The last he saw of the creature was the tip of its tail as it scampered off in the direction of the wood.'

'It is a thirsty brute, an insatiable bloodsucker; there is nothing now in the forest for it to get, not even a drop of water. We shall probably find that it has come home again.'

'I hate ferrets,' said Mrs. C——; 'they are odious beasts. I wish, for my part, it may never come back.'

'I dislike them, madam, as much as you do; still, we are obliged to make use of them occasionally. If it do not come back, C——,' continued Davies, 'to get rid of the nest of rats, you had better lock up Minet four-and-twenty hours in the granary, with just a pint of milk as his stock of provision, and he will probably succeed in dislodging your visitors.'

'No, you shan't,' interrupted Septima, with the prettiest of poutings,—'that you shan't! Minet is

Seppy's cat; and I won't let him be locked up all
night in the granary.'

'Hush, naughty child; don't talk so!' said Mrs.
C——, with the mildest of rebukes. 'You will
do whatever papa pleases. Come now, and be dressed
to go to Campagne.'

'Yes, mamma. And Seppy will wear her brown
round hat with grass-green ribbons.'

'No indeed, dear, you won't. It's much too shabby
for driving out, such fine weather as this is. Eliza,
dress Miss Septima, if you please, in a white frock
and her paille d'Italie bonnet with primrose ribbon.
I am determined to have my own way, this once at
least.'

'I should think so, indeed,' said Madame Van
E—, with a smile half-incredulous and half-amused.

IV.

At half-past-five in the afternoon, the forest of
Guines was stiller than it might be at midnight.
The dry, slippery grass rustled under the feet; not
a leaf stirred on the topmost branches; every bird
was mute, every insect hushed. Overhead, the sky
was of the deepest blue, and in it floated a few
immeasurably lofty clouds—Pelions of white foam
heaped to the utmost upon Ossas of wide-extended
snow. These clouds had a hard, menacing, decided
look, as if they were not sailing in the firmament for
nothing, with an inky tinge in their deepest shadows,
while their rounded cauliflower summits were espe-

cially bright and fleecy. The sun scorched, as if it shone through a burning-glass.

French forests under government management differ considerably from an English wood. They exhibit the struggle of natural wildness rebelling against the yoke of periodical cropping and methodical arboriculture. In this locality, the hilly surface and irregular area of the entire forest is pierced through, at wide intervals, by parallel open grassy glades, of the breadth of an ordinary highway road. At right angles to these, very narrow alleys, just wide enough for people to walk in single file, run across, thus dividing the whole superficies of the land under wood into squares or parallelograms of moderate extent in respect to acreage. The entrance of each valley, at either of its ends, is marked with a low borne, or boundary stone. Therefore, any one past childhood, knowing this, might, were he to lose his way in a thicket, decide to walk straight forward in any direction, which would lead him to an alley; by following the alley, he would reach a glade; while the glade would take him to the open fields.

But this arrangement was probably adopted, not with any view to the guidance of strayed wanderers, but for the convenience of cropping the wood in regular succession. Suppose that one of these alley-enclosed squares has acquired the growth that fits it for fire-wood, and France is a wood-burning country, principally; it is clean cut down, every stem and stick, leaving nothing but the stools remaining to sprout again, and the trees which stand, to survive several generations of coppice, till they have finally attained the rank of timber. Now, different portions of the forest are always in different stages of growth. The ground cleared last year, is this spring covered with primroses, violets, woodruff, and other wild flowers, the delight of children. There is fruit also ; strawberries, such as they are, grow in great abundance, and are brought into the town of Guines in large bouquets, more pleasing, however, to the eye than to the palate. On one side, perhaps, of our free and flowery expanse, is a field of brushwood (for such it is) which was cut three years ago. Here the flowers are beginning to be choked and to disappear ; while of fruit there is little else than the blackberry, in its season. On the opposite side may be a division of the forest which has remained untouched by the axe for the last eight or ten years. It is a thicket, whose degree of penetrability depends much on the species of wood of which it is composed. In no case is it easy to make your way through it ; and, once fairly in, to follow any given direction is hopeless, unless you carry a pocket-compass with you, or have an accurate knowledge of the slope of the ground. In such portions of the wood as these, flowers are almost able to prove their alibi, while fruit is represented by hazel-nuts.

The old oak, the rendezvous of the picnic party, stands at the edge of one of the open glades, which was to furnish the grass-plot for the entertainment ; opposite, around, and within an easy distance, are specimens of almost every stage of woody growth, from the coppice nearly ready to cut, to the ground only cleared during the passing winter, the densest thickets being the nearest at hand.

v.

At a quarter to six, with the aid of Alphonse and another helping hand, the sylvan repast was ready. The ladies were on the spot, awaiting the gentlemen. Two carpets were spread on the grass; a large Kidderminster that had never been used was destined for the service of the adults; a little way off, on the other side of the glade, a Persian rug was occupied by the children and their maid. Besides them, the minor group was increased by the presence of the three pet animals. Curly-coated Milor seemed more inclined to dozing than any other form of enjoyment; slender Flibbertygibbet yawned and stretched his delicate limbs, as though he intended to be very active shortly; while faithful Minet set up his tail bolt upright, unceasingly rubbing his silky coat against the legs of his patroness, little Septima.

'So here you are at last,' said Mrs. C——, as she saw her husband and Mr. Davies emerge from an alley. 'We hope your afternoon's occupations have given you an appetite for our lamb and salad, in spite of the heat.'

'They have; we have been busy gardening. We could do nothing in the way of dislodging the long-tailed family. The ferret is gone, and has not been seen or heard of since.'

'Eliza, come and fetch the children's dinners.'

'I was afraid, my dear madam, how it would be,' said Davies. 'You could not refuse the young folks dining on the grass.'

'Why should I? They are not in the way, where they are. Eliza will attend to them there; and you never object to young people at dessert.'

'It is not that I was thinking of. I don't like children in the forest.'

'But why not, Mr. Davies, if they cause no interruption?'

'I can hardly tell you. For a woman's reason; because I don't. The forest is not the place for young children.'

'Now, is that reasonable, Aunt Van E—? I did not think that Mr. Davies had been of so apprehensive and timid a disposition. We have no Cruel Uncle here, to get up the tragedy of the Babes in the Wood; nor have we any cunning Wolf to repeat the catastrophe of Little Red Riding-Hood.'

'But there are wolves in some French forests,' observed Mademoiselle Van E—.

'Certainly,' said Davies; 'but I am not afraid of them, just now. Still, only last winter, in one of the southern departments, a little girl was killed by a wolf on her way to school; and in another department, a woodcutter who happened to be without either tools or weapons, was found horribly mangled by wolves in a thicket.'

'But there are no wolves within many miles of this spot,' remarked Mrs. C——, turning pale.

'Probably not. But that is nothing; a famished

wolf will travel forty or fifty miles at a stretch to find
a breakfast; so that distance is scarcely a safeguard
from accident. It is true, such things happen only in
very severe winters. Nevertheless, I confess, I do not
like the forest for infant children, even in the height
of summer.'

'If a wolf were to dare to show his face here,'
said Mrs. C——, with forced gaiety, 'we should
soon put him to flight with our pack of animals.
Flibby and Milor would commence the attack; and,
backed by Minet, they—'

'Listen, my dear!' said Madame Van E—, pointing with her forefinger upwards. 'What is that I
hear?'

'It   sounds   like   distant   thunder,' answered
C——, uneasily.

'That's what it is,' said Davies in an undertone,
raising his eyebrows. 'As to your dogs, my dear
madam,' he continued, 'they would certainly render
us one important service in such a case. Were we
attacked by no more than a couple of wolves, Milor
would serve as a mouthful for one of them, and
Flibby for the other; the rest of the company might
thus get off scot-free. Your dogs would be very
acceptable substitutes for other live eatables; but as
for fighting, shut them up in the granary with the
rats to night, and Milor will be found dead with
fright in the morning, while Flibby would jump out
of the wicket instantly. Minet looks like a better
champion than either of them, whether against wolf
or rat.'

Meanwhile, the sun was declining. Suddenly, one of the great white clouds, now almost turned to black, intercepted his sinking rays. Till the eye got a little used to the change, it seemed as if total darkness had fallen.

'Really, Adelaide,' said Mr. C——, 'I think you had better send the children home to Campagne. They will be just as happy on the grass plot in the garden, as here. Let them have half this excellent West India pine-apple, which Davies has kindly brought, to amuse themselves with.'

Mrs. C—— was on the point of uttering her assent, when little Septima who had overheard the conversation, shouted, 'No; Seppy won't. Not yet, mamma. Seppy will go home soon, but not quite yet.'

'Let them stay just another ten minutes,' pleaded Mrs. C——.

'When will you cease to ruin your babies?' asked Madame Van E—, shaking her head.

'I suppose, when I have no more babies to ruin,' her niece replied, endeavouring to hide beneath a smile a rising compunction of self-reproach. Mr. C—— heaved a slight sigh, with the air of a man who tries to make up his mind to a misfortune which he cannot avoid. Davies purposely took no notice of the little domestic incident which he had so often witnessed, but devoted his attention to the two lady guests.

'Come here, my darling Septima,' said Mrs. C——, calling to the junior party without looking in that direction. 'Here is a plate of beautiful garden strawberries for you and Charley, as you have been good children, and have not eaten those that grow in the wood. Come for them, dear, and mind you give Eliza her share.'

Another very low but very long muttered rumbling of thunder was heard in the distance.

'Miss Septima, ma'am? I thought she was with you,' answered Eliza, starting to her feet from her seat on the ground. 'She ran across the glade, just now; I thought she was gone to kiss you and her papa, previously to returning to the house.'

'We have seen nothing of her,' said Mr. C——. 'She cannot be far,' he anxiously added.

'Septima! Septima!' shouted the alarmed mother, at the top of her voice, till it was almost a scream. 'Septima! My love, we want you. Make haste, dear! We want you. Septima!'

The appeal was fruitless. No Septima answered or returned to the summons.

'Let us all try and find the child, without delay,' said Davies, as the party were regarding each other with stupefied looks of wonder and alarm. 'Charley, my dear, go home with your aunt, and tell Alphonse I want him here. Eliza, you and Mademoiselle might walk along the glade in the direction of the valley, looking carefully to the right and left. If Mr. and Mrs. C—— will do the same in the opposite direction, uphill, I will search the neighbouring thickets. We will meet again, at this spot, in twenty minutes from this time, by our watches.'

VI.

The counsel was adopted without debate. Davies hunted right and left in the underwood, while the other two parties explored along their appointed track. Before the twenty minutes had elapsed, the cloudy twilight deepened almost into darkness. Sheet-lightning flickered all around the horizon, and muffled sounds of threatening were continually audible from some far-off battle of the elements. The ladies returned after an unavailing search, and were staring at one another with bewildered countenances, when Alphonse arrived, saying that he had come, according to orders, to fetch the things back to the house, he supposed, and also to take the cat Minet, to shut him up in the granary.

'The cat is not here, though the dogs are,' said Mr. C——. 'He is gone somewhere; home, no doubt. Did you see anything of Septima as you came?' he inquired, catching at a sudden hope. 'We cannot find her. We don't know where she is.'

'Mon Dieu, no!' exclaimed the man, with terror in his face. 'I saw nothing of her. And what a night it is likely to be!'

Davies was the last of the searchers to appear. He had exceeded the appointed time by two or three minutes. He was pale with fatigue and serious alarm, and both his face and clothes bore marks of rude contact with twigs and brushwood.

'Where's my child?' gasped Mrs. C——. 'Haven't

you found her? No? oh! What a foolish, what
a wicked woman I have been! I see it all now,
as clearly as if I were on my deathbed. Why did
you let me persist in my folly? You, Mr. Davies,
ought to have positively forbidden me to bring the
children to this dreadful wood. You should have led
me back to the house, like a mad woman as I was,
and clothed me in a strait-jacket, if necessary, rather
than allow what has happened to—'

'My dear friend,' said Davies, 'your husband is
here; and he, you know, alone has the right—'

'He! He is too good, too kind to me. He has had
no sorrows nor losses, like you. He has no experience
or forethought of evil, nothing to hold in check a
wilful creature like me. Poor little Seppy!' said the
despairing mother, sinking to the ground in the pros-
tration of grief, 'she is lost for ever. She is dead
to us. If she were but dead without suffering!'

'Come, dear madam,' said Davies, seeing that it
was requisite for him to assume the authority which
he was reproached for not exercising; 'this will not
do. This will not help us to recover little Seppy.
You must be more of a woman. Swallow this glass
of cognac at a draught. Yes, yes; I insist upon it.
You must. That's right. Lean on your husband's
shoulder. Summon all your presence of mind by an
act of self-control; and let us look the position
resolutely and calmly in the face.'

'I will,' she faintly said. The glare of the lightning just served to show the depression impressed on
her every feature.

'Seppy will be found again alive, I quite believe, and, I trust, well; though it is impossible to predict by what means, or where. She cannot be far. Almost any other dogs than those we have, would help to find her; these are useless, as I proved during your absence. If my friend Walter were at Calais now, we should probably succeed with his half-bred blood-hound. But he and his dog are both at Hazebrouck; we will telegraph for him, and he will be here in the course of to morrow forenoon. If the storm would but hold off, I should be under no great uneasiness. At daybreak we can organize a methodical search, which will probably be successful before Walter's dog arrives. To night we can do nothing. The child is doubtless fast asleep under the shelter of some bush or tree. It will soon be so dark that we might pass within a yard of her, without seeing her. There is no moon till four in the morning. Were we to blow horns or trumpets, or to beat drums, they would frighten her away, rather than attract her to us. Do you see the force of what I am saying?'

'Thank you; yes.'

'But we, C——, must not quit this spot. We ought to burn a light here, and keep watch till day-light.'

'Certainly. You, my dear wife, must now go home. Leave us the carpets and the rest of the provisions. Send Alphonse with umbrellas and macintoshes, in case of need. Let us have the brightest of the lamps, too. Afterwards, let him have the awning that shaded the tulip-bed. It will be almost as good as a tent.

We will then arrange with him about the people for
the search to morrow.'

'Am I, then, to leave you here?'

'There is no help for it. If by chance any news
reaches the house, ring the bell. You may return
hither as soon as daylight breaks. Meanwhile, go to
bed, and to sleep, if you can. Take Charley for your
bedfellow to night; he will be some comfort to you;
and pray that the tempest may delay its coming only
four-and-twenty hours.'

Mrs. C—— kissed her husband, and shook hands
with Davies, in a manner that betokened the resignation of helplessness, and walked home accompanied
by her relatives and the maid, with the step of
resolute though sorrowful obedience.

VII.

The gentlemen passed the night,—long to them,
though happily short in reality,—as nights of anxiety
and watching are passed, mostly in silence, after
they had once settled the programme of to-morrow's
beating the forest by Alphonse and the assembled
sportsmen of the neighbourhood. In one of the few
intervals of talk, C—— said,

'I confess I do not like the notion of that vicious
ferret being at large. Do you believe that ferrets
ever attack young children?'

'Of course, you must be aware,' Davies answered,
'that instances of such horrid facts have occurred,
though rarely. But do not exaggerate the dangers to
be apprehended; remember that the forest is large.'

'Indeed it is,' replied C——, with a sigh. 'The tempest keeps aloof longer than I anticipated; but when it does come, I firmly expect, it will make up by its violence for its forbearance now.'

'Never mind, so·it does but hold off long enough for our purpose. In another hour and a half, we shall be able to set to work. Did you hear that?'

'Yes; I hear continually that it is thundering severely somewhere.'

'I don't mean that. Listen again. Put your ear close to the ground.'

In the absolute silence of very early morn, something like a distant struggle was audible. There were two or three distinct sharp screams, a savage growl, a crackling of sticks, a rustling of leaves, a noise of wrestling, and then all was still. The two friends looked at each other without uttering a word.

'If we could but find out where those sounds came from!' said C——, at last.

'Impossible, for the present!' Davies replied.

VIII.

Mrs. C—— fulfilled her promise. She partially undressed, and laid herself in bed by the side of little Charley, who was fast asleep. Sleep she had no hope of attaining herself; but the sight of the boy's lovely and tranquil face, and the collapse of her feelings, brought on, what had been before impossible, a fit of weeping. Tears induced, first relief, and then slumber—not a sound repose such as she was accustomed to enjoy, before trouble had ever come near her, but a tossing, semi-conscious half-sleep, full of dreams, in which Septima was sometimes floating, a beatified angel, on clouds of light, and then was lying at the bottom of a dark pit, torn limb from limb by wild beasts, in sight of her father, Alphonse, and Mr. Davies, who all tried to render assistance, in vain. The impression of dawning day upon her eyelids awoke her to the realities of the case. There was a leaden grey morning flushed with crimson gleams; the wind was rising; the branches in sight of her window were heaving to and fro; while dust, sticks, and straws, beat against the panes. Her first impulse was to be up and away, to rejoin her husband. The sight of little Charley, still sleeping, once more aroused her tenderness. She clasped him tightly in her arms, covering his face with kisses and hot tears.

'Why do you cry so, dear mamma?' asked the child, opening his eyes wide with astonishment. 'You have nothing to cry for! I am your sleeping-companion here, and I'll not leave you alone at night, until papa comes back again.'

'I am crying, my love,' said Mrs. Carpenter, scarcely able to articulate, 'because we have lost dear sister Seppy in the forest, and we cannot find her; we don't know where she has wandered to; and she cannot get back to Campagne alone.'

'Ah! Is that all?' said Charley, sitting up in the bed, his eyes brightening, as if with sudden inspiration. 'I think, then, I know where Seppy is. I think, mamma, if you will let me get up, I can show you where Seppy is gone to.'

The mother's heart leapt within her for joy; but she mastered herself. By an effort on her will, she reined in her impatience, conscious that she might spoil all by any precipitate outburst.

'So you shall, my darling. Mamma will dress you herself. We will walk there directly, before breakfast, because I fear it is going to be a stormy day. Some big drops of rain are falling already. If Charley will show mamma where Seppy is, mamma will give him anything he asks for;—that is, anything reasonable,' she added, checking herself at the bitter remembrance of the consequence of her yesterday's indulgence.

'Oh, mamma! I'm reasonable now, you know; I'm more than five years old. I'm not like Seppy. This way, mamma. Come along!'

The gallant little guide proudly led the way to a point very close to the scene of the picnic. They passed within sight of the watchers, who were preparing to separate to pursue their search. At a signal from Mrs. C——, they made a halt. There was a breathless pause. It was clear that some clue to the fugitive had been found. The mother and son crossed the glade without pronouncing a syllable. Charley dived into an alley between two tall hornbeam coppices. Suddenly he said, 'Give me hold of your apron, mamma. Now, stoop, and follow me.' He penetrated the thicket in a diagonal direction by a scarcely-visible track worn by the poor women who are permitted to gather dead sticks, and then he came out into a large recent cutting, where the ground was carpeted with gay tufts of dog-violets, wood-strawberries, and the rest of the sylvan flora.

'I think, mamma,' he said decidedly, 'that Seppy must be somewhere not far from this. But how oddly the light shines from those red clouds! The flowers look of such a different colour to what they did yesterday! The leaves are greener! There's a great yellow flower, behind that bush;—there, mamma; close to the tuft of tall grass—'

''Tis my child! 'Tis Septima's bonnet!' screamed Mrs. C——, rushing to the spot.

She caught up the sleeping truant in her arms and covered her with kisses.

'Only think, mamma, here's Minet too!' said Charley, caressing the animal, who arched his back and tail, purring with pleasure. 'He has hurt himself though, I fear; he is lame in one foot, and the skin about his neck is torn.'

'Never mind that. We have found your sister. Let us make haste back to papa and Mr. Davies.'

Before the rejoicing party could reach the house, the storm burst overhead. The lightning flashed, and the thunder rattled and cracked instantly afterwards. In a couple of minutes, they were drenched to the skin; it was as nothing. They were hardly conscious of the wetting. The house-bell was sounded long and loud in the midst of the storm, to communicate the good tidings to neighbours around. In the confusion of their arrival, Minet was observed to be dragging something heavy after him across the garden, which he finally laid on the step of the front

door, before entering by the back way, to warm
and dry himself at the kitchen fire. C—— and
Davies were curious to see what game it might be
that Minet had brought home. It was an enormous
ferret, which evidently had not succumbed without a
fierce and bloody resistance.

IX.

'And now, my dear boy,' said Mrs. C——, when
she had put Septima to bed, and had re-dressed
Charley after his shower-bath in the storm; 'tell
me, my love, how it was that you knew so exactly
where to find Seppy in the wood.'

'Why, mamma, you know, you told us we were
not to eat wood-strawberries. When we went down
the glade with Eliza yesterday afternoon, Seppy
pointed to the place and said, "Seppy will!"—And at
dinner, when she left us, as Eliza thought, to go
across to you, she again laughed, looking in the way
you know, mamma, and whispered to me, "Seppy
will, Charley! Yes; Seppy will!"'

When Mrs. Verney ended, a vote of thanks to her
was gracefully proposed and seconded, and unani-
mously carried; and Scott was called upon to award
his prize. It was quite certain, after Scott's dogmas
about the impropriety of love-tales and the like, that
neither Angerstein nor Graham nor Rebow would
have it. D'Aubrey had been already condemned.
It was manifest, too, that there was much in Verney's

narratives which Scott disliked. There only remained Duvernoy's 'Diamond Clasp,' Mrs. Verney's 'Seppy Will,' and his own, or rather Rebow's tale, 'Marriage by Lottery.'·

Scott declared that 'Seppy Will' had won the prize. He confessed that he did not know much about children, and could not perhaps judge very accurately whether childish life was depicted with entire truth; 'but,' said he, 'the tone of the tale alone entitles it to 2000 marks; it would certainly win an Essay-prize in the University, and I now award to it this prize; and now,' said he, going up to Verney and whispering in his ear, 'I have given Mrs. Verney the prize, will you ask her for my coat?'

The next morning there was a general break-up. D'Aubrey was off to the Circuit, and was presently engaged in establishing his client's right to a ditch; Angerstein was off to the Continent; Duvernoy went to town to receive the slippers from Hampton Court and elsewhere. Graham's return enabled the suspended affairs of Europe to go on again in the usual course; Rebow carried up his articles to the magazine publisher, and got a new task set him; Scott got his coat, and returned to Trinity, and vowed that nothing should ever induce him again to go into the society of persons who had not learnt, as life advanced, to throw aside those low under-graduate manners which were so repulsive to his more correct nature.

Verney relapsed into his ordinary life, instructed and amused by the Tales he had heard ; and so, I trust, reader, are you.

Two or three days aftewards, Rebow came blundering in unexpectedly to Verney's house, which had then resumed its wonted quiet, and slipping a roll of paper on the table, said :

'I beg your pardon, Verney, about that tale of mine. It really was very shabby of me to give you only a translation. I—I didn't mean it ; but the tale which I had meant to read was one written some years ago—when—alas ! I *could* write tales—only I did not dare to read it before D'Aubrey and Angerstein ; for it contains something about barristers and their profession, and I was sure that pair of persecutors would come down upon me if I made a single false step in some of their fidgety etiquette. You know I kept Terms myself at the Temple, and ought to have known all about the proprieties of their profession ; but I feared to read out even the title before them ; and so—pray excuse me for giving it you now instead—'

'My dear fellow, I am intensely indebted to you,' replied Verney ; 'but now you've come, you must pay toll, and stay and read your tale, and dine with us *en famille.*'

Rebow made no demur to this ; and so, after the repast, he read to Verney's domestic circle the following tale :

WILLIAM REBOW'S SECOND STORY.

A LAWYER'S FISHING ADVENTURE;

OR, HOOKING A CASE.

I DESPAIR of conveying to any save one in populous city pent for three-fourths of the year, and that amid dusty papers and mouldering records, only ex-changed for the din and jargon of some over-crowded court of law, the bounding delight (akin to that of the great house-dog when released from the thral-dom of his chain) with which we sons of Themis shake off from our feet the dust of London, and plunge, after our several fashions, up to the very neck in rural joys!

To a few of the quieter and more contemplative sort, the 'woods and fields' *per se* seem to be a source of inexhaustible refreshment—a long walk in a shady lane, or a lounge under green trees sufficing to wrap them in a rural Elysium. But for the greater part of English trained youths, school and college have laid in a stock of more stirring tastes and recreations; boating and cricket, hunting and shooting realize for such the *summun bonum* of holiday existence.

Now it so happens that my vacation paradise—though pulling a stroke oar at Oxford, and as a man of Kent, a bowler from my very cradle, no bad rider cross country after hounds, and a tolerable shot at grouse, for partridges and pheasants I rather despised

—consisted in none of these; but rather a *melange* of the contemplative enjoyments aforesaid, with the keenest possible relish for the beauties of nature, and the inexplicable to all save brethren of the craft, but engrossing passion for fishing!

As surely as with the long vacation lawyers rush from town, and undergraduates pour forth from the deserted universities, did some stream or other lure me into its vortex the first moment I could call my own, after family claims had been impatiently satisfied. Sometimes it was one of North Devon's innumerable streams, renowned in song—the dark Teign, clear Tamar, or rapid Dart or foaming twin torrent Lynn. Sometimes, when time permitted, I wooed my favourite sport amid the sparkling Derbyshire brooks, or becks and tarns of Cumberland. And one privileged year, marked with a white stone on my calendar, I owed to the kindness of a college friend a long bright autumn among the mossy streams and mountain lochs of Scotland; and felt, in my first victorious contest on his native waters with a huge salmon, as I suppose little Sayers did while encountering the gigantic Heenan.

I did not condescend to trout, I remember, all the following season, but consoled myself by a foreign tour with my mother and sisters. By another season however my appetite for such small fry was restored; and acting on the Scottish proverb, (often quoted to me during my first infant essays on salmon,) ' better sma' fish than nane '—I betook myself, as a sort of compromise between them and minnows, to North

Wales, then not so perforated as now with railways, or infested with tourists, but where, in some privileged spots at least, a fisher might spend some weeks, 'the world forgetting by the world forgot,' living chiefly on the produce of his rod, and as completely released from all the etiquettes of society as the primitive Welsh-speaking people around him.

Chance, rather than choice, directed me to the village of W——, where a fine trout-stream, and no one to dispute or even share my enjoyment of it, induced me to take up my quarters. And never surely was locality more happily selected for a lover of the picturesque, as well as piscatorial sources of delight. The little hamlet, nestled in a cleft or coomb, or narrow valley, with only space in it between perpendicular wooded banks for the few scattered houses (of which the inn was one) and the brawling foaming river by whose mountain melody (sweet in its very hoarseness to a fisher's ear) my slumbers were only rendered more profound.

For some miles, from its birth-place in the far hills to where it joined just below the village the lovely western sea, it held its headlong course amid such a profusion of wild rocks, and fern-clad cliffs, and fantastic giant-tossed boulders, that but for the deep still pools formed by those very obstacles, a fisher might have despaired of catching anything save a sprained ancle or a violent cold. But of such hitherto uninvaded haunts of patriarchal trout, there were abundance; and I was not long at W—— without astonishing its simple denizens by luring from their darkest depths fish of such fabulous dimensions, that I verily believe I was imagined to have introduced the race, or conjured them by magical incantations, from some more favoured stream. These plaudits, albeit easily won, and from gaping rustics, were to a fisher as the approving nod of a Chief Justice to a junior counsel, and only stimulated me to farther efforts.

I was trying to throw my line towards a very promising pool which, somewhat retired from the rush and foam of the mountain stream, lay in its glassy gloom beyond a projecting headland fringed with hazel bushes. That under such circumstances it should get caught was not very wonderful. But on looking upward with a view to disentangle it, as I supposed from one of the overhanging shrubs, I was not a little startled to encounter, kneeling on the brink of the cliff, and gazing steadfastly into the pool, a tall, thin, ghostly-looking female, whose large eyes, on closer inspection, seemed rather fixed on vacancy than either on the fisherman or his operations. There had been beauty once in the regular though now gaunt features, but in expression they were deficient; though a singularly sweet smile played about the mouth, as, reaching confidentially down from her dizzy elevation, the lady (for such spite of her scanty odd attire, she evidently was) exclaimed with a childish glee strangely at variance with her weird appearance, 'Caught! caught! fairly caught!'

'Caught indeed! Madam!' cried I, casting a

rueful glance at my unhappy line, dangling from the branch of an alder not to be reached, and that with difficulty, but from the spot on which was now perched erect my tall white guardian of the stream. Recover it I must, or give up all chance of sport not only for that day, but in future. Yet wishing to do so without alarming the strange lady (on whose premises I should probably be at the same time trespassing), I, in the blandest and most courteous terms I could muster, begged her permission to scramble up and unhook my unlucky gear. She nodded a pleased, though mute assent; and availing myself of it I swung myself, with considerable effort, up the fern-clad rock, and stood on a bit of emerald sward at its summit, beside the supposed mistress of the demesne, who stood watching, with an infantine interest, sad to contemplate, the progress of the operation.

I was preparing (ashamed of my intrusion, and not very comfortable in my strange vicinity) to return— easier said than done—by the way I had come, when my weird Undine, uttering a shrill scream of terror, and seizing me by the arm, dragged me away in the opposite direction towards some more eligible way of egress. The sound of the cry, shrill and unearthly in itself, and echoed by the surrounding rocks, brought to the spot two other beings, as little apparently of the matter-of-fact, working day world, as the apparition by which I had been at first startled. In a dress as peculiar in form and homely in material as the elder lady's, there stood behind me on the cliff, a youthful *fac simile* of herself in height and figure, but with all the unimaginable difference between them which could be created by the contrast of youth with age, and still more by that of the utmost depth and intensity of expression on the one countenance, and its painful absence from the other. To the dress of the younger, though not absolutely youthful member of a possibly *unique* group, clung a boy of some six or seven years old, beautiful as Cupid, but alas! in spite of the magnificence of as fine a pair of eyes as ever graced a human head, evidently blind.

There was in the air and aspect of the last comer something so inexpressibly sweet and touching, and at the same time lofty and dignified, that an un-authorized intrusion on her, humble as were her homespun garments, would have been simply im-possible. I could only hastily explain the accident which had brought me (with the sanction of, no doubt, a relative) within their precincts.

'Oh!' said she, courteously, with a smile of sur-passing sweetness, matched by a voice I learned to prefer to music, 'you were very welcome to come and fetch your line! aunty and I are not churlish enough to refuse such a trifle, though,' with emphasis on the word, 'we cannot, situated as we are, receive strangers.'

'Something tells me, however,' said I, borrowing courage from her gentle manner of dismissal, 'that you will not refuse even a stranger two slight requests—one, that you would honour him by accepting

the contents of a basket filled from, and soon to be
replenished by, your own river, the other, that you
would charitably indulge him, in this hot day, with
a draught of milk or water.' 'Oh! yes! yes!' cried
the elder lady eagerly, 'we love fish, and have no
one now to catch us any, and I'm tired of potatoes!
and see Philly's gone already, dear child! to milk
Nanny for you. 'Tis Nanny feeds us all, God bless her!'
So saying the old lady once more drew me towards
what I afterwards found was the abode of two women
of gentle nurture and ancient family, though I then
merely took it for a neglected outhouse. Apart from
extensive ruins of what must at one time have been,
a splendid mansion—whether desolated by fire or
mouldering away from slow decay I could hardly at
a glance decide—and the debris of still more extensive
stabling and out-offices, stood what might have been,
while these subsisted, a rude gamekeeper's lodge or
fisherman's hut, whose thatch of heath dilapidated
by the rains, and weather-stained tottering walls,
constituted it a mere shelter, not a very efficient one,
from actual exposure to the elements. From this
issued to meet us the young lady and her inseparable
companion the child, who, as with unaffected courtesy
she apologized for the unpretending draught, said, in
tones rivalling hers in kindly cordiality, 'Redmond
stroked Nanny all the while to make her be good and
stand: for 'twas not milking time she knew, and you
know Aunt Philly always puts me to bed first.'

From this and various hints it would have been
impossible not to infer that this strange *trio* lived

under peculiar and sadly straitened circumstances; and the scanty particulars I gathered on returning to the little inn from the landlord, afforded abundant food for sympathy as well as conjecture. The ladies, he said, descended from one of the oldest families in Wales, and the rightful heiresses 'twas thought, if they had their due, to untold wealth, had lived some years on sufferance in the hovel I had seen, literally on the produce of their garden and goats, with the help in the way of potatoes, and turf, and other necessaries, which the mingled compassion and respect of the tenantry induced them to insist on affording. To my inquiries respecting the boy, the landlord replied that shortly before that dispersion by death of their relatives by which the ladies had been cast out on the wide world, this helpless addition to their cares and burden had been sent home from India, where his father, a gallant young officer, had been killed in battle, and his young mother (sister to Miss Philippa and niece to the elder lady) had died in giving him birth. How calculated all this was to excite the deepest interest and wish to improve the acquaintance I need not say; but the parting words of the younger, yet evidently leading member of the primitive household, though courteous were not encouraging, and I had not felt courage at the time to ask if I might call again.

Curiosity, however, I fear, begets cunning, and it were a poor lawyer who could not frame some device for making good his point. So, on a certain morning, when I learned from the landlord's child that young

Madam Gwynne had been seen going in a chaise-cart with farmer Morgan to S——, no doubt to see the doctor about little Redmond's eyes, I caught up line and basket, and filling the latter on my way up the stream, availed myself of my knowledge of localities to achieve a surreptitious entrance into the otherwise inaccessible premises.

I could not but pause a moment on their threshold to contemplate the scene of profound desolation amid which age, youth, and infancy seemed unpiningly to vegetate. Avenues, shrubberies, nay parterres once had been, but of them all no relic survived—save one little carefully tended spot in a corner where roses and a few favourite flowers attested the hand of taste. Forcing a path (different from the opener one I had missed) from the river side, through a thicket of tangled shrubs, I came suddenly on the ruined dwelling (if such it can be called) before mentioned, and tapping gently, not to alarm its lone inhabitant, at the door, it was opened, as I had hoped, by my original 'Lurline', whose weird and wasted countenance lighted up on seeing me with a degree of unexpected intelligence. 'I thought you would come back some day!' said she, 'and told Philly so; but she thought you had left, and *she* never wishes to see any one. But I am lonely at times, especially when she is obliged to go once or twice a year to S——; and we have lived many a weary year alone. Now! I wonder,' added she, with the quick transition of an unstable intellect, 'where we shall go next? I'd rather stay here than go wandering elsewhere, when

Lawyer Slack turns us out, as I suppose he will. Philly's gone,' she whispered confidentially, 'of course you know, to ask him if it is all true, and we really must go?' Under any other circumstances, and in my private capacity, I think I should have been incapable of taking advantage to gratify an idle curiosity of the unreserve of a weakened mind. But the words 'lawyer' and 'turn us out,' seemed to give so legal and legitimate an aspect to my inquiries, that in the real hope of being enabled to advise and to watch over, if not control, the movements of the village attorney (a class against whom London barristers are said to cherish considerable prejudices), I felt absolved from treachery in putting a leading question, likely to bring forth perhaps the whole family history. 'If these, as I suppose, are your own grounds, (though the mansion I see, has fallen into decay), how can any lawyer have power to "turn you out" of your present residence?' 'Oh! you see, it fell to my father somehow, (only he never lived here and went abroad, and we never heard from him and it was nobody's business,) so we thought we might as well find shelter here as elsewhere. But he's dead, it seems—I don't think so'—added she mysteriously, 'else he would have been sure to let us know—and Cousin Howell says it is his now, and *he* won't let us live here, I'm sure, even if Philly liked him enough to stay.' The ground on which the good lady was advancing was delicate enough for me to shrink from eliciting more unofficial information; so I shifted it by asking if her father had left no son? 'No! poor

Gryffith died, else things would have been very different. Papa doated on Gryffith, and never cared for us girls. Indeed I think,' she added in one of her whispers, but with a visible shudder, 'he quite hated us !'

'Unfortunate topics again!' thought I, and was trying to talk of indifferent matters, when the latch of the little garden, in which I felt a guilty intruder, was suddenly lifted, and hours before her probable reappearance, the younger lady (niece I had gathered to my harmless companion) stood before me.

She did not start, or manifest any symptom either of surprise or displeasure. Her air was rather that of one to whom Providence, in an hour of trial and difficulty, has sent unexpected aid; she seemed to take my being there for granted, and without other notice of it than her habitual melancholy smile, she said, as if regardless of a stranger's presence, to her aunt, 'Lawyer Slack was from home, I was told, making somebody's will, so it was no use to go on to S——. I suppose we shall hear it all soon enough!'

Emboldened by the word 'lawyer' which afforded so fortunate an opening, and still more by the air of patient resignation painted on the sweet face before me, I ventured to ask if it was a case in which one lawyer might not do as well as another; and if so, expressing my readiness to be employed. 'It is quite a God-send,' I added, playfully, 'for us briefless barristers to get a little work in the holidays. It keeps our hands in, and, I assure you, is quite as good sport as fishing, especially for such tiny prey, (showing as I spoke my filled basket, as my warrant for being there at all). 'Seriously however,' I added, (for with the sad realities before me, I was in no mood for jesting,) 'if I can be of the smallest use, in the way either of advice or active exertion in your behalf, I shall view my sporting excursion henceforward in the light of a providential interposition. My legal experience, such as it is, was never, I am sure, more heartily at any one's service.' 'Well,' said she, in reply, 'never perhaps was it more needed by a couple of lone helpless women. But as it cannot be given without your knowing something of our strange family history, and as' (with a glance of unspeakable fondness towards the two equally dependent objects of her tender care) 'little Redmond here I am sure wants his milk, to help down the huge lump of cake which Dame Morgan handed into the cart after him, perhaps Aunty will go and get it for him, while Philly will sit here and rest.'

So saying, she sunk really exhausted into the mossy stone seat, almost, from its imperishable nature, the only relic of civilization the quondam garden afforded. The sweet, simple frankness with which she made room on it beside her for a stranger, was, with a man of any feeling, a greater guarantee of profoundly respectful demeanour than the most prudish affectation of reserve. Utterly guileless, ignorant as a child of conventional proprieties, there was about Philippa Gwynne a nameless dignity which hedged her round like a queen; and made me listen to her strange tale of family wrongs and sorrows with a courtier's deference, and all a brother's sympathy.

In reply to some expression of the latter feeling, which I threw out to pave the way for the narration, she said, 'We have indeed had our share of family sorrows; though to me they have rather been a wild ghostly tradition, than an actual stern reality. My grandfather, whom I never saw, was by all accounts one of the handsomest and finest gentlemen of his time, as well as very learned—two things which I believe do not always go together. He married my grandmother, whose birth was not equal to his own, for love, in the hope, I believe, that by after education, on which he spared no pains, he could make her as clever and accomplished as himself. I fear he only made her very miserable; for though gentle and amiable as she was lovely, God had denied her capacity for learning, and the more she strove to take it in, the less she was able to succeed; and in losing, through vexation, her natural sweet cheerfulness, lost of course much of the charm which first drew my proud grandfather to demean himself by marrying, while still quite young and heir presumptive to a great estate, a small farmer's daughter. This very heirship itself came to be a source of additional disappointment and mortification; for girls could not inherit, and my poor grandmother had for many years, nothing but daughters. Alas! too, these as they grew up inherited, with her failing health, her limited intellect, two at least of the three (my poor dear aunt yonder, and an elder sister, now dead) dependent, as you may have perceived, on others for support and guidance. Some parents, I believe, feel for children so visited a double portion of love and tenderness; and so it was with my poor grandmother. But it was far otherwise with her husband. He hated, I have been told, the very sight of what he called (it was harsh and cruel of him) his 'idiot daughters,' while, as you see, sir, it had only pleased God to make them deficient in head. Their hearts, thanks be to Him! were all right; and I would not give the true love of my poor Aunt Winny for me, or my fondness for her, for many a showier and less enduring bond.

They were happier, too, I should humbly think, in their ignorance of life and its evils, than my dear mother, the long-idolized third child, who combined her mother's beauty with her father's talents. That both could not entitle her to inherit the estate (not yet fallen however to her father) was, I have heard, the only drawback to his doating injurious fondness. But lavishing on her all the advantages his hobby—education, could bestow, he looked to a high marriage for her, as a compensation for his own folly in marrying beneath him.

But example, they say, is stronger than precept. My mother was wilful as beautiful; his indulgence towards her as boundless as his severity to others; and a regular struggle between two headstrong wills was commencing, when the birth of a baby boy—the long-coveted heir—threw his sister too much into the shade to make her doings for some time an object to any one.

Cast down at once, like a broken trampled toy, from her dangerous elevation, the idol of every one became suddenly nobody in parlour or in nursery; thrust out from every spot where she had so long reigned, except that last refuge of every ill-used, neglected child, her mother's heart and bosom. There she continued to keep her place unrivalled even by the baby heir, who I believe from his birth was more a source of dread and anxiety than happiness to my poor grandmother. His health was delicate, his temper high and unruly, and his excessive preciousness in his father's eyes precluded one happy moment when out of her own sight; while all efforts at controlling him were during infancy forbidden, and even in childhood, soon beyond her power.

She had prayed—no doubt fervently prayed—for her own sake and others, to have a living son. Perhaps it was well for both that her prayer was answered in the merciful way of her being taken away, before the strife which arose among so many stronger spirits had marred her comfort in her darling daughter, and poisoned the troubled joy with which she clasped her too precious son. She died, blessing all her children alike; perhaps with yearning tenderness, (reluctant to forsake those nestlings never to be fully fledged here below!) more deeply and fervently, her two afflicted elder girls, at woman's age still children, needing some tender yet firm hand to lead them through life's rugged way, yet probably doomed to unkindness and neglect.

For my mother she had fears and misgivings of another kind; and clever and beautiful as she was, when at seventeen to be deprived of a mother's care, it was with a feeling of relief amid presages of great suffering for all, that a dying parent perceived a growing attachment between this proud, and wilful, and no longer valued girl, and the young Curate who came to read with the boy; whom her change of position in the eyes of the family could not escape, and whom it emboldened to aspire where some time before he could not have ventured to hope.

The storm of indignation with which the bare suspicion of such a connexion was received, only hastened it. From mere parental severity, my dear father was too right-thinking and unselfish to have helped her he loved to escape—by sharing his poverty especially. But when cruelly turned out of her unhappy home what could he do but open to her the best he had to offer? And a happy home it was! in my childish remembrance of it, and still more so in poor Aunty's; for she (her other sister had happily soon followed her mother to a better world) was turned out too, on the plea of connivance!—She, to whom God had granted the simplicity of the dove without the wisdom, or rather cunning, of the serpent —to cast in her lot with the already straitened couple. But somehow it seemed as if the widow's cruse was once more filled for these immediate pensioners on Heaven's bounty. We lived from hand to mouth, and from day to day, but never actually knew want; perhaps because my father was too humble, and my

mother too proud, to live one iota beyond their very
limited means, and conformed cheerfully to the econo-
mical ways of a very cheap remote country. Money,
I remember, we seldom saw—(I have since learned to
forget its very colour)—but 'Parson' (for with the
rectory-house my father enjoyed the privileges of
the absent incumbent) was a favourite with young
and old in the parish; and many were the plump
fowls, and fat geese, and crocks of butter—ay and
homespun webs of clothing—which found their way,
as Christmas approached, to the clergyman's fireside!
In summer we had the produce of a huge kitchen
garden, which not only fed the children, happily confined to a sister and myself, but the cow—the only
relic of better days for which I own I pine, and for
which the goat we only now can manage is but a
poor substitute.—Well! if I dwell thus on past times
I shall never get on; but while father and mother
were spared to us, we were so—so happy!'

'May I ask,' said I, after listening with breathless
interest to a tale at once so strange and simple,
'what during these years of domestic enjoyment,
became of your grandfather and his beloved boy?'

'I was unwilling to come to that sad part of my
story. Gryffith I fear was not naturally dutiful, and
he had been terribly—terribly spoilt. My grandfather
expected implicit obedience in great things from one
never thwarted even in trifles; and had set his heart
on making a scholar of his clever son, who I believe,
if inclined, had every requisite to become one. But
study, of which from a boy he had heard too much,

was his aversion; and when the time for going to College came he horrified his father by saying he would be nothing but a soldier, and if not indulged with a commission was determined to enlist. Grandpapa thought this an idle threat, and had actually gone to Oxford to see about rooms in his own old college for his son; when, on coming back from a trip in which he had met many former friends, whose good will he had bespoken for his heir, he found the object of so many fond speculations had left home without a clue to his destination, and with only a brief note to say he preferred destitution and liberty to wealth with imprisonment within College walls. From that day to this I don't believe father and son ever met; and we only know from hearsay that on ascertaining, or at least hearing rumours of Uncle Gryffith's death somewhere abroad, Grandpapa left England himself, and never inquired after or took possession of the property to which he had so long looked forward, but which came too late for him to care about.

'No one ever seemed to know exactly whether he was alive or dead (if alive he must be very very old), but as, if alive, the ground all round here belonged to him, and there was no one to dispute it, we were advised—poor Aunty and myself and little Redmond, my eldest sister's orphan child, when it pleased God to take my father and mother from us in one week by the cholera—to come and inhabit the only shelter on earth we had a right to; and here we have lived in peace and quiet on our garden and our goats— the kind tenants now and then helping us with a little labour and wood and fuel, and a bite of hay for Nanny in the winter—for half a dozen years or more.'

'And what, if I understood your aunt properly, now threatens you with removal from this most unique of possible domiciles?'

'The turning up of a claimant who is as little likely to permit our continued sojourn, as we should be to avail ourselves of the permission. A cousin, the male heir certainly supposing Gryffith dead, to my grandfather, has come home from abroad, furnished, he says, with evidence of the deaths of both; and lays claim not only to the estate—which no one could in that case dispute with him—but the twenty years', at least, arrears of the rents, which Chancery has been drawing for the missing proprietor.

'Of Gryffith's death I fear there can be no doubt, for Grandpapa, after endless inquiries, I know, was satisfied of it. And he himself, I think, must also be dead, else he would surely have entered into possession somehow or other of the estate, even if he could no longer take pleasure in it. No certain tidings however of his death have ever till now been received. But Lawyer Slack writes that my cousin Howell has all the proofs, and is to bring them forward immediately; and that he fears getting into trouble if he lets us remain any longer, as the heir is a very strict and hard gentleman, and thinks he has been shamefully long kept out of the property already.'

'Do you know anything of this relative?' asked I, remembering one or two expressions of disinclination to owe even shelter to him.

A slight blush crossed the marble pallor of the sweet, still face beside me : 'I did once know him; and at a time when I believe he thought a daughter could inherit, he would have taken the estate with the incumbrance on it (a faint smile displacing the blush) ; but I soon put him right on that point, and happily heard nothing of him afterwards. Papa, I believe, thought him a bad man, and poor Mamma could never be persuaded he belonged to the family, his ways were so unlike them ! I only know I preferred starvation, to wealth through his means.'

'Have you any clue to where your grandfather chiefly resided after he left England ?'

'Oh! he was a great wanderer for many years, in hopeless quest of my poor Uncle Gryffith. At last some one said, he settled down fairly worn out in a little Swiss town, where I believe Uncle Gryffith was buried; and changed his name, and lived like a hermit and saw nobody.'

'Can you tell me,' asked I, rather abruptly, what name he went by ? But indeed, strange to say, I have yet to learn his real one.

'Gryffith was his and my mother's — his assumed one I never heard.'

'And the town in Switzerland—do you recollect it ?'

'Saint W—— I think; at least that is the place from which Lawyer Slack writes my cousin brings the parish registers.'

'And how far back, do you know, are these registers dated?' asked I; haunted by a vague recollection every moment assuming shape and consistency.

'Oh! near twenty years back I believe ; very shortly indeed after the succession to the property opened to my grandfather—so there will be great accumulations.'

The conversation, I believe, at least on my side, dropped here, for I was so busy conjuring back the stray threads of a very vagrant set of reminiscences, that I dare say my companion thought my absence denoted want of further interest, when, God knows, every word of her singular narrative had inspired the deepest. She rose, and said, in her sweet, frank way, 'I fear I must have tired you sadly ; but perhaps if you are still here when the regular notice comes, you might tell us how soon we are obliged to quit, and even what would be best for us to do.'

'I doubt if I can be here,' said I, my heart full of a scheme for being a thousand miles off; 'but keep yourselves easy. Not only must your cousin establish his claims to the satisfaction of a court not proverbial for expedition, but if he even did so, so many forms will have to be gone through that I guarantee your not being disturbed for some weeks, perhaps months. Meantime I'll see the lawyer you speak of on my way—but don't you have any communication with him except through me your legal adviser. Here is my name and address, —handing my card—'and for a retainer,' added I, cheerfully—'you must give me one of your roses,' a luxuriant bush of which grew over the seat. 'Depend on hearing from me, ere long ; and till then let nothing induce you to leave this place, or at least the neighbourhood. Mrs. Jones, down at the inn below, would only think it an honour and a pleasure to take the dear ladies in—but you won't require her hospitality yet awhile!'

Afraid that, if I again encountered the sad resist-less smile, I should be tempted to betray the nature and extent of some tolerably chimerical visions and projects, I hurried abruptly away to the village inn ; and in a very few hours my portmanteau and myself were in the sole gig of the establishment, and far on the road to town.

I resisted a strong impulse to digress a few miles to S——, to suck the brains of the country attorney'; balancing the risk of showing my own game ; with the very slight chance of eliciting his client's; and deterred by the vague nature of the suit which had as suddenly displaced my piscatorial propensities, as if I had not, from my early taste and proficiency in them, gone from a boy in my own neighbourhood by the significant *soubriquet* of 'the Otter!'

Some five years before, I had made on the circuit the acquaintance of a brother of the craft; I don't mean the fisherman's, though he could throw a tolerable line, and when, from the bridge of Laufen on the Rhine we pulled out the trout faster than the gaping rustics could count them, we astonished the natives with a specimen of fly-fishing not dreamt of in their philosophy! But I am forgetting how we came to be there together.

This youth—a clever young fellow, as he showed in a cause we were on together—asked me what were my holiday plans; and if I should dislike joining him in a pedestrian tour in Switzerland, on which,

he added he could. scarcely have ventured on his
own resources, but that his expenses were to be partially paid; conditionally on his going out of the
beaten track to ascertain the fate of a young
Englishman, supposed to have perished on a mountain
excursion, many many years before.

This formed, of course, a very small drawback, or
rather none at all, on the projected tour—the locality
(in German Switzerland) being one seldom explored
by travellers—and some weeks after we started ; and
I remembered accompanying young Stephens to the
town nearest the village where the object of his inquiries lay—though from idleness, or finding metal
more attractive, I did not actually make the pilgrim-
age. It was a successful one however, I recalled to
mind, as far as ascertaining the melancholy fate of
the headstrong youth, who, despising all admonition,
and trusting to his mountain experience (for he was,
I understood, a Welshman), would venture on hitherto
untrodden and dangerous ground.

His grave, with a simple inscription commemorat-
ing the event, was pointed out to Stephens, and
here, having copied it, so far as its immediate object
his commission ended. But what rose before my
memory as connecting it with my present source of
interest, was the almost forgotten ghost story which,
over our evening glass of Kirchen wasser, my somewhat superstitious Irish comrade made the most of,
by his *con amore* and half-believing recital.

He had, it seems, forgotten to note some small
particular of the inscription, and on returning before

leaving the village to verify it, had been startled
by perceiving in the dim twilight a tall, dark, unearthly looking figure, bending as if in the same act
of investigation over the grave,—an apparition with
which (though the party was far too gaunt and thin
to be mistaken for his own 'fetch') he confessed he
was too much disturbed in mind to execute his purpose of a nearer approach; the more so, as on apparently becoming aware of the vicinity of a stranger,
the ghost had suddenly disappeared.

This spectre, in my more prosaic and matter of
fact view of the case, it struck me could only have
been the fleshly reality of the repentant father,
lingering (as represented by his descendant) around
the resting-place of his unfortunate long-lost son.
If so, he was unquestionably alive at a period long
subsequent to the date assigned for his death by the
heir-at-law. And this it became a paramount object
with me to establish; because even in the event,
rendered probable by his very advanced age, of Mr.
Gryffith having actually since died, his being alive so
recently as five years before, if it could be ascer-
tained, would not only give the lie to the falsified
register, but, what was of more consequence, would
secure to the survivors of his own family a sum of
unclaimed arrears sufficient to maintain them in
affluence for the remainder of their lives.

I had a clear three weeks' holiday still before me,
and how could it be half as well expended as in
tracing, dead or alive, and if the latter, (which was
most unlikely,) producing in court the *bonâ fide* pro-

prietor of Wynnecoat? This, I confessed to myself
would be a stage *denouément* utterly beyond probability; even in a novel. But recovering even five
years, accumulations of £4000 per annum for desti-
tute females and a blind child was an object worthy
of double the exertion, not to mention the professional pleasure of disconcerting a deep-laid scheme
to defraud them.

In the days of which I am writing steam was in
its infancy and railroads were not; yet a resolute
traveller, a young and active man, might find his
way in something less than a week to the obscure
point in German Switzerland among whose overhanging cliffs poor Gryffith junior had met his fate.

I rushed through Holland and up the Rhine in a
haste and mood which made me thankful that I saw
neither for the first time; and reached the little
primitive *bourg* of W—— at the rather *mal à propos*
moment when the old-fashioned town itself was in all
the very opposite excitement of the annual burghers'
ball. To escape from its monopolizing influence—as
from the antdiluvian hour of five o'clock every room
in the house would overflow with guests of all ages,
from six years old and under to threescore and
upwards—I asked if the 'Herr Pastor' was a likely
person to afford the quiet of his roof for a few hours
to a traveller so circumstanced; and who, moreover,
had come all the way from England to prosecute
inquiries on which no one else could probably half
so well enlighten him? 'Oh! Gewiss!' was mine
host's ready reply, 'the Herr Pastor, is never so glad

as when he can entertain a stranger, and speaks
English too, *sehr gut, sehr gut!* he had such practice
with the old English Herr that lived here so long.'

'Had?' exclaimed I, eagerly—'is the old gentleman
dead then?'

'No, not that I know of, but he was annoyed at
being dogged by some countryman, and he went
and hid himself somewhere. But Herr T—— I
believe knows where to find him if still above ground,
and will tell you all about him. He must be terribly
old, and people say he is doing penance for some
great crime—but the Herr Pastor probably knows
better. Here Hans! show the gentleman the way to
the *Pfarr haus!*'

I found the occupier of the thatched cottage which
rejoiced in the above sonorous name walking in his
garden, culling, with all the pride of an *amateur*, the
smiling fruits with which it abounded. Prefacing
with the offer of a tempting basket of October
peaches such farther hospitalities as he evidently
meditated—the good man listened at first with
politeness, which soon warmed up into interest, to my
hasty and not very intelligible account of my motives
for intruding on his solitude.

He smiled at mention of the ball, and assured me
that, under less pressing circumstances, it might have
amused me to see, whirling simultaneously in one
interminable waltz, the entire population of three
generations of his primitive flock. But on my
naming young Gryffith and his melancholy fate, while
a cloud stole over his benevolent face, a slight tinge

of reserve and suspicion seemed to mingle with it, as
if placed on his guard by some previous inquiries, and
justly sceptical as to their precise nature and object.

To get over a state of things so uncomfortable in
itself, as well as unfavourable for eliciting information, I felt there was nothing to be done but to make
a confidant of the worthy '*Pfarrer*,' and tell him exactly all I knew or suspected. I painted, *con amore*,
the distresses and deserts of the natural heirs to the
wealth of the long-missing old man ; stated what
advantage would accrue to them from a knowledge
of even the precise time of his demise ; and hinted a
suspicion that the latter had been antedated by some
means or other for fraudulent purposes—as a burial
register, I had reason to believe, dated as far back as
twenty-five years ago, had been procured, and was to
be exhibited in Court.

I drew, from the subdued smile which flitted over
the pastor's face—soon chased thence by an indignant
flush—the inference that any burial register, as regarded my adopted elder client, whensoever dated,
would have been premature. And though not quite
sure whether, judicially, I should not have preferred
the old man's death (well attested as having occurred
recently) to the inconvenience of his resuscitation,
still the latter would afford such an immeasurably
more telling reply to the allegations of the would-be
heir, that I should have been a recreant disciple of
Themis not to rejoice in the irresistibility of so very
valid a contra plea.

My only fear and by no means an unnecessary

one, was lest this most eccentric of mortals should, by making some fantastic disposition of his back rents, deprive my dear ladies of their indubitable succession to them if he had died intestate. I hoped much, however, from the mild influence of the good clergyman, with whom he had evidently lived on terms of friendly intercourse, and whom I now implored to let me into all he knew of past circumstances, as well as of the present state of the recluse's mind as regarded his unoffending and helpless family.

The worthy man, who saw that my heart was in the cause, and whose sympathies I had thoroughly called forth, after insisting on my partaking his early repast, and being his guest for the night, gave me, during a long mountain ramble, the fullest answer to my inquiries.

And first as respected the younger Gryffith, whose stay at W—— previous to the accident had been too brief to admit of personal acquaintance (though the pastor recollected his athletic form, lofty confident bearing, and striking likeness to the father, whose *fac simile* in early life his niece had been assured he presented), and the puzzling circumstance to all of his having met his death in Switzerland so shortly after his disappearance.

This, the pastor had subsequently learned from his sorrowing Swiss comrade, had arisen from the persuasions of the latter, whom Gryffith had casually known in London when at school, and who was returning home, that instead of flying to America—a voyage which might in those days be an affair of mouths, and was proportionably expensive—he should accompany him to his native country, where he might indulge his three ruling predilections—for freedom, mountains, and soldiering—without the possibility, as in the case of America, (supposing him to obtain service in her limited army,) of being called upon to bear arms against his country. For Gryffith was too much of a Briton, as well as too much of a gentleman, to carry into effect his threat of enlisting at home. But the prospect of fighting side by side with the countrymen of William Tell though even in some foreign quarrel, had nothing in it repugnant to boyish honour; and with this view the young men were proceeding through the canton of Aargau to Berne (where the influence of Reuter's family would be exerted to effect the enrolment), when, to beguile the temporary absence of his companion, the daring Welshman lost his life in the manner before mentioned.

The long-overwhelmed survivor was first unable, and then afraid, to communicate the dreadful tidings to the bereaved father, of whose address he was but imperfectly informed; and ere the clergyman on whom the sad duty devolved could fulfil it, old Gryffith, misled by some false clue, had set out in frantic quest of his son for the United States.

To traverse these on a worse than cold scent was in itself the work of many months; but when in addition I strove to realize that disabled by an engagement, dismasted by a gale, and driven to refit into an obscure port in Spain, seven months passed ere the very goal of his inquiries was reached by the unhappy father, it was no wonder that years had elapsed ere the tardy rumours of his boy's fate reached the conscience-stricken parent.

It might be some seventeen or eighteen years ago, and several after the catastrophe—with which at that time Europe did not ring as now within a week of its occurrence—that the father had arrived to have his fears corroborated, and his life-long remorse excited, at the grave of his mismanaged heir; round which he had ever since hovered, in a spirit, alas! rather of increased hostility toward mankind in general (including himself) than of softened feelings towards the innocent remaining portion of his family. Women he persisted in considering mere cumberers of the ground, and unworthy of care or solicitude; while he seemed resigned to live, chiefly as barring the succession to his landed property against the cousin and heir at law, for whom in that capacity he felt a double portion of dislike.

Of his pecuniary affairs or family matters in general he spoke very rarely, while freely unlocking in the clergyman's favour his vast treasures of classical and general knowledge; and the latter, ignorant till I came of what precise female relatives might survive to be benefited by the old man's neglected wealth, deemed it wisest not to provoke discussion, but leave it to descend in due time in the ordinary channel.

The present destitution, however, which I feelingly represented, of those amiable ladies awoke corresponding sentiments of compassion in the good man's breast; but when I spoke of the little interesting blind boy, I could see that his hitherto faint hopes gathered immediate strength from the sex of the orphan.

A grandson would, he knew, prove a wonderful spell to evoke the long-dormant pride and interest of the strange misogynist; and though even, as descended from a despised female, incompetent to succeed to his estates, there were arrears sufficient to endow him with a goodly heritage.

So it was not without hope of a successful issue that the pastor—leaving me meanwhile to prosecute my fishing rambles in the neighbourhood of W——, under the guidance of his deputy the parish clerk—betook himself to the old cynic's hermitage.

Whether from indifferent success arising from miserable fishing appliances or the engrossing nature of my present quest, piscatorial were once more speedily merged in professional interests, when I found that my old cicerone could throw some light (now, however, rather curious than important) on the mode in which the falsification of the extract from the register under his care had been accomplished.

He remembered about six or seven months before, the arrival of a silent, reserved, middle-aged gentleman, supposed to be from America, who, the pastor being absent on one of his visits to the English recluse, requested permission to copy an entry in the *livre de paroisse* regarding, he said, the poor young man who was killed among the Alps. It was already dusk when the request was made, and on the plea

z 2

that the stranger was obliged to go off early next morning, the clerk, whose sight was failing and his spectacles left at home at the other end of the village, confessed to having signed without more than a very cursory inspection the certificate that the 'Herr' with the two unpronounceable Welsh names had been duly interred in the Cimetière of W——. In what year of grace, or in what month of that year, the interment had been stated to have taken place, the clerk owned had been left pretty much (from utter absence of suspicion as to his motives) to the discretion and honesty of the copyist—a supposed *bonâ fide* friend of the deceased's surviving family; all knowledge of the connection between the old man who had so long haunted W—— and him who had perished there being confined I found, from the clerk's unconsciousness of it, to the clergyman alone.

To him and his benevolent exertions it is time to return. At first he failed, as he expected, in awakening any deep interest in the forlorn state of the two 'unprotected females' whom the old man's monomania had condemned to such long and unmerited hardships and privations. When he learned that in the midst of these they had contrived to maintain and rear a precious boy, they rose at once in his estimation, and he swore their cares should be duly rewarded. But it was when the pastor, having exhausted his eloquence in endeavouring to instil sentiments of a more lofty and Christian kind, appealed to the sterner and less amiable features of the old man's character, by relating the attempts about to be made by the heir-at-law to ignore his existence, and step at the expense of fraud and falsification into possession of both estate and arrears, that the sunken eyes of the nonagenarian once more kindled with angry fire, and his shrivelled hands were clenched in wrathful agony.

The pitying but sorrowing clergyman half feared the storm of indignation would shake the frail frame of the now bed-ridden man, and thus- preclude a tardy act of justice to his kith and kin; but under the stimulus of unhallowed passion the needful strength was afforded to execute without delay a formal document, bequeathing to his great grandson not only all the arrears of rent (small legacies to his aunts excepted) of the seventeen years which had elapsed since his own succession, with their accumulated interest—a sum amounting to not far short of 100,000*l.*, —but the fee-simple of the estate itself, the limitation of which to heirs male it had suited his ideas too well to question hitherto, but of which doubts had been expressed to him by an eminent lawyer, at a time when it was thought the descent of it to his daughters might have been peculiarly acceptable.

I am afraid *my* lawyer-like instincts arose within me at this prospect of a possible '*cause celébre,*' not to mention the delight of defrauding the 'cousin' of his prey; and as the sweet object of my yet unconscious homage could by no possibility (as the younger daughter) derive any advantage from the 'law point,' I felt I could argue it all the more boldly and disinterestedly. The old man I also instinctively felt (being too infirm for me to produce him in court)

had nothing now, in a legal capacity, to do but to
die. And he apparently took the same view of the
case; for partly from the excitement, so trying at his
great age, he rapidly sunk after executing the important deed; though not (and it *was* a satisfaction
to be able to tell them so) without bequeathing,
through the efforts of the good pastor, his tardy
blessing to his neglected and desolate children.

Furnished with the precious will, and a record
more authentic than some others of the precise
date of the demise of one whom, for his offspring's
sake, I decorously assisted in laying beside his son,
I returned to England time enough before the opening of the law courts to make a run into Wales,
and communicate to Philippa Gwynne at least the
success of my mission; a result, the advantages of
which to her darling little nephew were, in her loving
and unselfish soul, sadly damped and marred by the
unholy frame and tardy, scanty relentings of her
hard grandfather. 'He did bless us, however, you
say,' added she, 'and for that I am so thankful
for our sakes and his own, poor man! It will be a
great comfort to dear aunty. She did so pine under
the thought of his hating her! I wish I might tell
her that much.'

'Not a word, my dear Miss Gwynne,' said I; 'for
a short time only, I must bar all communications to
one so little trained to secrecy.'

'But why should there be any secret to any one?
Will not just showing the will and register privately
to my cousin, or his lawyer, stop the lawsuit, and
save him the exposure? I should not like to dis-

grace one of our name, especially when I owe him a
grudge !'.

'Your sentiments are very praiseworthy, and do you
honour' (I could have fallen down and worshipped
the sweet, serene impersonation of mercy !), but with
those your cousin has already manifested, I should
be very sorry to trust him with the originals in my
possession, and I confess, even to spare him the
ignominy of setting up his unfounded claims.

'But I have a far deeper and more interesting
lawyer's reason for postponing all disclosures, and
keeping even your own kind self in the dark about
what I am anything but sure of myself. Meantime
I must hurry up to town, and commence operations;
but before I can do so, I must see your family papers.
Do you think you could manage this for me, through
the old attorney at S—? Is he likely to have the
custody of them ?'

'I don't well know where else they could be,
grandpapa went away so suddenly. But,' (recollect-
ing herself,) 'as he never lived here at all, or troubled
himself about the estate, I don't see how the papers
could have come into his possession.'

'True—they are probably with the Master in
Chancery under whom the property is administered.
I know two or three of them, and can perhaps find
access to them, if I only knew which. Much depends
on my doing so—more than you are aware of. Do
you remember any legal friend your grandfather had,
likely to give him an important advice ?'

'I don't, of course—but Aunt Winny may; her

memory is wonderfully good for things which happened long ago.' So saying, she went in quest of her aunt, giving little Redmond, who had joined us, a kiss of exulting affection as she passed.

Aunt Winifred, with the tenacious grasp of those whose events in life have been few, *did* remember a visit at G—, shortly before her indignant expulsion along with her offending married sister, from an old college friend of her father's—a keen, black-browed, quick-witted gentleman, who looked like a judge, and she was told was in the fair way to become one.

'Could she recollect his name?'

'No, but she was sure it was an odd one, for it began with a Q, and yet sounded like Welsh, and was not unlike Philly's.'

'Oh!' thought I, 'Quin, probably! Judge Quin, if alive, must have been much the same age as Mr. Gryffith; and he has a son a Master in Chancery, and I know him very well. By Jove, won't it be lucky, as well as strange, if he is the man?' (All this was muttered *sotto voce*, but indeed little better than Greek to my audience, even supposing it overheard.)

On this scent, albeit a somewhat cold one, I entered with more alacrity on my chase; and with the aid of my former *compagnon de voyage*, the young solicitor, (whose tombstone evidence I found was the duplicate testimony relied on for proving, from separate and apparently distinct parties, the deaths both of father and son,) I succeeded in ferreting out the depository of the title-deeds of the Welsh estate.

By one of those coincidences as frequent to the full in common life as in fiction, the son of Judge Quin was the judicial administrator of the unclaimed property; an appointment due chiefly to his connexion with the Principality, and also to that acquaintance on the part of his late father with the family and its affairs which had enabled him to insinuate doubts regarding its tenure.

Strengthened by this bond of hereditary good-will, I had no hesitation in making myself and my purpose known to the 'Master'; and gained not only easy access to the necessary documents, but the benefit of his experienced judgment as to the validity of the plea I was about, in another Court, to adduce in favour of the unfettered entry of the lost heir.

I will not weary my legal readers, nor mystify the far greater number of those to whom law is as algebra, by entering into the particulars of the case. Suffice it that I obtained a brief (which for aught they knew of its contents might have been an assignation to the property) from the natural heirs; furnished with which I confronted at W— assizes the consequential and confident claimant not only of the entailed estate (to which he might really believe himself entitled), but the fraudulent tamperer with dates and records, whom it was a duty, as well as a pleasure, to expose.

His game—the singular Christian and surnames of father and son being the same—had been to produce the *extract mortuaire* of the former as that of his unhappy son. But as the death of the latter some five and twenty years previous, would have been too far back for the probable decease of his missing parent, the figures in the extract had been skilfully altered to fifteen—a period during which, certainly, no tidings had been authentically heard in England of either.

To confute these *cooked* certificates, I was of course provided with the affidavit of the pastor that twenty-five years previously he had officiated at the funeral of the younger Gryffith Gryffith. And, in addition, to his equally valid attestation to the recent demise (within two months) of the man asserted to have been dead for·fifteen years. I was ready to make oath that I too had assisted at the funeral ceremony, and witnessed (though to avoid agitation to the dying man I had passed for the clerk to the Swiss *procureur* who drew it up) the last will and testament of the long-absent Gryffith Gryffith, senior, of Wynne-coat Hall.

This will—proved both according to the forms of Swiss and English law—bore that, in addition to all his accumulated monied property (subject to the legacies before mentioned), he bequeathed to his grandson Redmond Phillips, on taking the name of Gryffith, the estate of Wynnecoat, if, as he had been advised by one eminent in the law, it should be found that as last-named heir in the entail the restriction to male heirs terminated in his person.

On this point, also, I had not failed to obtain the opinion of counsel. And having in the exordium of my speech enlisted the sympathies of an over-

flowing Welsh auditory in the sad privations and
heroic endurance of the helpless females whom a
father's cruel prejudices had induced him, even in
the tomb, to set aside—and appealed to all their
clannish feelings on behalf of the blind infant heir
whom the tardy though sure march of justice was
about to invest with a noble heritage—I made good
my law point to the satisfaction of the learned judge,
with whom declamation, or even sympathy, would
have gone for nothing.

Foiled, discomfited, and shunned, Mr. Howell
Gryffith was, in turf phraseology, nowhere! and
slunk, like a beaten hound, out of court.

The victory gained, it remained to be seen what
would be its consequences to the victors. If I may
be egotist enough to begin with those to myself, I am
ashamed to say how I secretly rejoiced (knowing how
purely indifferent to Philippa would be the involuntary and unforeseen result of my interposition)
that instead of the large amount of arrears which,
had her grandfather died intestate, would have fallen
to her as one of his heirs at law, the small sum bequeathed to her as a legacy would exonerate me
from all suspicion of mercenary motives in seeking
to appropriate to myself (as I felt I must do) the
sweetest and rarest specimen of female humanity
which had ever crossed my bachelor path.

I had previous to the decision enlisted my mother
in the cause of the lonely ladies; and on the double
plea of their being within reach while drawing up the
case, and of having first-rate consultation regarding

the little blind boy—I persuaded them to accept the comforts of at least that temporary home of which they had been so long and cruelly deprived.

In the hope of restoring to the blessing of sight their interesting young charge (who, not having been born blind, had it was supposed become so in early infancy from the privation of all suitable nourishment during a protracted passage in a troop-ship from India) we were unhappily disappointed. Wealth to palliate the evil would be amply his—but proved itself powerless to put him in possession of that wide world of enjoyment in which the beggar boy might unconsciously revel.

I felt this blow severely—far more so than the meek and chastened spirit of her whom I somehow feared it would estrange from me, and prove the death-knell of my trembling hope. I was too anxious—too wretchedly anxious—to ascertain this to defer long bringing on the crisis. When consulted, in the unreserved confidence of friendship, on the arrange-ments consequent on the child's accession of fortune, and the plan most eligible for his peculiar educa-tion—I seized the opportunity, to obviate all diffi-culty, by proffering my life-long services in sharing the interesting office, and my hand and heart to her whom I felt sure nothing would ever divorce from it.

Little flurried out of her wonted calm serenity by a proposal (which she said was 'very kind,' and 'just like myself') to be 'encumbered for life with two helpless women, and a blind child,' she gave me

one of her ineffable smiles, and said, 'No, Mr.
Vivian! were I capable of taking advantage of your
romantic fancy for your poor client, I should not be
the Philippa Gwynne you have endowed with ideal
perfection. My vocation in life has been chalked
out for me by One, who has denied sight to my little
Redmond that I might serve him by being 'eyes to
the blind,' as well as a guide and support to the
wavering footsteps of my mother's afflicted sister.
With these duties—performed with heart and soul,
as they ought, and, in God's strength, will be fulfilled
—a wife's hourly devotion is incompatible; and it
would be but a bad return to cheat you out of a
partner,' added she, again smiling, 'when you have
saved us from being cheated out of an estate!

'To qualify myself for being of all the use possible
to my darling boy, I shall place him and myself near
a blind asylum; and when he has there mastered
all the means of instruction open to him, you shall
advise how further his education can be carried on.
Dear child! I as yet must be with him wherever he
is; he would pine out of the sound of my voice, and
yet he must have companions like himself to cheer
and amuse him; the only playfellow of his childhood
has been poor Nanny!'

There was something in this concentration of
future views and feelings on one object, more quietly
and completely fatal to the hopes of another than
the most vehement protestations and denials. Large
and loving as was Philippa's heart, it had room—at
present at least—for none but her foster-child; and I
was obliged to be content with silent hopes, which

borrowed a little strength from her unhesitating acquiescence in my appointment by the Court of joint guardian with herself to the infant orphan.

On the income of their legacies, and a handsome allowance for the child out of the estate, she and her aunt, before submitting as infallible to the fiat of the English oculists as to the incurable nature of Redmond's blindness, established themselves for some time in a lovely spot in Switzerland (congenial to their retired tastes and mountain habits) to try the skill of a German renowned throughout Europe, and to whom monarchs had resorted, for successful, though often tedious cures of disorders of the eye. That of little Redmond had chiefly baffled the regular faculty from its anomalous character—referrible to none of the common types of disease—and on this his devoted aunt founded her not very sanguine hopes. Of the slightest favourable change I might depend on being immediately informed, and with this I was obliged, for the present, to be content.

I had recourse in my disappointment (or rather the remedy was happily forced upon me) to the sole specific for such heart complaints, an overwhelming press of mental labour. The 'cause' had brought me into a certain 'celebrity;' business flowed in upon me, and during Term time and circuit I contrived to cheat painful recollections, and fill up with legal technicalities what would otherwise have been the 'aching void' within. But it was in vacations that I pined for what had robbed fishing of its zest, and Nature of its beauty, and existence—unoccupied existence at least—of its spring and sunshine.

I had lounged out part of my second autumn list-
lessly in town, and not having heard for a longer
time than usual from G——, was half meditating a
trip thither, from which reason whispered I should
probably return more tantalized and unhappy than
before; so I compromised the matter and wrote,
under the saddened feelings of the moment, what
must have been a very disconsolate letter to Philippa.

Wealth, unshared and unprized, I told her, came to
me unsought, and of the 'bubble reputation' (though
not acquired at the 'cannon's mouth') I had a daily
increasing portion, sufficient to satisfy a more ambi-
tious mind. But what was all this to one, who in
the dull old house in Westminster, with only her
retainer, the rose, next his heart, found all 'vanity and
vexation of spirit?'

I was still sitting, two or three weeks later, over a
smouldering wood fire, in the dusk of a resolutely
rainy autumnal day in London, when a letter with a
foreign post-mark aroused me from my reverie. Too
impatient to wait for lights, I stirred the glowing
embers into a blaze, to peruse what I half longed,
half dreaded to open. I read as follows:—

'It gladdens my heart to be able to tell you that,
thanks to God's mercy and the skill and perseverance
of Herr N——, Redmond sees! not perfectly indeed
or sufficiently for an artist or a marksman, but
enough to follow out an ordinary course of study, and,
with God's blessing, to turn out in time an English
country gentleman. To make him this we must come
at once to England; and as my grandfather was

brought up at Westminster, and sent his own son there, no doubt he would have liked his heir to go there also. So if there is room in the "old house in Westminster," perhaps he might do so from under his guardian's roof, and then it would be "dull" no longer. You will let him build me a cottage on the old spot at Wynnecoat, and then in the holidays you can teach him fishing, without trespassing this time on any one's property.'

The little archness of the last sentence, and the accompanying smile which it enabled me to conjure up, sent me, not altogether miserable, to G—— to escort home Philippa and her little nephew: he, wild with all the nameless and unimagined delights of vision, she, radiant with his joy, and sweetly roused out of her habitual serenity by the first taste of positive felicity her life of devotion to others had yet afforded—a state which I schooled myself to abstain from disturbing by one premature word, trusting to the resistless influence of the boy when hereafter exerted on my behalf.

We digressed on our homeward *route* to visit the quiet church of W——, where some months before poor Aunt Winifred had been laid to rest beside her father and brother, and charm the heart of the good old pastor with a sight of the boy whose claims he had successfully advocated.

It was he, as I had fondly anticipated, who, ere long, triumphantly carried mine, from the simple impossibility of his ever imagining that Aunt Philly could live at Edmonton and he at Ware; at the bare idea of which he nearly cried his precious recovered optics blind again.

So the old house in Westminster ('dull' no longer) became the winter abode of the trio. By Redmond's tenth birthday the fishing-lodge was built out of the carefully husbanded allowance from the estate, of which his aunt was now happily independent. And at his coming of age (not so very long ago) a modern mansion, large enough for hospitality but not too large for comfort, replaced in its smiling readiness the desolation of Wynnecoat.

We are looking out for a wife to share and embellish it; but the gay, handsome, and (better still) good and grateful owner says, unless the world can produce him a second 'Aunt Philly,' he fears he must live and die a bachelor!

THE END.

LONDON: PRINTED BY WILLIAM CLOWES AND SONS, STAMFORD STREET.

www.ingramcontent.com/pod-product-compliance
Lightning Source LLC
Chambersburg PA
CBHW021749110726
47902CB00006B/1459